SHADOWS OF THE DEAD

SHADOWS OF THE DEAD

An Inspector Stark Mystery

Jim Eldridge

CRÈME de la CRIME

This first world edition published 2017
in Great Britain and the USA by
Crème de la Crime, an imprint of
SEVERN HOUSE PUBLISHERS LTD of
19 Cedar Road, Sutton, Surrey, England, SM2 5DA.
Trade paperback edition first published
in Great Britain and the USA 2017 by
SEVERN HOUSE PUBLISHERS LTD

British Library Cataloguing in Publication Data
A CIP catalogue record for this title is available from the British Library.

ISBN-13: 978-1-78029-095-9 (cased)
ISBN-13: 978-1-78029-577-0 (trade paper)
ISBN-13: 978-1-78010-857-5 (e-book)

Typeset by Palimpsest Book Production Ltd.,
Falkirk, Stirlingshire, Scotland.

To Lynne, for ever

ONE

'**F**ire!'

He was falling backwards, bullets tearing in to him, ripping through the khaki of his uniform. He hit the mud, sinking, and as he disappeared beneath it, he was suddenly elsewhere, watching as the boy in the khaki uniform was tied to a chair, strong ropes binding him as he struggled and screamed and screamed for his mother . . . until a cloth was tied over the boy's mouth, cutting off his frantic cries.

'Fire!'

This time he tried to step back but he couldn't move; the mud was clinging to his ankles, then to his calves, holding him in one place, forcing him to watch . . .

'No! No!'

'Paul! It's all right! I'm here! It's all right!'

He woke, shaking, her arms wrapped right around him, the scent of her body filling his nostrils, replacing the smell of mud and blood . . .

'Paul! I'm here. You're all right.'

He looked up at her, at Amelia, felt the sheets and blankets around them, the warmth of her as she hugged him close, rocked him back and forth . . .

He fell back into sleep, still wrapped in her arms. The next time he woke, she was sitting up in bed next to him, watching him, her face concerned.

'You had a nightmare,' she said.

'I'm sorry,' he apologized, pushing himself up and slipping back against the pillows.

'Don't be silly,' she said, and she leant across and kissed him on the mouth. 'I love you. I love everything about you. Even your nightmares.'

'No one can love them,' he said. He looked at the clock beside the bed. Quarter to seven. 'I meant to get home,' he said. 'To see Stephen before he goes to school.'

'You still have time,' she said. 'What was it about? The nightmare?'

'An execution. By firing squad.'

'You were there?'

Stark nodded. 'His name was Harry Hawks,' said Stark. 'He was thirteen.'

'Thirteen!' echoed Amelia, shocked. 'Didn't anyone notice how old he was when he joined up?'

'Of course,' said Stark. 'I'm pretty sure he told them his age when he went to the recruiting office to enlist. But how it worked is that the recruiting sergeant would ask volunteers how old they were, and if they said they were sixteen, or fourteen, or even thirteen, or whatever, he'd say to them, "Sorry, you're too young. Come back when you're eighteen." And then he'd give them a wink and say, "Like tomorrow." And the next day they'd go back and he'd ask them, "How old are you?" and they'd say, "Eighteen", and they were in. Signed up.'

'But thirteen!'

'Harry looked older than he was. He was big for his age.' He shook his head. 'He should never have been there. I guess at that age he just thought it was a game, like playing soldiers in the park. But when the bullets and shells started flying and people started getting shot and blown to bits, it was all too much for him. He just went to pieces. He started crying for his mum. He was told to go over the top, and he refused, just curled up into a ball and kept crying and screaming for his mum over and over again.

'So they charged him with desertion and cowardice in the face of the enemy, and he was shot by a firing squad. He was in such a state he couldn't even stand up. They tied him to a wooden post, but he kept sliding down it, still crying, so they tied him to a wooden chair. He messed himself, of course, just like a baby – because that's all he was.'

He shook his head, haunted and angry at the nightmare that could so easily have ruined this night with Amelia. 'It's all about class,' he said. 'Harry Hawks died because he was just cannon fodder from the backstreets. If an officer, or someone from an important family, refused to go into battle, they were diagnosed with shellshock and sent home for treatment. A nice rest in a hospital in pleasant surroundings. Poor kids like Harry Hawks, they were shot as an example to others.'

'You sound like one of my Bolsheviks,' smiled Amelia.

'Not me,' said Stark. 'I do my best to avoid politics.'

'Not very successfully,' smiled Amelia.

The ringing of the telephone pealed through the house.

Amelia looked at the clock and frowned. 'Seven o'clock,' she said, pulling on her dressing gown and heading for the hallway. 'I can't think of anyone I know who gets up at this hour.'

Phone calls in the early morning and late at night usually mean trouble, Stark said to himself. He got out of bed and began to pull on his clothes. From the hallway he heard Amelia say in surprise, 'Redford?' Then she gave a little gasp, and as Stark came into the hallway he saw her fingers clutch at the telephone cord.

'When?' She stood, barefoot and white-faced, listening to the voice at the other end. Then she said, 'No, you did the right thing. Thank you for letting me know.'

She hung up and suddenly sat down heavily on the chair by the telephone table.

'What's wrong?' asked Stark.

'It's Johnny.'

'Johnny?'

'My former husband. Lord Fairfax. He . . .' She hesitated, then said, 'He's dead. Murdered.'

Stark stared at her. 'Murdered?'

'That's what Redford says. He's . . . he's Johnny's valet. It seems that Johnny sent him away for the night, and when he came back early this morning, he found Johnny and another man, dead.'

Stark headed for the drinks tray. He poured a measure of brandy and handed it to her. 'Here, drink this.'

She forced a weak smile as she looked at the glass. 'A bit early for it, don't you think?'

'Medicine – for shock.'

She raised the glass to her lips, then downed it in one gulp.

'Have the police been called?' asked Stark.

'Your sergeant, Bobby Danvers, has just arrived at his flat.' She shook her head. 'I can't believe it. Johnny always seemed so . . . indestructible.'

'I'd better get along there,' said Stark.

Amelia looked at him quizzically. 'How will you say you found out about it?' she asked. 'He'll know you must have been here with me.'

'My guess is that he'll have tried phoning me at my home and left a message with my parents,' said Stark. 'I'll tell him I got it from them.'

'Still not ready to be public about us?' challenged Amelia.

Stark hesitated. 'I need time to tell Stephen,' he said.

'I'm not asking you to make an honest woman of me,' snapped Amelia. 'Where does he think you were last night?'

'Here, with you,' said Stark. 'But once it becomes public, there are more things to think about. There's a moral clause for police officers. Consorting with a divorced woman – and a titled one at that – could put my job at risk.'

'Oh, for God's sake, Paul,' exploded Amelia. 'You don't think the Chief Constable or the Commissioner aren't off with a variety of women, none of whom are their wives!'

'Yes, but it's like I said about Harry Hawks: there's one rule for the rich and powerful, and another for those of us who aren't. I've upset quite a few important people, and there are some at Scotland Yard who'd like to see the back of me. Invoking the morals clause would be just the ammunition they want. I'm sorry.' He took his jacket and overcoat from the hallstand. 'The thing is, I do want to make an honest woman of you. But there are things to be sorted out. Like, where will we live? I can't imagine you slotting in easily into a tiny slum house in Plender Street.'

'It's not a slum!'

'The area is, however you dress it up.'

'Paul, you're rushing things. Yes, I said I love you because I do, but that's not the same as . . . well, getting married!'

'Why not?'

'My God, you are so old-fashioned! What's wrong with how things are now?'

'Haven't you heard what I said about the morality clause?'

'Is that the reason? So you don't lose your job?'

'No, of course not!'

'Look, Paul, we are what we are to one another, and these past two weeks have been wonderful. And I hope it will continue to be wonderful. But let's not tie ourselves down so soon! You don't know me properly yet.'

'I know enough.'

She shook her head. 'Do I want you? Yes, I do. Do I want to be with you? Yes, I do. And damn their morality clause! We'll just deny it. What are they going to do? Spy on us in bed? If anyone asks, we are friends. The very best of friends.'

'From two different social classes.'

'That's their problem, not ours.'

He fell silent, then asked, 'Don't you want to get married again?'

'Perhaps. But next time I want to be sure it'll last. I was married before and it didn't work.'

'Did you love him?' asked Stark.

'I thought I did,' said Amelia briskly. Then she dropped her head. 'No, I didn't. I did it to annoy my mother. And he was dashing and handsome and lively, and now . . .' And suddenly she began to cry. 'And now he's dead! Some bastard killed him!'

Stark went to her and knelt down beside her, enveloping her in his arms, pulling her close to him.

'And I'll find out who did it,' he promised her.

TWO

Stark settled into the leather seat of the taxi as it drove from Knightsbridge towards Chelsea, wondering what lay in store for him at Lord Fairfax's flat. This was something completely unexpected; he and Amelia had just recently become involved, and here he was investigating the murder of her ex-husband.

He knew they'd appear an odd couple if anyone found out about them. He, a detective chief inspector with the Metropolitan Police. A thirty-five-year-old widower with an eight-year-old son. A veteran of the war, having served the whole four years from 1914 until 1918 in the trenches of Flanders. He'd gone out as a private, a volunteer, and returned as Captain Paul Stark, DSM, his body torn apart by his injuries, and his heart empty when he discovered that his deeply loved wife, Susan, had died in the flu epidemic of 1918. It was said that a hundred million people had died around the world in the epidemic, but to Stark that was just numbers. Susan had been his heart, his life, and he never thought he'd ever meet anyone again who made him feel this way. And then Lady Amelia Fairfax had come into his life just a month ago, as part of a murder investigation.

Divorced. Titled. On the surface, it would seem that the only thing they had in common was their age, both thirty-five. But beneath her aristocratic veneer, Amelia Fairfax was a mass of contradictions. For one thing, to her own class she was a maverick for her social campaigning: equal votes for women, social justice for all, which went as far as being a volunteer administrator for the British Communist Party, working at their offices in the East End of London. Consequently, she was viewed with suspicion by her own class, and her activities were followed with salacious glee by the downmarket press.

It was a feeling that Stark knew well. Not the business of being a target for the press, but being seen as a maverick by his own class. He was viewed with suspicion by many in the police force because he wouldn't join in taking the bribes and pay-offs to keep certain 'important' people out of trouble. Stark believed in justice, regardless of social class, creed or race, and that put him at odds with some officers who had a dislike for the Irish, foreigners and Jews, or 'Micks, Wogs, Dagos and Sheenies', as they called them. No one said that in Stark's presence, though, not after he'd made his feelings known at a leaving party for a retiring superintendent. 'I gave four years of my life fighting for freedom and liberty,' he'd told a senior officer who'd made the remark. 'That means liberty and freedom for everyone. Not just the select few.'

Some had remarked – behind his back, of course – that he only expressed those views because his grandmother had been a poor Irish immigrant, escaping the famine. Stark didn't care. Let them think what they liked. He'd seen terrible injustices during his four years in the trenches, and he'd seen injustices just as bad in the three years since he'd been back from the war. Which is why he admired Amelia and the stands she took.

No, not just admired her. He *loved* her. It had hit him hard and unexpectedly. Those first few days when they'd become lovers had filled him with thoughts of her, and he had had to force himself to concentrate on his job.

The problem was: what to do about it.

Maybe she was right. Maybe he was rushing things. Yes, he

was old-fashioned – too old-fashioned. And even if he could break down her resistance to marriage, where would they live?

For all her declarations of social justice, and her identifying with the poor and socially disadvantaged, in all of which he knew she was sincere, he could not imagine her moving into his rented terraced three-up-two-down house in Camden Town. With no electricity, just gas for lighting. With an outside toilet at the end of the yard. No inside bathroom or running water, just a cold water tap in the scullery with a large old sink, and a tin bath that was brought into the kitchen on Friday nights and filled with pans of hot water from the coal range.

Her house, then? But he knew that his parents wouldn't agree to that. They deeply disapproved of his relationship with Amelia, his father in particular stating that it was 'against the natural order'. 'The different classes should stick to their own!' he had said. 'That's how things are meant to be!'

Which would mean taking Stephen away from his grandparents, whom Stephen loved deeply. They'd brought the boy up from when he was born, at first with Susan, and then, after Susan died, on their own. Stark had been in no fit state to be a parent to young Stephen. At first he'd been in hospital, being treated for his injuries suffered during the war, then convalescing. And after that he'd spent his time grieving for Susan, and to try to cope with it he'd thrown himself into his work as a newly promoted detective inspector. It had really only been in the last year that he'd started to form a relationship with his son. For the first seven years of his young life, his grandparents had been the mainstays for Stephen. Stark couldn't take Stephen away from them, not yet – it would be too cruel to the boy, and to them.

So what was left? Move in with Amelia and leave Stephen behind, seeing him as often as he could? After all, that's what the upper classes did with their sons, packing them off to boarding school almost as soon as they could walk. No, for Stark, that was out of the question. He loved his son and he desperately wanted Stephen to *know* that he loved him. He'd been absent from his young son's life for far too long already.

Maybe Amelia was right. Maybe, with all these problems and issues, it was better left as it was. Best friends. Who slept together. In secret.

'Here we are, sir.' The taxi driver's voice cut into Stark's reverie. 'Cheyne Walk.'

Lord Fairfax's home was in a smart block of flats close to the Thames. The red-brick building was surrounded by gardens resplendent with late-flowering plants and shrubs dotted between evergreen trees, to give colour and seclusion to the building. Two police cars and a police van were parked in the driveway, and as Stark walked towards the building, he was recognized by a uniformed constable standing guard by the main entrance, who saluted him and said, 'DS Danvers is inside, sir. Flat two.'

Stark nodded and stepped into the lobby with its overpowering smell of polish. The door to the flat was open, with another uniformed constable guarding it from unwanted visitors. The constable stepped aside to allow Stark to enter. DS Robert Danvers, Stark's sergeant, was in the hallway talking to a short, thin man wearing a black waistcoat over a crisp white shirt. Those, along with the man's neatly pressed dark trousers, marked him out as Lord Fairfax's servant. Possibly this was the Redford that Amelia had mentioned, Lord Fairfax's valet.

Danvers spotted Stark and immediately came over to greet him. 'You got my message, sir,' said Danvers. 'Your father said he wasn't sure where you were when I phoned.'

No, he wouldn't, reflected Stark. Too embarrassed.

'Superintendent Benson only phoned me because he couldn't get hold of you,' continued Danvers.

'You did absolutely the right thing, Sergeant,' said Stark. 'When did this happen?'

'According to Lord Fairfax's valet, he got in at six o'clock this morning and found the bodies.' He indicated the short man. 'This is him, sir. Mr Redford.'

Stark nodded at the man. 'So you were out last night?'

'Yes, sir,' said Redford. 'I went to stay with my sister. Lord Fairfax had given me the night off. When I returned this morning, I went to the kitchen to check the stove and prepare the hot water for Lord Fairfax's bath, that sort of thing. Then I went into the study to draw the curtains and tidy up, and that's when I found them.'

Stark registered that the man seemed very composed for someone who'd just discovered the dead body of his master. But then, that's the way servants were expected to be.

Danvers gestured towards a room off the hallway. 'Doctor Kemp's in there with them.'

Stark followed Danvers into the study, leaving Redford waiting in the hall. Dr Kemp, the duty pathologist, was bent over a man tied to a chair. A second man was tied to another chair, just a few feet away.

'Doctor,' nodded Stark in greeting.

'Ah, they tracked you down, did they!' said Kemp.

'What have we got?' asked Stark.

Kemp indicated the bodies of the two men tied securely to the chairs, their arms and legs firmly bound. The faces of both men were horribly distorted, their eyes bulging from their sockets, and dried blood and pus crusted their mouths down to their chins. One was dressed in outdoor clothes, a jacket and tie, and wearing patent leather shoes. The other had slippers on his feet. Lord Fairfax.

'I'll know more when I get them back to the mortuary,' said Kemp. 'But at first sight – and smell – it looks as if they were tied up and then some sort of poison was poured down their throats. It smells like weed killer.'

'When did it happen?'

'I'd say about eleven o'clock last night.' He shook his head. 'An excruciatingly painful way to die.'

'I'll leave you to your deliberations, Doctor,' nodded Stark. To Danvers he said, 'I think I'll have another word with the valet. I know you've already talked to him, but we can compare notes afterwards and see if his story changes at all.'

'I've got men asking questions at the other apartments to see if anyone saw or heard anything around the block about eleven o'clock last night.'

'Good,' said Stark.

He went back out into the hallway, where Redford was still waiting. 'Mr Redford,' he said, 'I'm Detective Chief Inspector Stark.'

'Yes, sir,' nodded Redford. 'The sergeant told me he hoped you'd be arriving.'

'It must have been a terrible shock to you. Finding the bodies.'

'Indeed, sir. But, unfortunately, I am not unfamiliar with death.'

'You served?'

'Yes, sir. The Somme and Arras.'

'And you entered Lord Fairfax's service after the war?'

'No, sir. I was already in Lord Fairfax's employment before the war. He kindly took me back after.'

Old soldiers together, Stark guessed. 'The other man . . . ?'

'He's a Mr Adams, sir. Mr Carl Adams. An American gentleman.'

'Have you seen him here before?'

'Very briefly yesterday evening, sir, when he arrived to see Lord Fairfax. He'd telephoned yesterday afternoon and asked to speak to Lord Fairfax, and they arranged that Mr Adams would call on Lord Fairfax in the evening. He arrived at about half past nine. Lord Fairfax took him into the study. I served them drinks on a tray, and then, as I said, Lord Fairfax told me I could have the night off. Because it was short notice I hadn't made prior arrangements, so I went to my sister's in Kentish Town. I don't see her and my niece and nephew as much as I'd like. My sister's a widow. Her husband was killed in the war.'

'Did Lord Fairfax tell you what the purpose of Mr Adams' visit was?'

'No, sir.'

They were interrupted by the ringing of the telephone.

'If you'll excuse me, sir,' said Redford. He went to the telephone and lifted it from its cradle. 'Lord Fairfax's residence.' He looked towards Stark. 'Yes, sir. Detective Chief Inspector Stark is here.' He held out the phone towards Stark. 'It's Chief Superintendent Benson of Scotland Yard for you, sir.'

'Thank you,' said Stark.

He took the phone. 'Stark.'

'Where the hell have you been, Stark?' demanded the blustering tones of his chief superintendent.

'Making my way here, sir,' replied Stark calmly.

'Well, you'd better make your way *here* at the Yard,' snapped Benson. 'Something's come up that needs your immediate attention.'

'Yes, sir. Can you tell me what it is, so that I can keep Sergeant Danvers abreast of events?'

'Not over the telephone, no. It's a delicate matter. Suffice to say, it's urgent. And it relates to the case.'

'Yes, sir. I shall be along immediately.' Stark replaced the receiver and went back into the study. 'Superintendent Benson just telephoned,' he told Danvers. 'He wants me back at the Yard.'

'Yes, sir. Did he say why?'

'No, just that something urgent had come up, and it relates to this case.' He gave a wry smile. 'You know the superintendent, Sergeant. I suspect politics are involved. That's what usually makes everything suddenly become urgent where he's concerned.'

'That is a very cynical assertion to make, Stark,' interjected Kemp, from where he was examining the victims.

'You disagree?' asked Stark.

'Not at all,' said Kemp. 'I think that is a very fair summing-up of the situation and refreshing to hear a senior officer declare it. Although, as a word of warning, if you want my opinion . . .'

'Your medical opinion?' smiled Stark.

'You won't get much further up the career chain if you say that sort of thing too loudly and too frequently. It can be thought of as subversive, and a bad influence on junior officers.'

'Am I a bad influence on you, Sergeant?' asked Stark.

'Not at all, sir,' said Danvers blandly. 'I've never heard you express anything other than praise for senior officers.'

'In that case, Sergeant, my medical opinion is that you are deaf,' said Kemp. He straightened up. 'I'm ready to take these back to the Yard.'

'Can you give me a lift?' asked Stark. 'The chief superintendent has summoned me.' He turned to Danvers. 'I'll leave you here to continue the investigation and we'll compare notes when you get back.'

'Right, sir,' said Danvers.

'It'll take me a few minutes to get them into the van,' said Kemp. 'That all right with you?'

'That's fine,' said Stark. 'I need to make a phone call.'

He went back out to the hallway and said to Redford, 'Would you mind if I used your telephone?'

'Not at all, sir,' said the valet.

Stark lifted the receiver, got the operator and gave her his home phone number. There was the sound of the ringing tone, and then it was picked up and Stark heard his father say, 'Yes?'

'You're supposed to say the number, Dad,' said Stark.

'Why?' demanded his father. 'People know which number they're calling.'

'In case the call gets connected to the wrong number.'

'In which case I wouldn't want them knowing the number. They might call it again.'

It's not worth arguing with him, Stark told himself resignedly. 'I'm sorry I never made it home this morning,' he said. 'I got called to a case.'

'Your sergeant found you, then.'

Suddenly, a harsh spluttering coughing erupted in Stark's ear. Stark waited until it subsided, then said, 'Are you all right, Dad? Your cough sounds worse.'

'It's nothing – just the usual bronchitis,' snapped his father, but Stark could hear the sound of his laboured breathing. 'I always get it this time of year.'

'You ought to go and see Doctor Lomax.'

'I don't need a doctor; I know what it is. I'll look after myself,' rasped his father. Then he coughed violently again. Stark waited until it eased and was about to press him again to go to the doctor, but his father snapped angrily at him, 'So, where were you? At her Ladyship's?'

'I can't talk about it, Dad. Not on the phone.'

'Ashamed of her, are you?'

Stark felt the anger rising inside him, but forced himself to keep it under control. 'It's not a situation for discussion now. I'm only calling to let you know I have to go to Scotland Yard now, and it's likely I won't be home before six. Is Stephen all right?'

'He's fine. He went to school as usual.' There was a pause and Stark's ear was filled with a phlegm-filled rattle, and then his father rasped out breathily, 'Your mother doesn't like this thing. This telephone. It upsets her. She doesn't like to think who might be calling.'

'Only a few people have got the number, Dad.'

'It's not natural,' insisted his father.

'I'll see you later, Dad,' said Stark.

Benson was hunched over his desk as Stark knocked at the chief superintendent's door, and entered the office.

'Where were you this morning, Stark?' Benson demanded. 'I telephoned your home and your father said he didn't know where you were.'

'I had a private engagement, sir.'

'The reason we had a telephone put in at your house was so that we could reach you at all times!'

'And I did get the message, sir. Sergeant Danvers had also

telephoned my home and left a message about the incident at Lord Fairfax's home.' To deflect any further questions, Stark continued, 'You said it was urgent, sir. Something to do with the case.'

'Yes. I received this letter this morning.' Grim-faced, Benson handed Stark a white envelope which had already been opened. Stark took out the letter, unfolded it and read it.

There was no address on the letter, just a simple few lines in neat handwriting.

Dear Sir,
Lady Amelia Fairfax murdered her husband, Lord Fairfax.
Yours faithfully,
A Friend of Justice.

THREE

Stark did his best to keep his face expressionless, but inside he was in turmoil. Amelia? To give himself time to gather his thoughts, he studied the envelope. It was addressed to Chief Superintendent Benson, Scotland Yard, and was marked *Personal. By hand.*

'Well, Stark?' demanded Benson. 'I understand both men were poisoned!'

'Yes, sir.'

'Poison is notoriously a woman's weapon.' He pointed a stubby finger at the letter in Stark's hand. 'And we all know that so often in the case of murder it's the spouse who's responsible.'

'True, but in this case the men who were murdered were both very fit, and they'd been securely tied up before they were killed. Hardly the work of one woman, I would think.'

'She could have had accomplices, Stark,' insisted Benson. 'That's obvious! And this letter was only delivered here within the hour. News about the murders hasn't yet been released. The sender of this letter definitely knows something, and he or she names Lady Amelia Fairfax as the culprit!'

Yes, agreed Stark silently, *my thoughts exactly. And as Amelia Fairfax was with me last night, that means the letter was sent either by the murderer or by someone closely connected with the murders.*

Stark put the letter back in the envelope and held it out towards Benson to return it, but the chief superintendent waved it away.

'You keep it, Stark. This is your case. You seem to have a way with the aristocracy. But be discreet! We can hardly have Lady Amelia arrested until you've got a strong enough case against her. Hard evidence, Stark. Find out who her accomplices are.'

'*If* the accusations in this letter are correct,' cautioned Stark. 'My hunch is that this is just likely to be a malicious slur.'

'That may be so, but – as I said – whoever wrote that letter knew about the murder before it became public knowledge.'

'*Murders*, sir,' corrected Stark politely. 'Two men were murdered.' He indicated the envelope. 'It's interesting that the letter only mentions Lord Fairfax, not the other victim.'

'Do we know who the other man is?'

'An American businessman called Carl Adams.'

'Well, whatever you turn up, I leave it to you to act with discretion, Stark. But keep me informed. Questions will be asked, and I need to be ready to answer them.'

Stark walked to his office, the envelope with the incriminating letter clutched in his hand. *Now I have a much bigger problem*, he thought.

He walked in, sat down at his desk and pulled the letter out of the envelope and studied them both again. The right thing to do would be to excuse himself from the case. But if he did that, the case would be given to another chief inspector, one who might be happy to follow the chief superintendent's direction, and Amelia would find herself having a case built against her, however tenuous. The papers would get hold of the story and would fall on her with relish.

I know she didn't do it because she was with me. But if I tell Benson that, then I might as well start writing my letter of resignation.

Right now his immediate problem was what to do about Danvers. He'd have to show him the letter, and he'd have to tell him the facts of the matter. But could he trust Danvers to keep that a secret? Stark liked to think he was a good judge of men. During the war, that sense of judgement – knowing which men he could trust and which ones to be wary of – often meant the difference between life and death. Yes, he trusted Danvers, even though he'd only been his sergeant for four months. Danvers was honest, straight, which was one reason Stark had determined to keep him as his sergeant. There were still times when Stark puzzled over why someone from Danvers' background had joined the police force, and at a relatively junior level, when he could have used his family's influence to get an inspector's position. Just as Stark had seen happen during his time in the army, when some young men from well-connected families had been made officers, even though they had little aptitude for the military.

Danvers was from a privileged background, educated at a good public school. His father was Colonel Deverill Robert Danvers CBE; his mother, Victoria Danvers, descended from a long line of landed gentry. Everything in Robert Danvers' background was anathema to Stark. But then, so was everything in Amelia's equally privileged background.

I am the worst kind of snob, Stark told himself. *I am a bigot, prejudiced against the rich and privileged. I am just as bad as those who unthinkingly look down on the working class.*

Do I trust Danvers? Yes, I do. Is he honest and straight? Yes, he is. And because he is honest and straight and not corrupt, how will he react if I ask him to keep quiet about my relationship with Amelia? Will he insist I confess it to Benson?

He looked again at the letter and the envelope.

There was only one way to find out.

He spent the time as he waited for Danvers to return in the records office, seeing if they had any information about the American, Carl Adams. He managed to find something in recently issued notes of entry, stating that one Carl Jefferson Adams, a citizen of Boston, had entered Britain in the company of Edgar Cavendish, a businessman from Indiana, two weeks earlier. The purpose of their visit was listed as 'business'. Which covers an awful lot, thought Stark.

He returned to his office, just as Danvers was taking off his overcoat and hanging it on the hook. 'All done?' he asked.

'For the moment, sir,' replied Danvers. 'Redford reported that when he returned there was no sign of the lock having been forced. No damage to the flat door at all. Which suggests that Lord Fairfax opened the door to the people who killed him. So, did he know them? Or did they just rush in and overpower the pair?'

'If the killers did that, they must have known why Lord Fairfax and Mr Adams were meeting.'

'And wanted to silence them,' agreed Danvers. 'It's early stages at the moment, sir. I've still got men canvassing the area, but I thought I'd return and report the basics.'

'Good,' nodded Stark. 'But before you do . . .'

He took the envelope from his inside pocket and held it out to Danvers.

Danvers looked at the address on the outside and took the letter out. He read it, then stared at Stark, a look of astonishment on his face. 'Lady Amelia!' he exclaimed.

'My thoughts exactly, Sergeant,' said Stark. He gestured at the letter and envelope. 'What do you make of it?'

'Well, if you want my opinion, it's nonsense!' said Danvers hotly. 'I mean, I've known Lady Amelia for years. And yes, her husband didn't treat her properly. Nothing violent, as far as I know, but he wasn't a good husband. My parents know them both—'

'I meant, what do you make of the letter and envelope?' said Stark.

'Oh,' said Danvers. He scrutinized the letter, and then the envelope, his brow furrowing. 'The envelope's marked personal for the chief super,' mused Danvers thoughtfully. 'Most anonymous letters are just sent to "The Person in Charge". This person knows the structure of command here at Scotland Yard.'

'I agree,' nodded Stark. 'And the fact that it was sent before the murders were public knowledge gives it authenticity. So, the writer is someone who's involved with the murders and knows the inner workings of Scotland Yard.'

'I think a woman wrote it,' said Danvers. He pointed at the writing. 'It's similar to the handwriting style of many of the women I know. My sister, my mother, my aunts.'

Because we move in different social circles, thought Stark. *Most of the women in my family can't read or write.*

'I bow to your particular knowledge, Sergeant,' smiled Stark.

Danvers looked at the letter and frowned again. 'Why would the writer name Lady Amelia, sir?' He looked unhappily at Stark. 'And although I think it's impossible . . .' He hesitated, then asked, 'Could there be anything in it, do you think?'

The moment of truth, Stark told himself grimly. 'Sergeant,' he said, 'there's something you should know.'

Something in Stark's tone made Danvers look at him quizzically. 'The fact is . . .' began Stark.

He was interrupted by the door being thrown open and the bulky figure of Winston Churchill, Secretary of State for the Colonies, crashing into the office. Churchill stood there, swaying, like a man in shock.

Always the dramatic entrance, thought Stark ruefully. He never just walks into a room; he bursts in.

'My God, Stark! What a mess!' exclaimed Churchill. He shook his head, then looked at Danvers. 'Will you excuse us for a moment, Sergeant?'

Danvers looked towards Stark, who said, 'See what you can find out about the other man. Carl Adams.' He passed him the sheet of paper on which he'd written down the sparse pieces of information he'd collected. 'This is all I've been able to find out so far from Records.'

Danvers nodded and withdrew. Churchill waited until the door closed behind the sergeant, and then he exploded, 'Fairfax murdered! And so foully! I came as soon as I heard.'

It was on the tip of Stark's tongue to ask why the murder of Lord Fairfax should involve a cabinet minister, but Churchill was driving on, pacing the floor agitatedly. He's always pacing, realized Stark. All that energy needs to be expended.

'I saw Benson first, of course. The chief superintendent. Protocol, naturally. He said you were in charge of the case. Capital! I told him. First rate! No finer man!

'He told me about the letter accusing Amelia. Absolute nonsense! Amelia's not a killer! Flighty, yes. Erratic, but most of the time she does things like this Communist Party stuff to irritate people. I like that. Shows good character. But she'd never do anything to harm Johnny. I'm sure she still had a soft spot for him, though he treated her abominably. Other women, you know. But that's soldiers for you.'

At least we are in agreement on her innocence, thought Stark.

'No, I'll tell you what this is about, Stark. Gallipoli!'

Stark frowned, puzzled. 'Gallipoli, Minister?'

'Yes, Goddammit! You fought. You of all people know about Gallipoli!'

'I know about it, Minister, but I don't understand—'

'They blamed me for it!'

Yes, they did, mused Stark. *And that's because it was your idea.*

In 1915, when Churchill was First Lord of the Admiralty and with the war going badly, Churchill had pushed for an attack on Germany's ally, Turkey. As a result, early in 1915, a campaign had been launched in the Dardanelles Straits along the Gallipoli peninsula, aimed at taking Constantinople. The first Allied landings by British, French, Australian and New Zealand troops had been made on the beaches of Gallipoli in April 1915. By the end of the year, it was obvious that the campaign was a disaster for the Allies and a victory for the Turks. The surviving Anzacs – Australians and New Zealanders – had been evacuated in December 1915, with the last British forces retreating in January 1916.

'A disaster, perhaps, but I paid the price for it! I resigned from the government! How many others would have done the same?'

Not many, admitted Stark. But the price that Churchill had paid for this disaster – the loss of his seat in the cabinet – wasn't as big a price as the 205,000 dead and wounded Allied troops had paid. The Australians and New Zealanders, especially, had suffered the most in terms of casualties as a percentage of their small populations – 34,000 dead and wounded Anzacs.

But then Churchill had redeemed himself. Gone off to fight in the trenches, adopting the distinctive blue helmet of the French forces. Again, Stark couldn't imagine any other politician doing the same thing. Whether it had been done as a kind of atonement, or for some other reason, Churchill had never lacked guts.

'Johnny Fairfax was my number two in planning Gallipoli,' continued Churchill. 'They blamed us both. The relatives, that is. Most saw what we were trying to do. To be frank, we were let down by those in the field. They should have carried out proper intelligence about the conditions on the ground. We expected the Turks to just crumble, but we were wrong, I'll grant that. But no one could have foreseen how good a commander Ataturk would turn out to be.'

He stopped pacing and turned to face Stark. 'Both of us received death threats from relatives of those who died. Me and Johnny.'

'Gallipoli was six years ago,' pointed out Stark.

'War casts long shadows,' replied Churchill. 'There had been other attempts on Johnny's life before, and on mine, claiming vengeance for what happened at Gallipoli.'

'But what about the other man who was murdered with Lord Fairfax? The American, Carl Adams?'

Churchill shook his head. 'Incidental. He just happened to be in the wrong place at the wrong time. They came for Johnny and found this American chap with him, so they had to silence him as well.

'Mark my words, Stark. This is about Gallipoli.' He looked at his watch. 'I have to go. I have a cabinet meeting.'

As Churchill opened the door to leave, past him Stark saw Danvers waiting in the corridor. Stark waved for him to come in as Churchill marched off. 'Back so soon, Sergeant? Surely you haven't found out what we need to know about Mr Adams so swiftly?'

'No, sir. I've been thinking about that letter, sir.'

'So have I,' said Stark. He hesitated, then said awkwardly, 'Sit down, Sergeant.'

The embarrassed tone in Stark's voice made Danvers give a puzzled frown. He sat down in the chair opposite the chief inspector and waited.

'Sergeant, I have an admission to make,' began Stark.

He hesitated again, racked by indecision. As he'd said to Amelia, there was a morals clause in his contract, and if it came out that he and Amelia Fairfax were lovers, his career would be at risk. He didn't have enough influential people who would protect him. And there were certain top officials, especially in Special Branch, who would like to force him out if they could. And now, with Amelia named as a suspect in the case he was investigating . . . At the very least he'd be removed from the case. His career might be saved with a demotion to constable, but he'd never be able to regain chief inspector status.

He took a deep breath and looked at the waiting Danvers.

'You're going to tell me that you are Lady Amelia's alibi for last night, sir,' said Danvers. 'I apologize for interrupting, but I thought it might make it easier for you.'

Stark stared at his sergeant, thunderstruck. 'How the hell did you know?' he demanded. 'Have you been having me watched?'

'No, sir. It was deduction on my part. The fact that you appeared at Lord Fairfax's home so soon after Redford had telephoned

Lady Amelia to let her know what had happened. The fact that you hadn't been at home last night, as I discovered when I phoned very early this morning. And then I began to remember looks that passed between you and Lady Amelia towards the end of our previous investigation.'

'Looks?'

Danvers nodded. 'Looks where you were both doing your best to pretend indifference to one another.'

Stark fell silent, mulling this over. Then he said, 'You should have been a detective.'

'Thank you, sir,' said Danvers.

'Who else knows?' asked Stark.

'No one, sir. At least, as far as I know.'

Stark thought it over. 'You do understand that this has to be completely between ourselves,' he said. 'If it gets out—'

'It won't be through me, sir,' Danvers assured him. 'You have my word.'

'You realize you may well be charged with suppressing evidence if it does come out?'

'If I believed that Lady Amelia was guilty, I wouldn't be a party to it, sir. But I believe this to be a smokescreen to try to divert attention away from the real murderers.'

'Murderers?' repeated Stark.

'Yes, sir. From my inspection of the scene, I am sure there was more than one person involved in the murders.'

'Go on.'

'Before I do, sir, my thought about the letter. I've got a friend whose father is a graphologist.'

'A what?'

'Someone who can tell about a person's character by their handwriting.'

'An old school friend?' enquired Stark with the gentlest hint of friendly mockery.

'Yes, sir. His father works in the manuscript section of the British Museum.'

'What's this graphologist's name?'

'Sir Bernard Wallis.'

Of course, thought Stark wryly. Nothing as common as 'Mr'. Stark got up and headed for the coat hook.

'Right, Sergeant. Let's go and see this Sir Bernard Wallis.'

FOUR

The manuscript room in the British Museum had a musty smell to it, which was hardly surprising when every shelf was filled with books and papers, many of them centuries old. There was a reverential atmosphere in the large and ornately decorated room, similar to that felt in cathedrals and large churches. But that, too, was hardly surprising, reflected Stark as he looked around at the shelves rising up to the high rounded ceiling. That ceiling was adorned with paintings as grand and ornate as those on the ceilings of the Vatican: imposing figures from Greek and Roman mythology, intertwined with mythical creatures.

At ground level in the enormous circular room, amidst a sea of dark wooden tables, at which students and academics sat in silence as they pored over ancient texts, Stark and Danvers stood and waited for Sir Bernard Wallis. Then Danvers whispered, 'Here he comes.'

Stark saw a tall, thin man approaching, dressed in a tweed jacket. The most noticeable thing about him was his long and bushy white beard, which hid any evidence that he might have been wearing a tie.

'We used to call him Father Christmas,' whispered Danvers. 'But that was behind his back, obviously.'

Sir Bernard reached them and held out his hand to Danvers with a smile. 'Robert,' he greeted the sergeant warmly, but they noticed that he kept his voice down to a reverential level.

He turned to Stark. 'And you must be Detective Chief Inspector Stark. Welcome.' He glanced towards the tables, where some of those working were shooting venomous looks towards them in condemnation of this sound of the human voice.

'We'll go to my office,' said Sir Bernard, dropping his voice to a whisper.

Stark and Danvers followed him out of the circular room and across a black-and-white marbled floor to a door marked *Sir Bernard Wallis*. Inside, Sir Bernard gestured them towards two padded leather chairs, both of which were laden with piles of books.

'Just take those off and dump them anywhere,' he said.

Stark lifted a pile of books off and looked around for a suitable place to put them, but saw that every available surface – the desk, shelves and the tops of cupboards – seemed to be already filled with books.

'On the floor will be fine,' said Sir Bernard.

Stark dumped the books in his hands on the carpet, next to existing piles, then sat down in the now vacant chair, while Danvers did the same.

'Good to see you again, Robert, and looking well,' said Sir Bernard. 'How are your mother and father?'

'They are both well, thank you, sir,' replied Danvers.

Sir Bernard turned towards Stark and gave him a twinkling smile. 'And you, sir, as I recall, are the man who saved the life of the King! A hero for our times, a true Cicero, but with muscular power as well as intellectual!'

Stark looked uncomfortable. 'I am afraid the newspapers are prone to exaggeration, Sir Bernard. I was just doing what I was paid to do.'

'Mon métier et mon art, c'est vivre!' beamed Sir Bernard. 'Montaigne, 1533 to1592. "Living is my job and my art!" I think you are being too modest, Chief Inspector. But forgive me, you didn't come here to listen to an old man expend his knowledge. Robert – excuse me, Sergeant Danvers – said you wished for my advice.'

'Yes, sir,' said Stark. He took the envelope from his pocket, but paused before he passed it across the desk to the distinguished bibliophile. 'Unfortunately, this letter contains an allegation against a certain person. I would have preferred to have cut out the names of the people concerned, but to do so would have reduced the document to just the barest of words, which I don't think would have given you much to go on. If you would prefer not to be compromised with this information in this way . . . after all, you are not an employee of the police . . .'

'Do you have a penny?' asked Sir Bernard.

'A penny?' asked Stark, surprised.

'Yes. Or a halfpenny will do.'

Puzzled, Stark reached into his pocket, took out a handful of coins and selected a penny. He passed the coin to Sir Bernard.

'Thank you,' said Sir Bernard, taking the coin and putting it into his own pocket. 'I am now officially in your paid employment on this issue, the transaction witnessed by Sergeant Danvers, and as such I am sworn to confidence, just as if I were a solicitor acting on your behalf. Nothing that passes between us in this room can, or will, be passed on to any other parties.'

'Thank you,' said Stark. He handed the envelope to Sir Bernard, who opened it and took out the letter. He read it through silently, then took a pair of spectacles from a case on his desk, put them on and studied the letter through them in greater detail.

'We're hoping you might be able to get an idea of the kind of person who wrote this,' said Stark.

Sir Bernard nodded, still studying the letter. Then he announced, 'A woman. Educated, and from a good family background. Independent-minded. Attractive and she knows it. Used to being in control. Mid to late thirties, at a guess.'

'You can tell all that from just these few lines?'

'It's not just what she says; it's the style of the handwriting, the curves and loops of the pen, the words she chooses, even the quality of the paper the letter's written on.' He looked at the letter again. 'If you like, I can have the paper examined, see where it came from.'

'That's very kind of you, Sir Bernard, but I think the information you've given us is already of enormous help.'

Sir Bernard folded the letter and put it back in the envelope, then returned it to Stark.

'Glad I could be useful,' he said. 'I read about the murder in this morning's later edition. So fresh, the ink was still wet. They didn't say much, just that Lord Fairfax and some American chap . . .'

As he struggled to remember the name, Stark prompted, 'Carl Adams.'

'That was the name. Said they'd been found poisoned in Lord Fairfax's flat. Dreadful.' He looked at the letter again and frowned as he asked, 'You don't think there's anything in it, do you, Chief Inspector?' He tapped the letter with a long finger. 'I mean, I know it's none of my business, but I've met Amelia Fairfax a few times at social events here at the Museum, and I must say she seems the last person in the world who'd do such a dreadful thing.'

'We're keeping an open mind on it,' replied Stark blandly. 'But we do thank you very much for your assistance, Sir Bernard. It's been of enormous help.'

Afterwards, as Stark and Danvers left the silence of the museum and stepped out into the raucous, shrill sounds of Museum Street, Stark muttered, 'Yes, all right, Sergeant, I can guess what you're thinking. If Sir Bernard had added "red hair", it would have been a description of Lady Amelia.'

'It might be better if we don't pass that information to the superintendent, sir,' offered Danvers. 'In view of his opinion that Lady Amelia is connected with the murders.'

'But why would she name herself in a letter?'

Danvers shrugged. 'To lay a false trail? At least, that's how the super might interpret it.' As they walked through the gates towards their waiting car, he added, 'Still, that's two people who think that Lady Amelia is innocent. First Winston Churchill, and now Sir Bernard. Both pretty good character witnesses, I'd say, sir.'

'Possibly,' said Stark, although he sounded unconvinced. As they reached the car, he said, 'Sergeant, you take the car back to the Yard. There's something I've got to deal with.'

Lady Amelia, realized Danvers. 'Yes, sir,' he said. 'What do you want me to do?'

'We need to find out which of the two was the real target,' said Stark. 'You can start by digging through records – build up a picture of both Lord Fairfax and Carl Adams. Their backgrounds. People they might have offended.'

'Like Gallipoli,' nodded Danvers.

'It seems implausible after all this time, but you never know,' said Stark. 'There'll be less on Adams. All I could find was the most basic detail, saying that he was from Boston and was here on business accompanying a Mr Edgar Cavendish from Indiana, and they arrived two weeks ago.'

'Not a lot of time to make enemies,' observed Danvers.

'No, but it's surprising how swiftly some people can upset others. I agree it's a long shot, but we have to investigate them both. I'll see you back at the Yard.'

FIVE

As Danvers walked across the entrance hall of Scotland Yard towards the wide marble staircase, he saw that the desk sergeant was hailing him.

'Yes, Sergeant?' he asked.

The sergeant handed him a piece of paper. 'There's a telephone message for you, sir,' he said. 'From your mother. She said it was urgent.'

Danvers took the stairs up to the office he shared with Stark two at a time, his mind racing with dreadful possibilities. For his mother to phone him at work was unheard of. In fact, she hardly ever contacted him at all, letting his sister, Lettie, be the main conduit between him and the family. What had happened? Had something happened to Lettie? Or his father?

He rushed into the office, picked up the phone and gave the operator the number of the family's Hampstead home. It seemed to take ages for the connection to be made and he was tapping his fingers impatiently on the desk and muttering a barely silent 'Come on!' when the phone was picked up and he heard his mother give the number.

'It's Robert,' he said. 'What's wrong? What's happened?'

'It's nothing urgent,' said his mother.

'But you said it was. Or, at least, that's what it said on the note the desk sergeant gave me.'

'Yes, well, I wanted to make sure you got the message. The thing is, Robert, I wondered if you'd mind calling on us.'

An awkwardness in his mother's tone gave him a feeling of unease. 'Of course not. When? And . . . is it for anything special?'

'Not really. Although . . . it may be.'

'It all sounds a bit mysterious, mother.'

His mother gave a nervous laugh. 'I don't mean it to, dear. And I'm sure it's nothing, but your father said I should call you.'

'Oh?'

'Yes. We've just read in the newspaper about this American who was killed at Lord Fairfax's.'

Immediately, Danvers was alert. 'Carl Adams?'

'Yes. That's the man.'

'What? Have you got any information about him?'

'Really, Robert. You're talking to me as if you're a policeman.'

'Mother, I *am* a policeman.'

'Yes, but you know what I mean.'

Danvers did his best to hold his impatience in check. He picked up a pencil as he asked, 'What do you know about Mr Adams?'

'We'd rather tell you in person. I don't like talking about these things on the telephone.'

'Of course,' said Danvers. 'I'll come over right away.'

'If you're sure,' said his mother doubtfully. 'I don't want to think of you shirking your duties.'

'This is my duty,' pointed out Danvers.

'Yes, I suppose it is,' agreed his mother. 'Very well. We'll see you as soon as you can get here.'

As Stark rang the bell of Amelia's house in Cadogan Square, he reflected that when he'd left it just a few hours ago, everything in his life had seemed under control. Well, as much as it could be, in view of the difficulties he and Amelia faced. But now, with the arrival of that anonymous letter, everything had fallen apart.

The door was opened by Mrs Walker, who smiled happily when she saw Stark.

'Why, Mr Stark – my apologies, Chief Inspector . . .'

'Mr Stark is fine, Mrs Walker,' said Stark coming in. 'Is Lady Amelia at home?'

'She is indeed. And terribly upset at what's happened, although she's trying not to show it.' She took Stark's overcoat and hat from him and added, 'I know she was hoping you'd let her know what had happened.'

With Stark following, she began to walk towards the drawing room to announce him, but Amelia had already heard his voice and come running into the entrance hall. 'Oh Paul! I'm so glad!'

She threw herself at him, wrapping her arms around him, and Stark held her tightly, her head buried in his shoulder. He noticed that Mrs Walker made a discreet withdrawal.

'Was it horrible?' she asked.

'Yes,' he said. 'I'm not sure how much you want to hear.'

'All of it.' She pushed herself away from him and took him by the hand. 'Let's go into the drawing room.' Then she raised her voice to call out, 'Coffee, please, Mrs Walker!'

In the drawing room she pulled him down next to her on a large settee, still clutching his hand. 'I still can't believe it!' She gestured towards a copy of *The Times* that lay on the coffee table. 'The stop-press edition. They say he was poisoned. Is that right?'

'Yes,' nodded Stark.

'How? How had someone been able to poison him? Was it this other man they said was with him? This Carl Adams?'

'No,' replied Stark. 'They were both tied up, tied to chairs. Someone poisoned them both.'

'How?'

'It looks as if someone forced the poison down their throats.'

'Was it . . . painful?'

'Yes. I'm afraid it was.'

She let go his hand and put it to her face. 'Poor Johnny,' she said quietly. 'He was brave. Dying never seemed to worry him when he was a soldier, but I don't think he would have wanted to die that way.'

'No,' agreed Stark.

'Who did it? Do you have any idea?'

'No,' admitted Stark. 'We need to look into his life, see who might have anything against him.'

Amelia gave a bitter laugh. 'You won't find a shortage of enemies, I'm afraid. There were the women he abandoned. And political enemies, of course.'

'I had a visit from Churchill. He suggested it might have been revenge for what happened at Gallipoli. An angry relative. Thousands died.'

'But that was years ago!'

'Some people have long memories. In Ireland they still want revenge for what Cromwell did at Drogheda. And that was nearly three hundred years ago.'

She fell silent, then asked, 'So where do we start?'

'With everything you can tell me about him. You were married to him; you'd know him better than most.'

She gave a rueful sigh. 'I'm not sure about that,' she said. 'He was dashing and gallant when we met, every inch the handsome hero soldier. My parents didn't like him – thought he was too flashy. My parents and I didn't get on. Sometimes I think I married him just to upset them.'

She stopped as Mrs Walker came in bearing a tray with coffee in a silver pot, cups, sugar, cream and a plate with assorted biscuits.

'Thank you, Mrs Walker,' said Amelia.

Mrs Walker gave a little bob of a bow and left. Amelia poured the coffee, added cream to hers and settled back into the settee holding the cup and saucer, her face showing her sadness as she lost herself in memories.

'Are you sure you want to hear all this?' she asked. 'After all, it's my ex-husband we're talking about. And you're my . . . well, my lover.'

'Would you feel happier talking to Sergeant Danvers?' asked Stark.

'Bobby? Good God, no!' She sipped at her coffee, then said, 'It would be like talking to some infant relative. I knew him when he was just a child.'

'He's a very intelligent infant,' commented Stark.

She shook her head. 'There's only one person I can talk about this, and that's you. In fact, sometimes I feel you're the only person who knows the real me. The only person I've ever met who does.' She fell silent for a moment, lost in thought, then she asked, 'So, what exactly do you want to know? If it's about what Johnny's been up to recently, I'll have to disappoint you. We were divorced in 1914, the year the war started.'

'How long were you married?'

'Six years. 1908. A whirlwind romance. I was twenty-two, he was forty. As I said, I think I did it as much to upset my parents as because of any feelings I had for him.'

'You must have loved him at one time,' murmured Stark.

'I'm not sure,' admitted Amelia. 'When we're young, we do things, feel things, and we put labels on them. Love. Hate. Rebellion. But half the time we don't know the real meaning of the words. They're surface emotions. When you're young, they can change overnight. Or, in my case, over a few months. I realized that the dashing hero-type that Johnny presented to the world was all there was, and suddenly I found myself wanting some depth in a relationship. That wasn't Johnny's way. Thinking, emotions – these were anathema to him. He was Mr Action. Daring, tests of physical courage. That's why the army suited him so well, as long as there was a war on somewhere he could get involved in.

'I know he was terribly upset that they wouldn't let him go into action when the war started. That was Churchill, of course. He wanted someone like-minded with him at the War Office. An old soldier.'

'So he didn't see action?'

'I think he did, but not as much as he'd have liked. He managed to persuade the War Office to let him inspect how the action was going, and – knowing Johnny – I'm fairly sure he did his best to put himself right at the front. He was like Churchill in that respect. Remember how, after the debacle of Gallipoli, Churchill went into the trenches?'

And made sure everyone knew he'd done it, thought Stark. A very public penance, seeking to resurrect his reputation with the great British public.

'I know many people blamed Johnny for Gallipoli as well. But he was the junior in any decision-making at that time. It really wasn't his fault.' Then she added sadly, 'But then again, the kind of full-frontal assault the Allies made at Gallipoli was exactly Johnny's style. Straight into the action and caution be damned.'

'Did you see much of him during the war?'

'No. Nor after it. By then I'd got deeply involved in socialist politics, votes for women, fighting for better conditions for the poor and the vulnerable. All the sorts of things that were like a red rag to a bull as far as Johnny was concerned. He was fiercely anti the Red Menace as he called it.

'Our paths would cross occasionally, at social gatherings, but I didn't really know what he was up to. We had nothing in common.'

'But it was you that his valet telephoned this morning.'

Amelia hesitated, then said, 'He still had a soft spot for me. And, I must admit, I did have fond memories of our time together at the beginning. There had to have been something there. And I know that Johnny did remark now and then to mutual acquaintances that he wished we could get back together.' She gave a light laugh. 'I don't think he really meant it, and I'm sure he only said it when he'd had a few too many brandies and got a bit misty-eyed about the past.'

'He didn't marry again?'

Amelia shook her head. 'He said I'd been his destined one.'

She shrugged. 'If you ask me, he just used that because he preferred to live a life of unfettered bachelorhood. Women still flocked to him.' She gave Stark a sad smile. 'I'm afraid that's all I can tell you. I'm sure you'll be able to get much more information about his social life from Redford.'

'Yes,' Stark said. He finished his coffee and stood up. 'I'd better get back to the Yard and see what Danvers has come up with about the other man, Carl Adams'

Amelia got up. 'Will you come back tonight?'

Stark hesitated. This was really why he'd come. Finding out from Amelia about Lord Fairfax had been important, but they were facts, and a lot of those facts he could pick up from Lord Fairfax's social circle. Especially as Amelia and Fairfax hadn't been together for some years, and it was possible that the motive for the murder might lie in recent events. No, he'd come to tell her the bad news, and he wasn't sure how she'd take it. No, he *did* know how she'd take it, and it wasn't going to be good.

'There's a problem,' he said.

'Stephen?'

'No. This.' He took the envelope with the anonymous letter and gave it to her.

Puzzled, she took the letter out and read it. As she did, a flush of anger spread over her face. 'What the hell . . .'

'That was sent to my boss, Chief Superintendent Benson, this morning.'

'But . . . but this is nonsense! Absolute nonsense!'

'I know.'

'But at least you showed it to me,' she said, giving him the envelope back.

'I had to because of what it means.'

'I can see what it means! It states it in simple terms. It accuses me of having murdered Johnny!'

'I meant because of what it means for *us*. Until we crack this case, we can't be . . . together. You and I. As lovers.'

Amelia stared at him, stunned. 'What? Why?'

'Because, as far as Scotland Yard are concerned, you are a suspect. And I'm the officer investigating the case.'

'This is ludicrous! We became lovers when you were investigating a case that I was involved in!'

'That was different. You weren't a suspect.'

'You didn't know that!'

'I did.'

'So you're saying that you suspect me. That you think this letter might be right?'

'No . . .'

'For God's sake, Paul, we were in bed together all last night. What do you think happened? That I crept out in some way without you knowing . . .'

'No, of course not!'

'Then *what*?'

'Even if I stood up and told people where you were last night, that you were with me all night, suspicion would still fall on you, suspicion that you might possibly be involved. At worst I could get demoted; at best I'd be taken off the case and replaced by another DCI – someone who might take this ridiculous allegation seriously. I can't let that happen. I have to protect you.'

'By abandoning me?' she demanded bitterly.

'It's only until we solve this case,' he said.

She shook her head, her face flushed with anger now. 'No,' she snapped. 'I know what this is really about. It's because I said I wouldn't marry you.'

'No!' he protested.

'You can't fool me, Paul Stark! You're getting rid of me because I said no.'

'That is ridiculous!'

'Is it?'

'Yes! For God's sake, Amelia, I love you! The last thing I want to do is hurt you, but this situation—'

Abruptly, she stood up. 'Get out!' she said, and he could tell she was doing her best to hold her fury in check.

'Amelia, please, calm down . . .'

'I said get out!' she repeated, and this time she said it through teeth clenched tightly in anger.

Stark sighed wearily and got to his feet. 'I'll let you know how the investigation goes,' he said.

'No need,' she almost spat at him. 'Sergeant Danvers can keep me informed.'

'If that's what you wish,' said Stark.

'That's what I wish.'

Stark hesitated, then headed for the hallway. He hoped all the time that she'd rush after him, or at least call him back, but she didn't.

He collected his hat and coat from the hallstand, put them on and let himself out. He cast one final look back towards the drawing room, but Amelia had gone.

SIX

D anvers sat in his parents' drawing room, a cup of tea balanced on a saucer in his hand, and studied them, concerned. Despite his mother's insistence that everything was 'perfectly fine', the fact that she perched stiff-backed on the edge of her chair, and his father stood by the fireplace, staring moodily into the flames as they flickered around the hot coals, told Danvers that they were both worried.

'You said you wanted to talk about the American who was murdered. Carl Adams.'

'Yes,' nodded his mother. 'Yes, we do.'

'Did you know him?' asked Danvers.

'No, but Lettie met him.'

'When?'

'About a week ago. She told us about him.'

'Why did she meet him? Was it an arranged meeting?'

'No, no, nothing like that,' said his mother. 'A social gathering.'

'It was through this character Edgar Cavendish,' said his father, speaking for the first time. 'To be honest, that's why I asked your mother to call you. I don't like Cavendish, and if there's any suggestion that he may be involved in what happened to this Adams and Johnny Fairfax, then we have to nip it in the bud before it gets too messy.'

'Nip what in the bud?' asked Danvers.

'Your father means Lettie,' said his mother. 'She seems to have got herself rather . . . involved with this man Cavendish.'

Involved? thought Danvers. Did they mean . . . ?

'If you ask me, she seems to be obsessed with him,' grunted his father unhappily, and he moved away from the fire and began to pace backwards and forwards before it, deliberately avoiding looking directly at his son. 'She can hardly have a conversation without waxing lyrical about him, as if he's some sort of demi-God.'

'Do you think there's . . . anything between them?' asked Danvers.

'There'd better not be!' growled Colonel Danvers. 'But, as I said, I don't trust the man.'

'What about the man who was murdered? Carl Adams?'

'Lettie told me she met Mr Adams with Cavendish at an art gallery, a preview of an exhibition by some painter whose name I can't recall,' said his mother.

'The Bright Young Things, they call themselves,' growled his father. 'A fast set. Loose morals.'

'Perhaps I'd better have a word with her,' said Danvers. 'I'm trying to find out all I can about this Carl Adams. She might be able to point me in the right direction. The best people to talk to, that sort of thing.'

'Perhaps you could have a word with her about Cavendish while you're at it,' muttered his father. 'She listens to you. You might be able to talk some sense into her. Heaven knows, she won't take any notice of your mother or me.'

'What do you want me to say?' asked Danvers uncertainly.

'Warn her about him, obviously,' said his father irritably.

'But I don't know him,' protested Danvers. 'I've never met the man.'

'Well, I have and I can tell you he's a bad lot,' insisted his father.

'Perhaps if you just suggested that Lettie . . . calm herself down a little over him,' suggested his mother. 'Especially in view of this murder. After all, we don't know what Mr Adams may have been involved in.'

'Someone has suggested that he wasn't the real target,' Danvers said. 'They seem to think that Lord Fairfax was the real target and that Mr Adams just happened to be in the wrong place at the wrong time.'

Suddenly, he stopped and listened as he heard the noise of familiar footsteps from the hallway.

'Lettie's home,' he said.

'Right, we'll leave you to her,' said his father curtly, and headed for his study.

Danvers looked at his mother, who shrugged helplessly. 'I'm

sorry, darling,' she apologized. 'You know what he's like. He doesn't like confrontations.'

'He didn't seem to object to them when they were with me,' commented Danvers with a hint of bitterness.

'That was different, darling. He can do man talk. Lettie's a different kettle of fish for him, especially now she's started mixing with this arty crowd.'

'What arty crowd?' demanded Lettie, coming into the room. Then she saw Danvers and rushed over to him, throwing her arms around him and giving him a big kiss. 'Bobby! What brings you here?'

'I came to see you,' said Danvers, gently disentangling himself from his sister's grasp.

'What about?'

'An American called Carl Adams. I was talking to mother on the telephone and she mentioned that you'd met him.'

'Carl!' smiled Lettie. 'Yes, indeed!' She gave a mischievous smile. 'Why, what's he been up to? Driving a car on the wrong side of the street? It seems the Americans drive on the other side of the road.'

Danvers regarded his smiling sister with a concerned look. 'You haven't seen today's newspapers?' he asked.

'No,' said Lettie airily. 'There's never anything in them but politics.' Then she stopped and looked at her brother, suddenly worried. 'Why? What's happened? Has something happened?'

'I'm afraid that Mr Adams has been killed,' said Danvers.

Lettie's hand flew to her mouth and her face went pale. She swallowed hard, then managed to stammer out, 'Wh–what about Edgar?'

'Edgar?' asked Danvers. 'If you're talking about Edgar Cavendish, nothing's happened to him. Why? Do you think it might?'

'If Carl was killed, he and Edgar were often together, so I just thought . . .' She tailed off. All the happy gaiety was gone from her now. She crumpled on to a settee, pulling a handkerchief from her sleeve and wiping her eyes. 'What . . . what happened?' she asked, her voice hoarse.

'I'll leave you two together,' said their mother gently. She went to Lettie and put a hand on her shoulder. 'I shall be in my room if you want to talk, Letitia. After Robert's gone.' With that, she withdrew.

Lettie finished dabbing at her eyes and looked piteously at her brother, her eyes brimming with tears.

'Why?' she demanded. 'Was it an accident?'

'No,' said Danvers. 'He was murdered.'

Lettie shuddered. 'Who did it?' she demanded.

'We don't know,' said Danvers. 'That's what we're trying to find out. So, for a start, we're trying to find out as much about him as we can.'

'How?' insisted Lettie. 'How was he murdered? Where?'

As gently as he could, Danvers told her of the events that had taken place at Lord Fairfax's apartment and the discovery of the bodies. He told her they'd both been poisoned, but omitted the part about the weed killer.

'We don't know who the real target was; Carl Adams or Lord Fairfax.'

'Perhaps it was neither of them. Perhaps they caught someone burgling the flat and they were killed to silence them.'

'Possible, but it doesn't look as if anything was taken.'

'Then it must have been Lord Fairfax! Carl hasn't been here long enough to make any enemies. And he was the sweetest person! No one would want to hurt him!' She began to knead her handkerchief between her hands. 'Does Edgar know?'

'I expect so,' said Danvers.

'Poor Edgar!' She got up. 'I have to go to him. Make sure he's coping!'

'Of course,' nodded Danvers. 'But before you do . . . please, Lettie, I need to know everything you can tell me about Mr Adams.'

'Hardly anything!' protested Lettie. 'I only met him a couple of times because he was with Edgar.'

'So you and this Edgar Cavendish have become . . . close?' asked Danvers tentatively.

Lettie shot him an angry look. 'What have Mummy and Daddy been saying?' she demanded.

'Very little,' said Danvers. 'I asked about Carl Adams and they said he was a friend of this Mr Cavendish, but apart from that—'

'Daddy's horrible about him!' burst out Lettie angrily.

'About Carl Adams?'

'No! About Edgar! It's because Edgar's everything that Daddy isn't. Charming, handsome, young, dynamic.'

'And what about Carl Adams?'

'As I said, I hardly knew him. He was just in the background. He was a friend of Edgar's. A business associate.'

'What sort of business?'

'Moving pictures.'

'Oh? That sounds interesting.'

'Not to Daddy. To hear Daddy talk, you'd think poor Edgar was promoting Sodom and Gomorrah.'

'Mother mentioned that you met Mr Adams at some exhibition last week.'

'Well, I think "met" might be an overstatement. We only talked briefly. He seemed to spend most of the evening talking to a young actor who was there.'

'Oh? What was his name?'

'Noël Coward. He's appearing in a play in London at the moment. *The Knight of the Burning Pestle*. It's on at the New Theatre. He plays Rafe.'

'I don't know it,' admitted Danvers.

'Rafe is the starring role, and Noël is so good in it. He's tremendously witty. An awful gossip. He's a writer as well. Daddy can't stand him.'

'I'm surprised they move in the same circles.'

'They don't,' said Letitia. 'Noël came to pick me up to escort me to a party once, and he and Daddy got talking. Or, rather, Noël did the talking while Daddy sort of glowered at him. You'd like Noël. You'd like Edgar, too. They're such fun.' She turned and looked at her brother. 'Are you investigating Carl's . . . m–murder?'

'Yes,' Danvers told her. 'That is, along with Detective Chief Inspector Stark.'

'I remember him,' nodded Lettie. 'He's nice.'

'Yes, he is,' agreed Danvers. 'Look, is there anyone you can suggest I talk to, to find out about Carl Adams?'

'Edgar's the best person,' said Lettie. Then she thought it over and added, 'And perhaps Noël might be able to help. At least he'd be able to tell you what he and Carl were talking about.'

SEVEN

Stark was still feeling the turmoil as he walked along the corridor towards his office. Was it really over between him and Amelia? Perhaps it had been too fast, anyway. They didn't really know one another, and they were from different worlds, but he had felt alive when he had been with her in a way he hadn't experienced for years. And he knew that she felt the same way. Damn whoever had written that letter!

He walked into his office and saw the note from Danvers on his desk.

Gone to my parents' house at Hampstead. They may have some information. The telephone number there is Hampstead 863.

He took off his overcoat and hung it up.

Maybe she'd cool down after a while. But what then? The same problem still remained: what to do? Would she marry him? Definitely not at this moment, and from what she'd said earlier, it seemed unlikely in the future.

His telephone ringing jerked him out of his reverie. 'DCI Stark,' he said.

'Main reception, sir,' said the duty sergeant. 'There's an American gentleman to see you. Says it's urgent. His name is Mr Edgar Cavendish.'

'Thank you, Sergeant. Please have him brought up to my office.'

Edgar Cavendish, thought Stark. *Maybe we'll get some useful information about Carl Adams.*

He settled himself down at his desk, making sure the chair opposite was clear of papers and ready for his guest, mentally running through the questions he needed to ask his visitor. He didn't have long to wait. There was a tap at his door, then a uniformed constable was ushering in a tall, well-dressed man.

'Mr Edgar Cavendish for you, sir,' said the constable.

Stark got up and took the hand the man offered.

'I'm sorry to trouble you, Chief Inspector, but I came as soon as I heard about poor Carl.'

'I was intending to seek you out anyway, sir,' said Stark. 'It's a dreadful business.'

Cavendish looked unhappy, but there was something studied about him, and Stark wondered if his unhappiness was genuine or a symptom of how he should appear. Because there was no doubt that Cavendish was very much concerned with appearances. His clothes were impeccable, from the cut of his dark suit to his expensive patent leather shoes. Light glinted off his gold tie pin, and a matching pair of gold cufflinks were delicately exposed on the broad cuffs of his immaculate white shirt. The man's dark hair was slicked back, and Stark caught the scent of pomade. The illusion that Cavendish had modelled himself on a sophisticated motion picture matinee idol was completed by his pencil-thin moustache.

Stark gestured for Cavendish to take the chair opposite his.

'What a terrible tragedy! And an awful way to die!' sighed Cavendish.

'Can you think of anyone who might have wanted to kill him?'

'No! Absolutely not! Carl was a wonderful person, never hurt anyone. And he's hardly had time to make any enemies – we've only been here in this country for two weeks. I can only assume he must have been in the wrong place at the wrong time, when this man he was with . . .' Cavendish struggled to remember the name.

'Lord Fairfax,' Stark prompted.

'Yes, that's the name. When whoever did it murdered Lord Fairfax, and poor Carl was there at the same time and had to be silenced.'

'Possibly,' nodded Stark. 'I believe you and Mr Adams were here on business.'

'Yes, that's right.'

'What sort of business, if I may ask?'

'Moving pictures,' said Cavendish.

So I was right about the matinee idol look, thought Stark. 'Oh?' he said. 'In what capacity?'

'Nothing the public would know; I'm not in front of the camera, or even remotely near it. Co-production and distribution.'

'Financing.'

'That's right,' nodded Cavendish. 'You can have the most talented actors and the most brilliant directors, but unless you can find the money to put film in the camera and build the sets, you've got nothing.' His face softened and he smiled happily as he added, 'I love what I do! Getting those ideas and images on the screen, and knowing that thousands – no, millions – of people will be watching it, it's joyous!'

'What pictures have you been involved with?'

At this, Cavendish's face lit up with a wide and proud smile. 'Why, only the biggest picture that's ever been made. *The Birth of a Nation.* You must have seen it!'

'I'm afraid not,' said Stark. 'I've heard about it, obviously, but when it came out I was . . . busy.'

'Ah yes. The war,' nodded Cavendish. 'I mentioned to someone I was coming to see you, and they told me you'd been in the trenches. And decorated, I hear. A genuine war hero.'

'I survived,' said Stark. 'That was enough.' God knows, thousands didn't, he reflected. 'Out of curiosity, who told you about me?'

Cavendish frowned, thinking, then he gave a rueful shrug. 'I'm sorry, I can't remember. It was just a conversation I was having with a few people, and someone commented about you – about being awarded a medal in France. Is it important?'

'No,' said Stark.

'I tried to enlist once America entered the war, but our government decided I was needed at home, making propaganda pictures,' said Cavendish, his tone rueful, apologetic.

'We all do our bit in different ways,' said Stark. 'What about Mr Adams?'

'Oh yes, he served,' said Cavendish. 'He was with the AEF – the American Expeditionary Force – at the Battle of Belleau Wood, although he never talked about it much.'

No, thought Stark. People who fought in the war rarely liked to talk about their experiences, except to those who were there and suffered the same. 'Do you know why he was meeting Lord Fairfax?'

Cavendish shook his head. 'He just said he had a social engagement that evening. Meeting up with an old comrade.'

Which meant that Adams and Lord Fairfax must have met at some time during the war.

'I'd be most grateful if you could let me have a list of the people Mr Adams met during the time he's been here in England.'

'There have been so many,' said Cavendish, racking his memory. 'There have been a lot of social engagements. We're trying to do deals, you see. That means meeting the people who have the money – or know the people who have the money – to put the deals together. England is a new territory for us. I don't know if you're aware of it, Chief Inspector, but the film industry is mostly based in America, France and Germany. England has a strong theatrical tradition, but it hasn't yet made that big move into making pictures. Yes, there are the English greats like Charlie Chaplin, but, let's face it, they had to go to America to get on the screen.'

'So most of your meetings have been with moving pictures people?'

Cavendish gave a light laugh. 'Not really, mainly because – as I said – there aren't that many people here making pictures. We've met the actor Leslie Howard to talk about his film production company, Minerva Films. And we went out to a studio in a place called Islington to talk to the people there who are making pictures.' He grinned. 'We met with a really cute young guy there called Alfred Hitchcock. He writes the screen titles, but I know he wants to do more. I get the impression he wants to direct. Trust me, he's one to watch for the future!' His tone became serious again as he said, 'No, most of our meetings have been with the people who've got access to the money to set up new enterprises. Industrialists. The aristocracy. Society people. Politicians.'

The worst kind of people for any policeman to want to question, reflected Stark bitterly. All of them with 'contacts' in the hierarchy at Scotland Yard, or with very influential friends in high places who would step in to protect them if the questions became too uncomfortable.

The two men talked for a while longer, Stark making notes of the names of influential people Cavendish and Adams had met, while at the same time thinking, *This is just a brick wall*. None of these people will answer any questions honestly, and there is no way we can force them to. Finally, he said, 'Well, Mr Cavendish, I think you've told us all you can for the moment. We'll obviously look into all these people . . .'

Cavendish shook his head. 'I'm sure this isn't connected with Carl in any way. None of these people would have anything to gain by killing Carl. I'm sure the real target was Lord Fairfax, and Carl just happened to be caught in the crossfire. Wrong place, wrong time.'

'You may well be right, sir. But I do thank you for coming in and giving us this information. The more we can eliminate from our enquiries, the sooner we'll get to the truth of the matter.'

Stark got to his feet and held out his hand. Cavendish shook it with a firm grasp.

'I sure hope so, Chief Inspector. I hope you get the bastards who did this.'

EIGHT

Stark sat looking at the notes he'd made following Cavendish's visit. What had he learned from him about Carl Adams? Adams had seen action in France during the war. Effectively, that was it. The rest had been about the film industry. Somehow, he couldn't see a connection between Lord Fairfax and the film business. Cavendish had used the phrase 'meeting up with an old comrade'. Amelia had told him that Fairfax did his best to get to the Front when he could. So the connection had to have been the war.

He picked up the telephone and asked the operator to connect him with the War Office in Whitehall.

'This is Detective Chief Inspector Stark from Scotland Yard,' he introduced himself. 'I'm investigating the murder of Lord Fairfax, who, I understand, had an administrative role at the War Office during the Great War. I'm trying to discover if Lord Fairfax's duties included trips to France, especially during the summer of 1918.'

The Americans had only declared war on Germany in December 1917, and their troops hadn't entered action until early in 1918. Stark hoped that by only asking about this short period he would be able to get a swift reply. He found that he was wrong. At first he was frustratingly passed from one department to another, and when he finally thought he had located the right person who could give him the information he required, he was told, 'I regret that we are unable to supply you with any information concerning the activities of the late Lord Fairfax.'

'But this is a murder enquiry,' insisted Stark.

'That may be, sir,' said the crisp, detached voice at the other end of the telephone, 'but we are not allowed to give out any information about any War Office personnel.'

'Perhaps if the Police Commissioner approached the Minister for War with the enquiry?' asked Stark, doing his best to hide his anger.

'Providing the request was put in writing, it would be considered,' said the man curtly.

I'm hitting a brick wall, thought Stark angrily. 'Thank you,' he said. 'I will certainly initiate such a request. May I have your name, please, in order to make reference to this conversation in our request?'

'We are not allowed to give out names,' said the voice.

'Then perhaps you'd give me the name of your department,' suggested Stark.

'Nor are we allowed to disclose information about departments. If a written request is submitted, it will be passed to the relevant department. Thank you. Good day.'

Stark heard the hum of a disconnected call buzzing in his ear, then he slammed the receiver down. *Bastards!* he scowled. Typical War Office bureaucrat. Safe behind a desk, building a wall against any probing into their inner workings. 'Bastards!' he said again, out loud this time, just as the door opened and Sergeant Danvers came in.

'Problems, sir?' asked Danvers.

'The War Office,' grunted Stark. 'Doing what they do best. Hiding behind regulations.' He gave a weary and angry sigh, then said, 'I hope you had better luck. Your note said your parents might have some information about the case. Which aspect? Fairfax or Adams?'

'I thought it was going to be some information about Adams; as it turned out, though, they wanted to talk about Edgar Cavendish.'

'That's a coincidence; Mr Cavendish called earlier. What did they have to say about him?'

'They don't like him, sir. My father in particular. They're very concerned about my sister, Lettie, and her relationship with him.'

'Her relationship?'

'Not in that way. At least, they hope not. They asked me if I could intervene. Get her to back off from him.'

'Good luck with that, Sergeant. From my experience, the more people are warned against someone, the more attractive that person becomes.'

'Yes, sir.'

'Were they able to tell you anything about Adams?'

'I'm afraid we didn't actually get to talk much about him, except for them to say that Lettie had met him. And when I asked her about Adams, she wasn't able to tell me much either. She suggested I talk to an actor called Noël Coward. She said Adams was talking to him at some length at an art exhibition she went to with Cavendish.'

'Do you know him? This Noël Coward?'

'No, sir. But Lettie says he's a terrible gossip. Which might prove useful.'

'Yes, indeed, Sergeant. That's a good thought. Did your sister mention where we can get hold of him?'

'Lettie says he's appearing at the New Theatre in a play. I checked and there's a matinee performance this afternoon.' He looked at the clock. 'If we left now, we might be able to have a word with him before the performance.'

'Yes, let's go.' Stark took his coat and hat from the rack, and he and Danvers headed downstairs to the motor pool. As they walked, Stark filled Danvers in about Cavendish's visit, and the fact that Adams had seen action at Belleau Wood in the war.

'So it could have been an old soldiers' reunion,' said Danvers. He frowned. 'But I thought Lord Fairfax was in a desk job, directing operations, during the war.'

'Apparently, he also went to the Front when he could. That's the information I was trying to get out of the War Office, but I hit a stone wall.'

'Why don't I ask my father if he knows anything?' suggested Danvers. 'A lot of retired generals move in the same social circles. I'm sure they must have talked.'

'Good idea,' nodded Stark. He smiled. 'It'll also give you a chance to talk to your sister on the dangers of someone like Mr Cavendish.'

Danvers scowled unhappily. 'Thank you, sir,' he said sourly.

Stark and Danvers arrived at the New Theatre in St Martin's Lane half an hour before the performance was due to begin.

'Let's hope he's not one who needs hours to get prepared for his role,' muttered Stark doubtfully. 'Perhaps we should have telephoned ahead.'

'I get the impression from Lettie that he's not one of those serious theatrical types,' said Danvers. 'According to her, he seems to treat it all as fun.'

They interrupted the stage doorkeeper from reading his newspaper, showed him their warrant cards and asked for directions to Mr Noël Coward's dressing room.

'Down the corridor, first left, then first left again. It's the second door on the right.'

'Don't you need to check with him first that he won't mind us calling on him?' asked Stark.

The doorman shrugged. 'He won't mind,' he said. 'People are popping in and out of his dressing room the whole time. He seems to love it.'

Stark and Danvers followed the directions and found themselves outside the door of a dressing room coming from which they could hear singing.

'Is it a musical?' queried Stark.

'I don't think so, sir,' said Danvers. 'The poster says it's by Beaumont and Fletcher. From what I can remember, they were writing at about the same time as Shakespeare.'

Stark knocked on the door. The singing stopped and a voice called, 'Enter, whoever you are!'

Stark opened the door, and he and Danvers stepped into the dressing room. A thin-faced young man, wearing a dressing gown ornately patterned with Chinese designs, was sitting in front of a mirror applying white stage make-up.

'Mr Noël Coward?' enquired Stark.

'I sincerely hope so; otherwise someone else has stolen my dressing room,' said Coward. 'Let me guess. Reporters?'

'Police, sir. I'm Detective Chief Inspector Stark and this is Detective Sergeant Danvers.'

'Lettie's brother!' Coward put down his make-up and got to his feet, smiling at them. 'How wonderful to meet you! Lettie has told me so much about you! A policeman!' He smiled and winked. 'Sounds like social revolution to me! Joining the downtrodden lower orders! How wonderfully proletarian!' He gave Stark an arch smile. 'Not that I've got anything against the police! They've been involved in some of my most exciting escapades.'

'I'm glad to know that we have been of service, sir,' said Stark politely.

Coward let out a braying laugh. 'Why, what an outrageous thing to say, Chief Inspector!' he chuckled.

'You're sure this isn't an inconvenient time?' asked Stark. 'We do understand you have a performance to prepare for.'

'Hardly prepare for!' pouted Coward. 'Do you know the play, Chief Inspector?'

'Er . . . no, sir.'

'You have not missed a thing. Absolutely ghastly. It's supposed to be a comedy. Well, it may have had them rolling in the aisles in 1600 and whatever, but I can assure you it is absolutely turgid. Fortunately, the audience seem happy with it, so who am I to complain?' He sat down at his dressing table again, his expression suddenly serious. 'But enough of the dreaded Burning Pestle. Lettie phoned to tell me you might be in touch. I understand this is about poor Carl?'

'Yes, sir. Carl Adams. Miss Danvers said that you were engaged in conversation with him at a recent gathering at an art exhibition.'

'Art!' snorted Coward derisively. 'The Post-Vorticists, they were calling themselves. Though, if you ask me, it was just poor old Wyndham desperately scraping by on his fingernails.'

'Wyndham?' asked Stark

'Wyndham Lewis,' said Coward. 'Do you know his work? No, I don't suppose you do. Too, too outré! And, let's face it, Vorticism died with the war.'

'Mr Adams, sir,' prompted Stark. 'What did you talk about?'

'With Carl? Why, America, of course! I have already decided it is my spiritual home. And Mr Adams is – was – involved in the moving picture business! And that is the future for we creative types – you mark my words.'

'Was he helpful?'

'Very. But cagey, you know. I'd hoped to get an invitation of some sort. You know: "When you get to the States you must come and stay with us!" The Americans are like that, very friendly. But, alas, no such invitation was forthcoming. Perhaps it might have come later.'

'What about Mr Cavendish? Did you talk to him at all?'

Coward's face creased into a look of disapproval, as if his

nostrils had suddenly detected a bad smell. 'Briefly. Now, there's a dangerous creature, I said to myself.'

'Dangerous? In what way?'

'He's so *charming*, so *nice*. Have you met him?'

'Yes. He called to see me this morning.'

'Doing his best Douglas Fairbanks impression, I expect.' Stark did his best to hide his smile. Yes, that was Cavendish to a tee. A Douglas Fairbanks copy. 'Trust me, Chief Inspector, no one is that charming and nice, not in real life. He reminds me of a cobra – all hypnotic, the perfect smile, but just waiting for the right moment to strike and devour.'

'Getting back to Mr Adams, can you think of why he might have been meeting Lord Fairfax? Going to meet him at his flat?'

'Absolutely no idea! I'd have thought their two worlds were like oil and water: the moving picture business and the military machine. As far as I know, Lord Fairfax had no interest in anything to do with the arts. I've certainly never seen him at anything, and I go to most things. It's important to be seen.'

'So you've never met Lord Fairfax yourself?'

'Oh, of course I've *met* him. But not to socialize with. Especially with that dreadful harridan hanging around him whenever I see him, like some malevolent bodyguard.'

'Which harridan would that be?'

'Theresa Ambleton. Or *Lady* Ambleton, to give her her title. Because she *loves* her title. Now there's someone – if I had a suspicious mind – that I'd be taking a close interest in with relation to the poor dear departed Lord Fairfax. My God, the woman is Lady Macbeth personified! Beneath that elegant exterior, absolutely ruthless. Completely without ruth.'

'Would you say that this Lady Ambleton and Lord Fairfax were . . . close?' asked Stark.

'*Very* close indeed. Positively intertwined. But reflect on the black widow spider, Inspector, who kills her spouse after mating.' And Coward gave a little shudder of glee.

There was a tap at the door and it opened to reveal a small boy. 'Fifteen minutes!' chirruped the boy, then he vanished, on his way to alert the other members of the cast.

'Is there anything else?' asked Coward. 'Only I need to finish applying the cake so that I am ready for my public.'

'No. Thank you for your time, Mr Coward. Your help has been invaluable.'

'Always happy to be of service to the boys in blue,' said Coward. 'Do call again!'

Stark and Danvers left the young actor to complete his make-up.

'Well, what do you think, sir?' asked Danvers.

'I think Mr Coward will go far in his chosen profession,' commented Stark.

'I meant his opinion that Lady Ambleton might have had a hand in Lord Fairfax's death.'

Stark frowned. 'Motive?' he asked.

'A woman scorned?'

'We don't know if she was scorned. Or even what her relationship was with Lord Fairfax.' He looked at his watch. 'I suggest we divide our time, Sergeant. I shall return to Lord Fairfax's flat and talk to his valet and see what I can find out about his late Lordship's life, and also ask him about Lady Ambleton. You talk to your father. The period we're interested in is from early in 1918, once the Americans came into the action. See if Lord Fairfax was in the same part of France at the time of Belleau Wood. The summer of 1918.'

NINE

W hen Redford opened the door of Lord Fairfax's apartment to Stark's ring of the doorbell, Stark noticed the valet had the use of only one arm; his left arm was kept by his side. He mentally kicked himself. *Why didn't I spot that before?* Too busy looking at the scene of the crime, or too concerned about the implication that Amelia's ex-husband had been the victim.

I allowed myself to get too involved, he remonstrated with himself. *I need to keep myself detached if I'm going to solve these murders*. And that meant pushing the complicated situation with Amelia out of his mind. It wasn't easy.

'I'm sorry to trouble you again, Mr Redford,' he said, 'but there are just a few things I need to clarify.'

'By all means, sir,' said Redford. 'Do come in.'

Stark stepped into the flat, and followed the valet into the kitchen, which appeared to be Redford's base of operations.

'Do you know yet what will happen to you?' enquired Stark. 'I assume you live in.'

'I do indeed, sir. Fortunately, I have been informed by Mr Wright, Lord Fairfax's solicitor, that Lord Fairfax has made provisions for me under his will. Not enough to stay here, but enough for me to be able to rent somewhere reasonable. I'm glad to say Lord Fairfax was a very considerate employer. Many others would not have been so lucky.'

'That is true,' agreed Stark. 'You said before that you were with Lord Fairfax before the war, and returned to his service after it.'

'Yes, sir. I was with Lord Fairfax for nine years before the war, and the three years since it ended.'

'So you knew Lady Amelia?'

'I did, sir. A most wonderful lady, in my opinion. Very fair.'

'If you were in Lord Fairfax's service for all that time, you must have become familiar with his life.'

'Familiar to a certain degree, sir,' replied Redford cagily. 'He was the master, I was the servant.'

'Of course,' nodded Stark. 'I only meant that you would have known about people he mixed with socially.'

'Not really, sir. My world was here.'

'Then you would have known the people who called on him regularly.'

Once again, Stark was aware of a hesitancy in the valet as he answered guardedly, 'Yes, sir. To a degree.'

'Mr Redford,' said Stark, 'I'll put my cards on the table. Your master has been murdered in a most horrible fashion. It is obvious to me that you had the greatest respect for him and don't wish to say anything that might sully his memory. But unless I am in possession of all the facts, I cannot do my job properly and bring the people who committed this outrage to justice. You want Lord Fairfax to be avenged for what happened to him. So do I.'

Redford studied Stark for a moment, then he said, 'I heard that you served in the war, sir. That you were in the front line of the action for the whole four years. And that you received promotions in the field and medals for bravery.'

'Who told you that?' asked Stark.

'I recall reading it in the newspapers recently when you were investigating the death of Lord Amersham.'

'Yes, I served,' nodded Stark.

'And you commanded. You were a captain.'

'In wartime promotions happened. Dead man's shoes,' replied Stark.

'My point, sir, is that you understand about loyalty in the field. I didn't see action with Lord Fairfax because his war took him elsewhere, but he was loyal to me, taking me back into his service despite a disabling injury I received. He was a good man, sir. I would *never* sully his memory.'

'I can assure you I'm not asking you to do that,' said Stark. 'I'm not interested in gossip or tittle-tattle about his life. If I want that, I can always find it. What I want is information that might help me find out who killed him, and why. People he was close to. People who might have harboured ill will towards him. For example, I understand that you telephoned Lady Amelia this morning as one of the first people to be told.'

'Yes, sir. That is correct. In fact, she was the first person I contacted after I had informed the police.'

'Why was that? I understand she and Lord Fairfax had been separated for some years.'

'It was on the instructions of Lord Fairfax, sir. He told me that if anything should ever happen to him, I was to inform Lady Amelia, his solicitor, Victor Wright, and Lady Ambleton.'

'In that order?'

'Yes, sir.'

'And did you manage to get hold of his solicitor at that early hour?'

'Lord Fairfax had left me with Mr Wright's home telephone number, sir.'

'You'd better let me have that.'

'Yes, sir.'

'And then you telephoned Lady Ambleton.'

'Yes, sir.'

'Before or after I arrived this morning?'

'Before, sir. But I waited until the police had first appeared before I made the telephone calls.'

'No other people to contact? Relatives?'

'No, sir. That will be done by Mr Wright. Lord Fairfax had a younger brother, resident in Australia. But no other family.'

'Was Lady Ambleton a frequent visitor to this apartment?'

Redford hesitated.

He's weighing up his words, thought Stark. 'Mr Redford, we have already been told that there are suggestions of a relationship between Lord Fairfax and Lady Ambleton.'

'Lady Ambleton is a widow, sir,' said Redford quickly. 'There are no suggestions of impropriety.'

'Of course,' nodded Stark. 'I ask again: was she a frequent visitor to this apartment?'

'Yes, sir, she was,' said Redford.

'When was she last here?'

'That would be yesterday, sir.'

'When Mr Adams arrived?'

'No, sir. She'd left by then.'

'Why? Wasn't she interested in meeting Mr Adams?'

'She might have been, sir, but Lord Fairfax told her that Mr Adams seemed worried about something and needed to talk to him privately.'

'Worried about what?'

'He didn't say, sir. He told her he'd make contact with her today.'

'Apart from you and Lord Fairfax, who had keys to this apartment?'

'No one, sir. Lord Fairfax was very particular about that.'

'What about enemies?'

'Enemies, sir?'

'People who wished harm to Lord Fairfax. Winston Churchill told me that he'd received death threats over Gallipoli.'

'That was true shortly after the end of the war, but there have been none that I've been aware of these last eighteen months. There was a lot of anger and resentment immediately after the war. I believe much of it has dissipated. It is also my belief that Lord Fairfax has been unfairly blamed for what happened at Gallipoli; because he is an honourable gentleman, however, he has never gone public in his defence and laid the blame where it really lay.'

'And where did it lay, in your opinion?'

'That's not for me to say, sir,' replied Redford, declaring the matter closed with his firm tone.

'What form did these death threats take?'

'Anonymous letters, mostly.'

'Mostly?'

'Some were signed.'

'Have you got any of these letters?'

Redford shook his head. 'No, sir. Lord Fairfax tore them up.'

'All of them?'

'Yes, sir. All of them.'

'How many letters were there?'

'Quite a few just after the war. Possibly a hundred. But, as time passed, there were fewer letters. As I say, sir, I haven't been aware of any these last eighteen months.'

'Very well,' said Stark. 'I think that's all for the moment, but I may wish to talk to you again. Where can I get hold of you?'

'I have been advised by Mr Wright that I may stay here until Lord Fairfax's affairs are sorted out.'

'Thank you,' said Stark. 'One last thing: the telephone numbers and addresses of Mr Wright and Lady Ambleton.'

'Certainly, sir.' Redford wrote the details on a piece of paper and passed it to Stark.

'Thank you,' said Stark. He gestured towards the telephone. 'May I use the telephone?'

'Certainly, sir.'

Stark dialled the operator and asked to be connected to Lady Ambleton's number. There were the usual clicks, then a female voice said, 'Lady Ambleton's residence.'

'This is Detective Chief Inspector Stark. Is Lady Ambleton available?'

'One moment, sir,' said the woman.

Stark heard the clatter as the phone was laid down, and footsteps on a hard floor, then voices in the distance, before the receiver was picked up again.

'Lady Ambleton.' The voice was hard, forceful.

'My name is Detective Chief Inspector Stark—'

He was cut off by Lady Ambleton snapping brusquely, 'I know who you are.'

'I wonder if I might call on you?' asked Stark.

'When?'

'Now, if that's convenient.'

'Very well. I assume you have the address.'

'I do,' said Stark.

'I shall be expecting you.'

With that, the receiver was replaced and the call ended.

TEN

L ady Ambleton's residence was a large, impressive house in one of Regent's Park's more expensive terraces, a curving arc of fifteen three-storey houses adorned with white Romanesque columns in front of the dark oak front doors. Stark ordered his driver to pull up outside number eleven, then strode to the house and mounted the steps to the door. He pulled on the ornate black handle of the doorbell set into the wall beside the door and heard it ringing inside. The door was opened by a middle-aged, nervous-looking woman wearing a floral apron.

'Yes?' she asked, the tone of her voice apprehensive.

Either she's nervous by nature or Lady Ambleton is a fearsome task master, thought Stark. Or possibly a combination of both. Having recently spoken to the Lady herself, he decided it was the latter.

'Detective Chief Inspector Stark to see Lady Ambleton,' he said. 'She is expecting me.'

'Yes, sir,' said the woman. 'Madam is in the drawing room. Please follow me.'

She took Stark's hat from him and hung it on the coat stand, but made no offer to take his overcoat. *She's not expecting me to stay for long*, decided Stark.

He followed the housekeeper along a passageway oppressively painted a dark blue, taking in the very high ceilings decorated with frescos. Whoever had designed these houses had carried the ornate Italianate Renaissance look through every aspect.

The housekeeper arrived at a door and tapped timidly at it before opening it. 'Detective Chief Inspector Stark, ma'am,' she announced.

The housekeeper stood aside to let Stark pass into the drawing room, before withdrawing with a little bob of a curtsey and pulling the door shut behind her.

Lady Ambleton stood before the marble fireplace, which was again decorated with Roman figurines. She was an imposing and attractive figure, and she knew it. Tall and thin, in her late thirties, elegantly dressed and adorned with glittering jewellery, even for this visit by someone as lowly as a detective chief inspector. She regarded him coldly, a haughty, imperious expression on her face.

'Thank you for letting me call on you, Lady Ambleton,' said Stark.

'To be frank, I'm surprised at your being involved in this case, Inspector. I thought there was some kind of rule that the police didn't investigate cases where they were emotionally involved. Conflict of interest, or something like that.' She still hadn't moved, or offered for him to sit.

'I believe you're under a misapprehension, Lady Ambleton. Two murders have been committed, and my only involvement in this case is professional.'

'Really? I'd heard that you and Johnny's ex, Amelia, were a romantic item. Surely that puts you a little close?'

This is not a woman who appears to be grieving deeply, realized Stark. Her manner was light, almost flippant.

'I do know Lady Amelia, but I'm afraid gossip and rumour seem to have escalated our acquaintance into something else,' said Stark blandly. 'In a way, it is the same thing that brings me here. It has been suggested to me that you and Lord Fairfax were close friends.'

The ghost of a sardonic smile hovered around Lady Ambleton's mouth. 'How tactful you are, Inspector,' she said. 'Yes, we were. As I'm sure you know, life in society can be difficult for a woman when she is alone. I have been a widow ever since my late husband was killed at Gallipoli.'

'I understand you were informed of Lord Fairfax's death this morning.'

'Yes.'

'Can you think of anyone who might wish him harm?'

She shook her head. 'No, Inspector. I've been thinking about that ever since I heard the news. Johnny was a happy-go-lucky person. Harmless, really. I can't think of anyone who might hold a grudge against him.'

'I believe he told you he was due to receive a visit yesterday evening from the other man who died – Mr Carl Adams.'

'Yes, he did.'

'Did he mention the purpose of Mr Adams' visit?'

'No. He just said that they would be talking privately. So I said I would leave them to it.'

'How did Lord Fairfax seem to view Mr Adams' visit? Happy? Apprehensive? Concerned?'

'Hard to tell. Johnny wasn't one for displaying his feelings. The old soldier, I suppose. Why?'

'I'm just trying to build up a picture of their meeting.'

She snorted derisively. 'I think that picture is pretty gruesome, don't you, Inspector?'

And so their dialogue went on for another ten minutes, with Stark gently probing, and Lady Ambleton stonewalling or giving one-word answers. Finally, aware that he would get no useful information from her, he nodded politely and said, 'Thank you for your time, Lady Ambleton. And my condolences to you at this difficult time.'

'Johnson will show you out,' she said. She rang a bell, and the housekeeper appeared. 'The chief inspector is leaving,' Lady Ambleton said curtly.

'Yes, ma'am.'

As Stark followed the housekeeper out of the drawing room and across the hallway towards the front door, he spotted writing on a notepad by the telephone.

'I'm sorry.' He smiled apologetically at the housekeeper. 'I believe I left my warrant card on the table in the drawing room.'

'I'll get it for you, sir,' said Johnson, eager to prevent Stark from returning and upsetting her mistress.

As the housekeeper went back into the drawing room, Stark removed the top two pages from the notepad and slipped them into his pocket.

Mrs Johnson returned, a worried look on her face. 'I couldn't find it, sir,' she said.

Stark frowned and dug into his overcoat pocket, then produced his warrant card with a rueful smile. 'My apologies,' he said. 'I was looking in the wrong pocket. Do forgive me.'

Once outside, he got into his waiting car.

'There's a telephone box two streets away,' he told his driver. 'Make for it.'

As the car moved off, he took the piece of paper he'd taken

out of his pocket and studied the writing. He was sure it was the same as in the anonymous letter, but he'd be able to confirm that once he compared the two. He smiled at how accurate Sir Bernard Wallis's description had been of the letter writer. An educated woman from a good family background. Independent-minded. Attractive and she knows it. Used to being in control. Mid to late thirties. Everything fitted. There was one other aspect to her: her late husband had been killed at Gallipoli. Was there something in Churchill's theory of revenge after all?

The driver pulled up outside the telephone box. Stark went in, put coins into the slot, dialled the operator and asked to be connected to Amelia's number. He pressed the button when she answered, hearing the coins fall.

'It's Paul,' he said. 'May I come and see you?'

'Why?' she demanded coldly.

'I've received some information I'd like to check with you.'

'About Johnny's murder?'

'Yes.' There was a long pause at the other end of the line, prompting Stark to offer, 'I can send Sergeant Danvers along if you'd prefer.'

The silence continued for a moment longer, then Amelia said, 'No. You come. When?'

'I'll be there shortly.'

ELEVEN

D anvers had taken the precaution of phoning ahead to his parents' house to make sure his father was at home. His mother had not sounded pleased when he'd spoken to her on the telephone, and the warning look on the face of Bridges, his father's valet who opened the front door to him, suggested that he would not be receiving a warm welcome.

'Madam is displeased, Master Robert,' murmured Bridges as he took Danvers' hat and coat.

'Thank you for the warning, Bridges,' Danvers muttered back. He'd always been fond of Bridges, who'd been like a friendly surrogate uncle to him when he'd been growing up, tempering with sympathy his father's often austere and disapproving attitude towards him.

'Is that Robert?' called his mother from inside the house.

Before Bridges or Danvers could reply, she'd appeared in the hallway.

'Good afternoon, mother,' Danvers smiled at her.

'You didn't talk to Lettie,' said his mother accusingly.

'I did,' protested Danvers, adding awkwardly, 'but not, I have to admit, about Edgar Cavendish. I had to prioritize, mother, and this is a murder we're investigating.'

'Yes, I know, but we're very worried. Especially your father.'

'All right, I'll talk to her after I've spoken to Father.'

'She's out,' said his mother. 'She's gone somewhere with that man Cavendish.'

'Where?'

'Some social engagement. He's using her and the people she knows to gain entry to the best houses.'

'The man's a charlatan,' added Colonel Danvers, joining them. He, like his wife, looked accusingly at his son. 'You said you'd have a word with her.'

'And I will, I promise. But right now this murder has to be my priority.'

'More than your sister's good name?' demanded his father.

'I'm sure that people are talking about her and him,' added his mother, upset.

'Lettie's not that stupid,' said Danvers.

'Yes, she is,' snapped his father. 'That man has turned her head with his talk of moving pictures. And that dreadful-smelling hair cream!'

'I *will* talk to her,' Danvers repeated.

'When?' demanded his father.

'Tomorrow,' Danvers assured him. 'I'll telephone her tomorrow and arrange to call on her. But right now, I need your help, Father.'

'Mine?' asked Colonel Danvers. 'What about?'

'The murder of Lord Fairfax and Carl Adams.'

Colonel Danvers shook his head. 'I'm not sure how I can help. I never even met this chap, Adams.'

'But you knew Lord Fairfax.'

'Of course. Our paths sometimes crossed at The Rag. The Army and Navy Club. I'd be in there, chatting to old comrades, and he'd pop in for a hand of cards. Always sociable. A good chap and a fine soldier.' He looked at his wife, then back at his son. 'Look, if this is going to be one of *those* talks, then let's go to the library. Can't be having this kind of discussion here.'

As Danvers followed his father into the library, his mother called after him, 'What about Lettie?'

'I will talk to her,' Danvers assured her. 'I promise! I'll get in touch with her tomorrow!'

He was grateful when the door of the library closed and he was alone with his father, even though he knew he was only putting off the moment. And when that moment came, he just knew that Lettie would fly at him, accusing and defensive. It would not be a pleasant experience.

'So, what do you want to know about Johnny Fairfax?' asked his father, settling himself down in his favourite leather armchair, which creaked as it bore his weight. Danvers' mother always looked in disapproval at that particular piece of furniture, at the worn and scuffed leather, urging her husband to throw it out and replace it with a newer piece, something more in keeping with the smartness of the rest of the furniture in the room.

'Nonsense!' was the colonel's standard retort. 'It's comfortable. It's grown to my shape.'

Danvers sat down on a settee. 'What do you know about Lord Fairfax's activities during the war?' he asked.

'The war? Poor chap spent most of it desk-bound. Not his fault. I know he wanted to be at the Front, but the powers-that-be had decided they needed him back in London.'

'I understand he did manage to get into the action now and then.'

'Only when he could persuade those Whitehall wallahs it was important to the war effort. But they didn't let him go often.'

'Do you know if he was in France during the summer of 1918?'

'Why do you ask?'

'We're trying to find out when he met this Carl Adams, and we're pretty sure it can only have been during the war.'

'Was this chap Adams in the action, then?'

'Yes. He was with the AEF at Belleau Wood.'

'Then that's possible,' mused his father. 'I know Johnny was at Aisne. May and June 1918. That action was close to where the AEF and the French forces were at Belleau Wood. Different outcome, of course. The damned Germans smashed the British forces at Aisne. Scattered them. Lucky the AEF were there. The AEF and the French stopped the German advance. I believe there were remnants of the British forces fighting with them. I'm pretty sure Johnny Fairfax was with them at that time. Afterwards, he was recalled to the War Office. Sat out the rest of the war behind a desk.'

Then he looked at his son with great solemnity and asked, 'Seriously, Robert, *when* are you going to have a word with Lettie?'

Stark sat perched on the edge of a chair in the drawing room, Amelia reclining on a settee. *God, I want her*, he thought as he looked at her.

How swiftly things change. Just a few short hours ago we were in this house together, in bed, lovers filled with one another, passion and compassion, two complete beings, and now we sit as separate as strangers.

Mrs Walker had made a discreet disappearance once she'd shown Stark into the drawing room. They hadn't kissed; they hadn't even touched hands. Amelia had dropped on to the settee, her look at him suspicious and resentful in equal measures.

Stark had sat down on the chair. He felt awkward. Had he really needed to come here? He could have asked his questions over the phone, except for the fact that he would be aware of a telephone operator possibly eavesdropping. And he wanted to see Amelia again in the hope that she would be less aggressive than the last time.

'You said it was about Johnny's murder,' she prompted.

'Yes. Do you know Lady Ambleton?'

'Ha! Johnny's mistress! That fascist bitch!' snorted Amelia.

So she has kept up with her former husband's relationships, realized Stark. 'Fascist?' he echoed.

'She's part of that bunch of right-wing misfits, the British Union of Patriots.'

Stark shook his head. 'Sorry, that means nothing to me. I do my best to avoid politics.'

'Nonsense! You're one of the most politically aware people I know. You were very aware of the British Communist Party when we met!'

'Most people are aware of the communists, especially after what happened in Russia,' countered Stark.

Grudgingly, she admitted, 'Yes, you could be right. These people don't exactly publicize themselves. And they're not that big. Mainly, they're just a bunch of angry right-wing aristos. They claim to be pro-British patriots, but the reality is they're opposed to almost everything. They especially hate Jews and communists.'

'So you're working for the Communist Party . . .'

'A volunteer,' she corrected him.

'A volunteer,' he conceded. 'But to these people it's the same thing. You're a communist.'

'I'm a social reformer,' she corrected him again.

Stark sighed wearily. 'So many labels. The point I'm making is that people like Lady Ambleton would have a grudge against you.'

'More than a grudge. The woman hates me. I have seen it in her eyes on the few occasions we've been in the same room.' She frowned angrily. 'As I said, Johnny loathed my involvement with the Communist Party. It struck me that he only took up with that rabid fascist because he knew it would annoy me.'

'And did it?'

'Yes. He was too good for her.'

'Would she hate you enough to send an anonymous letter blaming you for your ex-husband's murder?'

Amelia let this sink in, then she said, 'You think *she* wrote it?'

'Yes,' said Stark. 'There's the timing of the letter. It was received at Scotland Yard at about eight o'clock, before news about the murders had got into the newspapers. At first I thought that suggested that whoever wrote it may have actually been involved in the murders.'

'But now?'

'After he telephoned you this morning, Redford phoned Lady Ambleton to let her know what had happened. Your ex-husband had given specific instructions to him on whom to contact if anything happened to him. Remember, the anonymous letter didn't say anything about the other man who was murdered. Just about your ex-husband.'

He produced the piece of paper he'd taken from Lady Ambleton's telephone table.

'This is her handwriting. It looks the same to me, but I'm going to get that confirmed.'

'The bitch!' said Amelia.

'I'm still not sure why . . .' began Stark.

'I am,' said Amelia. 'Theresa Ambleton was jealous of me. Johnny was still . . . fond of me. I told you, he kept dropping hints through mutual friends that he wanted me to go back to him.'

'Hints that you ignored.'

'Our marriage may have suited him, but it didn't suit me.' She looked at Stark. 'I seem to have a problem with the men in my life. First, I had to untangle myself from Johnny. And now I have to untangle myself from you.'

'No, you don't,' protested Stark.

'Yes, I do,' insisted Amelia sadly. 'And we both know it.'

TWELVE

Stark called out, 'I'm home!' as he let himself in. Despite the emotional turmoil of the day, he felt pleased that for once he'd arrived home early enough to be able to spend time with Stephen. He was heading for the kitchen when there was a bang on the front door. He opened it and saw his next-door neighbour, Mrs Pierce, looking worried.

'I saw you come in, Mr Stark,' she said. 'Just to tell you, not to worry, I've got Stephen with me.'

'Worry?' repeated Stark.

Suddenly, he saw a car pull up at the kerb and his mother, Sarah, got out with Dr Lomax.

'What's happened?' he demanded.

'Yes, well . . .' began Mrs Pierce, but she was cut off by Sarah Stark.

'It's your dad,' she said. 'He's upstairs, Doctor!'

Dr Lomax nodded and hurried into the house, clutching his large leather medical bag.

'I'll get back to Stephen,' said Mrs Pierce. 'Call me if you need me.'

Stark followed his mother into the house, stunned. 'What's happened?' he asked again.

'Your dad's been coughing up blood. It's more than just the usual.'

'So he called Doctor Lomax after all.'

Sarah shook her head. 'I did,' she said. 'He didn't want me to. But I knew he was really bad this time.'

'Why didn't you use the telephone?'

'I don't like that thing. Anyway, I didn't have Doctor Lomax's phone number. It was just as easy for me to run up the road and fetch him.'

'He's six streets away!'

'Will you stop going on about it! Your dad's badly sick!'

Stark subsided. 'I'm sorry, Mum.'

It wasn't his mother's fault. She was of a generation that didn't understand the new technologies. Like many, she was scared of them. And she was scared because of what was happening to her husband. So she'd acted the best way she knew: run for the doctor.

Henry must be really ill. He always adamantly refused to go to a doctor, preferring to treat any ailment with a patent medicine from the chemist, or let Sarah care for him.

'Doctors are a waste of money,' he insisted. 'All they do is charge you to tell you what you already know is wrong with you.'

It was no use trying to tell him, as Stark had often done, that modern doctors weren't like the quacks of Queen Victoria's time, when Henry Stark had been a young man.

'It's all right for you,' Henry had snapped at Stark during one of their arguments. 'You've got that medical insurance with the police. Us ordinary people have to pay!'

Stark stood with his mother at the bottom of the stairs, listening.

'I ought to go up,' she said. 'In case your dad can't speak.'

Stark put his hand on her arm. 'Let's wait and see if Doctor Lomax needs help,' he said.

They heard the sound of the bedroom door opening and closing, then Dr Lomax appeared down the stairs. He looked grave. 'He's got complications.'

'What sort of complications?' asked Stark.

'In addition to bronchitis, he's also got pleurisy and pneumonia.'

'Oh God!' Sarah Stark fell back against the banisters. 'He's going to die!'

'He has a chance, but he needs to go to hospital. Have you got a telephone?'

'In the passage,' said Stark, and he pointed Lomax towards it, then went to his mother and supported her into the kitchen, where he sat her on a chair. He'd never seen her in such shock.

'It doesn't mean he's going to die, Mum,' he said.

'Pneumonia,' said Sarah. 'That's the one that kills 'em.'

Yes, it did, Stark admitted silently to himself. Some even called it 'the old man's friend', because it usually ended the suffering of the elderly and frail. But Henry wasn't frail, Stark thought angrily. He was a stubborn, angry old bastard!

Sarah was doing her best not to cry, her face screwed up and her hands clenched tightly together. *She's staying strong for him*, Stark realized.

Dr Lomax returned. 'They're sending an ambulance. He'll be taken to University College Hospital.'

'Thank you, Doctor,' said Sarah, gritting her teeth in an effort to hold herself together. 'How much do I owe you?'

Lomax waved her away. 'We'll sort that out later,' he said.

'You know us, Doctor. Henry likes to pay as we go.'

'For this one, no charge,' said Lomax. He headed for the door. 'I'll check with UCH later and see what news there is.'

As the door closed behind him, Sarah turned to Stark. 'Stay here in case your dad calls. I'm going next door to tell Mrs Pierce what's happening and ask if she can look after Stephen till I get back from the hospital.'

'I'll go with Dad,' said Stark.

Sarah shook her head. 'I'm going with him,' she told him firmly. 'He'll be frightened in the ambulance without me.'

'Frightened?' queried Stark. 'Dad?'

'You don't know him like I do,' said Sarah. 'He's got his fears. Hospitals and ambulances is one. I'm going with him.'

'So am I,' said Stark.

She looked as if she was going to argue, but then nodded. 'All right. Just in case there's papers to fill in.'

She left the house, and Stark hurried up the stairs to his father. As he opened the bedroom door the smell assailed him: the overpowering odour of sickness mingled with sweat. Henry lay in the bed, propped up by a small mountain of pillows to try to stop him choking from the fluid in his lungs. The pillows and the sheet were stained red with blood, and Stark realized how much discomfort his father must have been in as he thrashed about, the pain from the harsh cough taxing his body. Henry's eyes were closed, but they flickered open as he heard Stark come in. His lips fluttered as he tried to talk, but no sound came out, just a rasping wheeze.

'Don't try to talk,' said Stark.

'I . . . don't want to . . . go to . . . hospital,' his father forced out, his face showing that every syllable was a painful struggle.

'You'll die if you stay here,' Stark told him.

'I'll die if . . .' Henry never completed the sentence. He was racked by a paroxysm of coughing that jerked his body violently around in the bed, and Stark saw more blood splutter out from his mouth and dribble down.

Stark took his handkerchief from his pocket and moved forward, wiping the blood from his father's chin. 'Rest,' he said.

A sound between a groan and a wheeze came from his father, and then there came a wet rattling sound from deep down in his lungs.

He's drowning, realized Stark. He'd seen it during his time in the trenches, heard that same sound, the lungs and the pleural sac outside the lungs filled with fluid, wet pus and blood clots. Stark took hold of his father beneath his armpits and tried to haul him higher up in the bed, trying to help keep the fluid down to the bottom of his lungs. It's what he'd seen the nurses do in the hospital he'd been in. Not that it saved them, but it bought time.

'Don't die, Dad,' he urged him. 'You've been a fighter and a miserable sod all your life. Keep being one now.'

THIRTEEN

Stark and his mother sat side by side on the hard wooden bench in the hospital waiting area. They'd been here for almost two hours, ever since the ambulance had pulled up and white-coated orderlies had unloaded Henry and, with a nurse in attendance, had taken the trolley bearing him to the lift and into the inner workings of the hospital. Stark and Sarah had been

told to wait and the doctor would be with them. It was now nine
o'clock and there had been no sign of a doctor. No, that was not
true: there had been many sightings of doctors, and nurses, and
sisters and matrons, but none apparently looking for them.

Stark rose and went to the reception desk and asked the nurse
on duty, who greeted him as coldly and stiffly as her starched
blue-and-white uniform, if there was news on Henry Stark.

'I'm his son, Detective Chief Inspector Stark,' he said, and he
produced his warrant card for her. Sometimes it helped. In this
case, she didn't even look at it.

'The doctor will report to you as soon as there's something
to tell you,' she said.

Stark returned to sit next to his mother. 'She doesn't know
anything,' he reported sourly.

'They're very busy,' said Sarah.

Stark was surprised at how calm she seemed. Her husband of
– what was it? – forty years was possibly dying, yet she sat
waiting patiently, as if she was waiting for a bus. But then, he
reflected, his mother had always been the quietly strong one.
Because Henry had the loud voice and the temper, people tended
to think of him as the dominant one in the marriage. And yes,
Henry did get his own way most of the time by scowling and
growling and dark looks. But on things that really mattered, Stark
remembered, especially where Stephen was concerned, his mother
usually got her way.

But why hadn't she got her way with Henry's bad health? Yes,
she had got an ambulance for him this time, but how many times
before had she tried to get him to see the doctor, and he'd flatly
refused?

'It's because of the money,' vented Stark in frustration.

'What is?' asked Sarah.

'Not seeing a doctor before!' said Stark, angry. 'Everything's
about the money with him!'

Sarah shook her head. 'He says it's about the money and
doctor's bills, but it isn't. When he was growing up, people who
went into hospital didn't come out. It was a place people went
to die. As happened with his mum and dad. And now he's old
like them, he's scared that's what going to happen to him.'

'He wouldn't be here if he'd seen Doctor Lomax before!'

'I'm not sure if Doctor Lomax could have stopped this

happening. Your dad's always had bronchitis in the winter. What with the damp and the fog lately . . .' She stopped and looked around the waiting area, and the other people sitting, like them, on benches, or standing, waiting.

'I should have come home this morning before I went to work,' said Stark, angry at himself. 'I meant to. I would have seen what was happening and done something about it.'

'He wasn't as bad first thing,' said Sarah. 'He went down about lunchtime. He couldn't eat anything – that's when I knew he was bad. And then he started to get worse. Sweating. Coughing.'

'I should have come home last night,' said Stark. 'I might have been able to persuade him to let me call Doctor Lomax.'

'You wouldn't,' said Sarah glumly. 'Your dad's too stubborn.' She looked enquiringly at Stark. 'So how's it going between you two?'

He nodded, but sighed. 'Up and down,' he said.

'Do you love her?'

'I do, Mum. If you met Amelia, I'm sure you'd like her.' He added sourly. 'Dad wouldn't, of course. All he can see is the class thing. She's upper-class and out of our league.' He snorted.

He heard a chuckle, and looked at her, surprised to see a smile on her face. 'When it comes to class, your dad's got a short memory.'

'What do you mean?'

'When he and I first met, his parents didn't approve of me. They thought I was low because of my family. Too low class for your dad.'

'Why?'

'We lived in Somers Town. Back then it was a real hole. The police would never come in there. Too scared. And my brothers were tearaways.'

'I know you said they were bare-knuckle boxers.'

Sarah laughed. 'They were, and a bit more. They were more fighters than boxers. Illegal. And that wasn't the only illegal thing they got up to. Nothing really serious, not hurting people, but there was thieving. They were wild. It comes from not having a dad to handle them.'

'But I met your dad,' said Stark. 'All right, I was young, but I remember him. He was a bit unsteady on his legs, but I remember you told me he wasn't well.'

'He'd been "unwell" all his life. Ever since he started drinking when he was a kid. He spent most of his time in the pub or in the street. So the boys grew up on their own. They were too much for my mum. Anyway, what I'm getting to is that my family had a bad reputation, and when your grandfather – your dad's dad, that is – heard that your dad wanted to marry me, he threw a fit. "No one from that family's coming into this one!" he shouted. I know, cos I was outside waiting for your dad to hear how he reacted, and I heard him. I reckon the whole street heard him.'

'So what happened? What made him change his mind?'

'He didn't. Not until he heard I was expecting you. Henry told him he was old enough to know his own business, and he was getting married to me with or without his dad's blessing. So your grandad said if that was the case, he didn't have a son no more.

'So me and your dad got married and set up in rooms near King's Cross station. And your grandad was as true as his word: he never came near us. But your gran did. She used to make secret visits to make sure we was all right. And then, when we found out I was expecting, we told her. And she went and told your grandad, which was pretty brave of her, because your grandad was a hard man and she knew he'd give her a hard time when he found out she was coming to see us behind his back.'

Stark remembered his grandfather, Jeremiah Stark. A huge intimidating figure, a blacksmith who smelt of soot and ashes and burning metal. Stark remembered, as a child, watching Jeremiah at his anvil, hammering at a red-hot piece of metal, sparks flying through the clouds of black curling smoke that filled the wooden barn of a forge.

'And did he?' asked Stark.

'As it turned out, he didn't. She told me later he just went quiet and left without a word. Next thing, he turns up at our rooms and asks how we are. Not a word about not having seen us or even mentioned us for a whole year.'

Stark nodded. 'Grandad could be stubborn.'

'And your dad's the same. And so are you. I've never known a family with such men as you three: stubborn and pig-headed. And I think Stephen's going to be the same.'

'It's not a bad thing,' said Stark awkwardly.

'It is when it means you don't talk to one another,' retorted his mother. 'So, are you going to marry her?'

'I would if I could.'

'What does that mean?'

'She doesn't want to marry me.'

'Why?'

'She says she wants to be sure before she gets married again. Her first marriage was a disaster. She says we haven't known each other long enough yet.'

'She makes sense,' said Mrs Stark.

'Maybe, but even if she agreed, where would we live? I don't want to take Stephen away from here and you and dad, but I can't see us living in her house.'

'Get another house, one close to us, and we can share Stephen.'

Stark hesitated, thinking it over. It was a possibility, one he hadn't thought of before. But how would Stephen take to it? Or Amelia?

Suddenly, he was aware of a doctor walking towards them across the marbled floor.

'Mrs Stark?'

They both stood up, and now Stark saw the anxiety etched on his mother's face.

'I'm Doctor Meek. We've stabilized your husband, Mrs Stark. We've drained the fluid from the inside and outside of his lungs.'

'Is he going to live?'

Meek hesitated. 'To be honest, it's too early to say. He's very weak. As you may know, pneumonia fills the lungs with fluid, and pleurisy adds more fluid in the pleural cavity outside the lungs. When you add in bronchitis, all three make breathing a very painful process and cuts down the amount of oxygen circulating in the body, which, in turn, affects the heart.' He gave an apologetic smile. 'I'm sorry if this sounds like a medical lecture, but I think you ought to know the reality of the situation.'

'Yes,' nodded Sarah. 'Should I stay here the night? In case . . .'

'It's hard to say, Mrs Stark. At the moment he's sleeping and comfortable. The testing time will come in the small hours of the morning. That's when the body's at its weakest. But, in your husband's case, it's hard to predict. What I will say is that he's one of the most stubborn men I've ever treated. To be frank, I would have expected him to be dead after what he's gone through, but he refuses to die. He must have very strong willpower.'

You can say that again, thought Stark.

'My advice is for you to go home and get some rest. If there is any change, we have your telephone number.'

'Thank you,' said Sarah.

'Can I also give you my telephone number at work,' said Stark. 'I'll telephone to see how he is in the morning, but this is in case you need to get in touch tomorrow.'

He handed the doctor one of his cards. Meek glanced at it and was about to put it in his pocket when he stopped and read it again. 'Of course! Chief Inspector Stark! You're the man who saved the life of the King!'

'I'm afraid the newspapers exaggerated my role in the situation,' said Stark apologetically.

'Nevertheless, that was a very courageous thing you did. It must have been nerve-wracking.'

Stark was tempted to say not as nerve-wracking as four years in the Flanders trenches, but he bit his tongue. 'Thank you for all you are doing for my father, Doctor,' he said. 'We'll be in touch in the morning.'

FOURTEEN

S tark made his telephone call to the hospital as soon as he woke at six the next morning, and was able to tell his mother that Henry had had a comfortable night.

'Though the hospital's idea of a comfortable night can be different from the patient's,' he added, remembering his own painful time in hospital recovering from the wounds he'd received in the war.

While Sarah made breakfast, Stark went next door to collect Stephen from Mrs Pierce's house, where he'd spent the night sharing a bed with her six-year-old son, Eric.

'He kept having these dreams and kicking me all night,' grumbled Stephen.

'Don't worry, you can sleep in your own bed tonight,' Stark promised him.

'Will Grandad be home tonight?' asked Stephen.

Stark and his mother exchanged glances, then Stark said, 'Even if he isn't, one of us will be at home with you tonight.'

When Stark's car arrived to take him to Scotland Yard at half past eight, he announced, 'We'll drop you off at school first, Stephen, and then I'll take your grandma to the hospital.'

'I can walk there,' said Sarah. 'It ain't far.'

'I've got the car,' said Stark. 'Let's use it.'

'But it's an official car,' Sarah pointed out.

'And I'm going to Scotland Yard on official business, and on the way I'm calling in at the hospital to see how Dad is. So, you might as well come with me.'

'Huh, you're as pig-headed as your dad,' grumbled his mother.

Stephen beamed. 'The other kids will be so jealous when I turn up in a police car!'

The latest report on Henry, when they got to University College Hospital, was the same as earlier that morning: Henry had had a comfortable night.

'Can I see him?' asked Sarah.

The nurse at the reception desk pointed at the notice listing visiting hours: ten to ten thirty, three till four and seven till eight in the evening. It was now ten to nine.

'I'll wait,' said Sarah, and she headed for the wooden bench where she and Stark had sat the night before. Stark followed her and offered her five shillings.

'What's this for?' she asked, looking suspiciously at the coins in his hand.

'So you can get a taxi home. There are always taxis outside.'

She shook her head. 'I'll walk,' she said.

'It's over a mile,' he pointed out.

'That's nothing,' she said. 'What do you think we did before you had money for taxis? I walked everywhere.'

'Yes, but you were younger then.'

'I can still walk as far as you can.'

Stark sighed and put the coins back in his pocket. 'You're as stubborn as Dad,' he said.

'And don't you forget it,' said Sarah.

Stark accepted defeat and returned to the waiting car.

'Trouble, sir?' asked the driver, Joe Brown, nodding at the hospital.

'Always,' said Stark with a sigh.

Stark sat at his desk, reading through the notes he'd made on the case.

'Gallipoli's the motive,' Churchill had said. Could there be something in that? Fairfax had received death threats because of what had happened at Gallipoli, though not for well over a year. But people with a burning desire for revenge had long memories. The problem was that those threatening letters had been destroyed; any evidence to identify potential vengeful assassins had gone.

There was Lady Ambleton, of course, whose husband had been killed at Gallipoli. What was it that actor chap, Coward, had said of her? 'If I had a suspicious mind, there's someone I'd be taking a close interest in with relation to the poor dear departed Lord Fairfax. Beneath that elegant exterior, absolutely ruthless . . . And reflect on the black widow spider who kills her spouse after mating.'

Was it possible that Lady Ambleton had been involved? There would have been no need for any break-in; she would have been admitted to the flat by Fairfax.

He shook his head. No, it was too convenient.

The office door opened and Danvers entered. 'Good morning, sir.' He looked at the clock, which showed ten past nine. 'Sorry I'm late, sir. I've been trying to get hold of my sister, but she's not taking my telephone calls. I think she suspects my parents have asked me to talk to her about Edgar Cavendish. However, I did talk to my father.'

'And?'

'Lord Fairfax was in the same area of France, and at about the same time as Carl Adams was at Belleau Wood. So it's quite possible they met there.'

'The link,' nodded Stark. 'But why would they be meeting up now? Carl Adams deliberately sought out Fairfax.'

'Was Lord Fairfax's man, Redford, able to throw any light on why they met?'

'No,' said Stark. 'But I then went on to call on Lady Ambleton.'

Stark produced the piece of notepaper he'd taken from Lady Ambleton's hall table and passed it to Danvers. Danvers frowned, then went to the evidence file and took out the anonymous letter.

'Yes, I've checked. The handwriting's the same,' said Stark.

'But why would she do that?' asked Danvers, puzzled.

'Jealousy,' said Stark. 'Apparently, she hated Lady Amelia and resented the fact that Lord Fairfax still harboured feelings for her.'

The shrill ringing of the telephone broke their thoughtful mood. Stark picked up the phone. 'DCI Stark.'

'Paul, it's Billy Hammond from Finsbury Park.'

'Yes, sir. What can I do for you?'

'You can start by cutting the "sir",' said Hammond.

'You are my superior officer, Superintendent,' Stark pointed out.

'In this case, Paul, I'm calling as an old friend. I've got a problem I'd like to run past you.'

'What is it?'

'It's a murder, and on the surface it looks clear-cut. We've got the man who's supposed to have done it in custody, we had a witness . . . but there's something that hits me as not quite right.'

'In what way?'

'I'd rather tell you about it face to face,' said Hammond.

The telephone operator, realized Stark. All telephone calls went through one of many switchboards spread around London, and it was well known that switchboard operators often listened in to telephone calls, usually for their own amusement and to pick up titbits of information and gossip, some of which they might be able to sell to the newspapers.

Stark hesitated. 'I've got a big case on at the moment, Billy . . .'

'I know. Lord Fairfax and the American. I wouldn't bother you but I'm sitting on a bit of a powder keg with this one, Paul. There's been a lot of trouble on the streets lately, and I'm worried it could all erupt into a large-scale riot if I make the wrong move.'

'I'll be there shortly.'

'Thanks.'

Stark hung up. 'That was Superintendent Hammond at Finsbury Park. He wants to see me about something.'

'To do with this case?'

'I don't know. But if Superintendent Benson asks where I am, tell him we think it may be.' He hesitated, wondering whether to bring Danvers into the situation with his father, but then decided he couldn't avoid it if things went wrong. 'The other thing is, my father was taken into hospital last night.'

'Something serious, sir?'

'Pleurisy, pneumonia and bronchitis.' Stark saw Danvers blanch at this, and nodded. 'Yes, it's not good. They removed fluid from his lungs, but they're keeping him in. I'm only telling you in case the hospital telephone for me while I'm out.'

'I'll take a message.'

'They might not leave one, if it's . . . bad news. Just give them the telephone number at Finsbury Park.'

'Yes, sir. I'm sorry, sir. If there's anything I can do . . .'

'Just hold the fort until I get back. Go through everything we've got again – all the notes, all the gossip we've picked up. We're still trying to find out which one of them was the real target. And get in touch with the War Office and see if they ever had any threatening letters about Gallipoli.'

'Gallipoli, sir?'

'Yes. Remember, Churchill said that he believed the reason for the murders was revenge for the disaster at Gallipoli. That he and Fairfax had both received death threats. Redford confirmed that Fairfax had received death threats over it, but not for eighteen months. And all the ones he'd received had been destroyed. There's a chance that whoever wrote to him may also have written to the War Office expressing their anger, and the War Office usually keeps every bit of paper that comes into it.'

'Right, sir,' said Danvers.

'One word of warning, Sergeant. If my experience earlier is anything to go by, trying to get the War Office to cooperate with us on this will be like getting blood out of a stone. It's highly likely they'll refuse to admit that there even was a battle at Gallipoli.'

'I'll do my best, sir,' Danvers promised.

In the car on the way to Finsbury Park, Stark thought about Billy Hammond. He and Hammond went way back. Hammond had been newly promoted to inspector at Camden Town station when Stark joined the force as a trainee copper. He'd been tough, but fair. Too fair for some who'd made a tidy sum taking bribes from thieves to avoid them being arrested, before Hammond stepped in. Taking bribes was banned. Anyone found doing it would be sacked – and also prosecuted. At first some of the older hands thought it was just a bluff, the new inspector throwing his weight about, or maybe doing it to get a slice of the action. They were wrong, and as some of those older hands left, or took early retirement, the nature of Camden Town station changed. They were thief-takers again. People who stopped crime, not those who took part in it.

Soon, Hammond's reputation grew. He was promoted again: chief inspector. But just when it seemed he would be moving to the hallowed halls of Scotland Yard, his career seemed to stall. Stark was one of the few who knew the reason. Hammond had caught a superintendent out in a corruption scandal, and tried to have him jailed. To the top brass, jailing a senior officer was unthinkable. It was one thing to dismiss lowly constables caught with their fingers in the till – it showed the police were taking action to root out the rotten apples in the force – but to prosecute a superintendent could ruin the reputation of the Metropolitan Police in the eyes of the public. And so the superintendent retired 'due to ill health', and Hammond was given a promotion, this one to superintendent of the North London Division, and based at Finsbury Park. It was as far as they could move him away from the centre of the action at Scotland Yard and still keep him in the boundaries of the Metropolitan area.

Hammond had accepted his fate. He wanted to be a policeman, a *good* policeman. Being a policeman, guarding society, he'd told his younger officers like Paul Stark, was the best job in the world. You protected the weak.

The force needed more officers like Billy Hammond at its heart in Scotland Yard, reflected Stark. But the powers-that-be weren't keen on mavericks who didn't toe the party line. *Maybe that's what lies in store for me*, thought Stark. Superintendent in some remote part of London bordering on the countryside. Well, maybe that wouldn't be too bad. A whole new life with Stephen, and possibly Amelia.

He shook his head. *Get real, Paul*, he told himself bitterly.

Billy Hammond greeted him warmly as he stepped into Finsbury Park police station. 'I'm glad you could make it,' he said.

'It sounds very mysterious,' said Stark. 'What's the issue?'

'Let's take a walk,' said Hammond. 'We can talk outside.'

Stark followed Hammond out of the building and waited until they were strolling along the High Street before he asked, 'Trouble in the station?'

'I don't know,' admitted Hammond. He took a copy of the *Daily Target* from his coat pocket and passed it to Stark. 'I don't know if you've seen this?'

Stark shook his head. 'It's a paper I do my best to avoid. Gossip, lies, half-truths and hate-filled propaganda wrapped up in a Union Jack.'

'True. And today it's anti-Jewish.' He gestured at the paper. 'Page two. A man called Israel Rothstein, a Jewish factory owner who the *Target* says brutally murdered a hard-working trade union official.'

Stark opened the newspaper and scanned the story. 'The *Target* taking the side of a trade unionist? Isn't that supporting Bolshevism in their eyes?'

'The *Target* uses whatever it wants to keep its message emotive,' said Hammond. 'Mr Rothstein is the owner of a small clothing firm who's supposed to have beaten a trade union official to death.'

As they walked, Stark read the report. According to the newspaper, Israel Rothstein, the Jewish owner of a clothing factory, had been heard having a fierce argument with a popular trade union official called Harry Jukes. The argument had got violent, and Rothstein had beaten Harry Jukes to death with a heavy iron doorstop. A witness who'd heard the argument had called the police, and when the beat constable arrived on the scene, he found Jukes dead, his head bashed in, and Rothstein unconscious, the bloodstained doorstop clutched in his hand. The constable presumed that Jukes had managed to get in one final blow that knocked Rothstein out, before collapsing and dying from his injuries.

'Who was this witness?' asked Stark, handing the newspaper back to Hammond.

'He was a tramp who said he'd gone into the factory to get warm. He said he didn't see the fight, but he heard it. Rothstein and Jukes shouting at one another in the office, and then he heard what sounded like a fight break out. So he left the factory and found a beat copper and told him what was going on.

'The beat constable went with the tramp into the factory and into Rothstein's office, where they found Jukes dead and Rothstein lying in a daze on the floor.

'The constable went to get help, and the tramp scarpered. The constable guessed he didn't want to get involved. Tramps do their best to avoid getting involved with the law.'

'But he made sure he got the law involved before he vanished.'

Hammond nodded. 'Exactly. It's all too pat. And it's not just this case. There's been some stirring up lately – having a go at Jews locally. Attacks on their shops, that sort of thing.'

'Organized?'

'Have you ever heard of an outfit called the British Union of Patriots?'

Stark frowned. 'Not before yesterday. Why? Do you think they're behind these attacks?'

'They've started to be active in the area, holding meetings, mainly about how the Jews are taking over everything. Officially, they're just another political outfit, like the communists, but they're a bit more rabble-rousing.'

'More rabble-rousing than the communists?' queried Stark with a smile.

'Yes, all right,' said Hammond ruefully. 'We've all heard the speeches about the revolution and blood in Park Lane. But this BUP lot seem more targeted.'

'Against Jews?'

'Jews. Chinese. Anyone who's not British.'

'Most Jews *are* British. They've been here for years.'

'True, but since the revolution in Russia there have been a lot more arriving. And, of course, they move into areas where there are already plenty of Jews.'

'I'm still not sure how I can help in this case,' said Stark doubtfully. 'I'm guessing, as we're walking, it's something to do with the station.'

Hammond nodded. 'My gut feeling is that the clothing firm owner has been set up. The question is, is anyone inside the station a part of it?'

'The beat constable?'

'Constable Danny Fields,' Hammond nodded. 'The business of the tramp is too pat. I'm not saying it's not possible – tramps disappear all the time. But there was something about Fields when I asked him for his report – something in his manner – that made me wonder if there wasn't something more going on.

'The thing is, Paul, Harry Jukes, the trade union bloke who was killed, was very popular around here. If I do the wrong thing, we could end up with riots in the streets, either from angry Jews or from an angry mob who hate Jews looking for vengeance.'

'So you want me to have a word with this Danny Fields and see if I reach the same conclusion.'

'Yes,' said Hammond. 'Or am I seeing bad things when there's nothing wrong?'

'I'll talk to him, but there's no guarantee I'll be able to do any better than you.' He looked questioningly at Hammond. 'What makes you suspect him?'

'Better I don't say anything because it might colour your attitude towards him.'

'You don't like him?'

'No, but I want to be fair. It may just be prejudice against him on my part.'

'All right, I'll talk to him,' said Stark. 'Is he at the station?'

'Yes. I've asked him to wait.'

'Before I talk to him, I'd like to have a word with this Mr Rothstein to get his version of what happened.'

'Gallipoli,' said Danvers wearily. This was the fifth person he'd been put through to at the War Office. He was now talking to someone from Correspondence Archives, who had refused to give his name, and was asking the reason Danvers had been put through to him. 'My name is Detective Sergeant Danvers from Scotland Yard and we are investigating the murder of Lord Fairfax, who worked at the War Office. We are trying to ascertain a motive for his murder. It has been suggested that the root cause may lay in the Dardanelles campaign.'

'I don't see how,' said the voice coldly.

'That is what we are trying to establish,' explained Danvers patiently. He turned as the door of the office opened and a uniformed messenger entered. Danvers held up a hand, asking the messenger to wait as he asked, for what seemed to him the umpteenth time, 'Do you have in your files any threatening letters that may have been sent to the War Office from relatives or friends of those who died at Gallipoli?'

The person at the other end of the telephone replied coldly, 'If any such letters were received, that information would be classified.'

'Then how . . . ?' began Danvers.

'I'm sorry, I am not allowed to discuss this matter,' said the voice.

There was a click, then the hum of the dialling tone as the very unhelpful War Office official hung up. Danvers sighed and replaced the receiver, then turned to the messenger. 'Yes?' he asked.

'I've been sent from Chief Superintendent Benson to find DCI Stark.'

'I'm afraid he's out at the moment. Can I help?'

'I don't think so. CS Benson specifically asked for DCI Stark.'

'He's gone to Finsbury Park police station,' said Danvers.

'Thanks,' said the messenger. He was about to leave, when he stopped and said, 'I couldn't help but hear you asking about Gallipoli.'

'The War Office,' sighed Danvers. He gestured at the telephone. 'No one there wants to talk about it.'

'If you want to know about Gallipoli, you ought to have a word with Ted Bell down in Records,' said the messenger. 'He was there. He'll tell you all about it.' He grinned. 'Once you get him started on it, it's hard to get him to stop.'

There were four holding cells in the basement of Finsbury Park station. An elderly man in a crumpled suit was sitting forlornly on a bench inside one. He had a bandage around his head, and Stark could see where the blood had dried and crusted at the fabric's edge.

'You come to let me go?' asked Rothstein hopefully, pushing himself to his feet as the turnkey opened the door to the cell and Stark and Hammond entered. Rothstein was short and overweight, and he swayed as he stood looking at them.

'Not yet, Mr Rothstein,' said Hammond. 'Please, you can sit down. How's your head?'

Rothstein put a hand to his bandage. 'It's not bad. I've had worse headaches. Have you told my Becky? My wife? She worries about me.'

'Yes, we've informed Mrs Rothstein,' Hammond did his best to reassure him. He gestured towards Stark. 'This is Detective Chief Inspector Stark from Scotland Yard. He's come to ask you some questions.'

'Scotland Yard?' echoed Rothstein, a touch of awe in his voice. 'This is that serious?'

'It's murder, Mr Rothstein,' said Hammond. 'It doesn't get more serious than that.'

'I didn't murder him!' protested Rothstein. 'I couldn't murder anybody!'

'Please, sit down,' urged Hammond.

Reluctantly, Rothstein sat down on the bench. Stark sat down next to him.

'You were found semi-conscious in your office,' said Stark.

'The body of Harry Jukes was lying nearby. He'd been beaten to death. The bloodstained iron doorstop that had been used as a weapon was found with your fingers wrapped round it.'

'I don't know how that was! As I said before, someone must have knocked me out, killed Harry, then left that doorstop in my hand. Someone is framing me!'

'You were heard arguing with Mr Jukes shortly before.'

'Harry and I always argued. That was how it worked. We'd been doing it the same way for years! He asked for more money for my workers; I said no. We'd shout at one another and then sit down and reach a deal.'

'Why would anyone want to frame you?' asked Stark. 'What about a competitor? Someone trying to put you out of business.'

Rothstein shook his head. 'No. The garment trade is very tight. Everyone knows everyone. Yes, we're rivals, but we never use violence against one another. Most of us are Jews. Why would we attack one another? Most of us had enough of that already in the old countries. Russia. Poland.' He shook his head again. 'This is against us Jews. That's what I think is behind it.'

They left Rothstein miserably locked in his cell and mounted the steps back to Hammond's office.

'Now for Constable Fields,' muttered Hammond.

They found Constable Fields sitting in the locker room, smoking a cigarette and reading a newspaper. He leapt to his feet when he saw Hammond, and looked suspiciously at Stark. Fields was tall and thin, with a narrow pencil moustache and slicked-back dark hair highlighting his very pale, pinched face. His uniform was meticulously neat. He was obviously a man who paid a lot of attention to his appearance.

'This is Detective Chief Inspector Stark from Scotland Yard,' introduced Hammond. 'They're taking an interest in this case.'

Stark smiled, doing his best to put Fields at his ease, but the constable remained wary. 'You've done a good job on this one, Constable, by the sound of it,' Stark complimented him.

'Thank you, sir.'

'There's just a couple of small issues to get clear, just in case the press or the top brass start asking any questions.'

'What sort of issues?' asked Fields, frowning.

'You can use my office,' offered Hammond. 'Less chance of interruption.'

'Thank you, Superintendent,' said Stark.

He and Fields followed Hammond to his office. Stark took the chair behind Hammond's desk and gestured Fields to the one opposite. Hammond left them to it.

'As I said, Constable, excellent work,' said Stark. 'By all accounts, it looks like an open-and-shut case.'

'That's what I thought, sir, when I saw the scene. Especially taking into account the evidence from the witness about the shouting and the bashing sounds and all that.'

'Absolutely,' nodded Stark. 'And that's the person we might need to sew this one up.'

'The tramp?'

Stark nodded again. 'You found them, but your evidence can only be hearsay, retelling what the tramp told you had gone on. Because when you found them, Harry Jukes was dead and Rothstein was unconscious. At least, that's what it said in your report. Is that right?'

'Er . . . yes, sir,' agreed Fields, slightly uncomfortable.

'You see the problem, Constable. A clever defence lawyer could claim that it wasn't Rothstein who did it at all. They could claim, for example, that it was the tramp who knocked Rothstein out and then killed Harry Jukes.'

'But . . . why would he? The argument was between Harry Jukes and the Jew.'

'Again, you've only got the tramp's word for that.'

'But if he did it, why would he come and get me to take a look?'

'To frame Rothstein.' Stark gave a rueful shrug. 'Again, I'm only saying what a good defence barrister will say. Which is why we need to get hold of the tramp.'

Fields looked doubtful. 'I can't see that happening, sir. These blokes aren't easy to find, unless they want to be found.'

'I'm guessing he must be local. After all, he knew enough to seek out Rothstein's factory as a warm place to stay.'

'Yes, that makes sense,' admitted Fields reluctantly.

'So I suggest we start a search for him. What did he look like?'

'Look like?' Fields was obviously uncomfortable with this line of questioning.

'Yes. Tall? Short?'

'Er . . . he was . . . about average.'

'Hair colour? Red? Black? Fair?'

'I . . . er . . . I'm not sure. He had a hat on.'

'What sort of hat?'

'Well . . . it was . . . like a gent's hat. But old and battered.'

'Colour? Black? Brown?'

'I . . . I can't be sure.'

'Beard? No beard? Moustache?'

'To be honest, sir, it all happened so fast. And I was more thinking about what the tramp had told me – that there was a murder being committed.'

'He actually said that, did he? There was a murder being committed? Not that there was a fight going on?'

Fields looked even more uncomfortable. 'I think that's what he said.'

Stark nodded thoughtfully. 'I understand, Constable. I've been there myself. It can be difficult to remember everything exactly in the heat of the moment.'

'Yes, sir,' said Fields, slightly relieved at these words.

And so it continued, Stark gently prodding and probing, the constable doing his best to come up with satisfactory answers. After another five minutes, Fields was relieved to be told he could return to his duties.

'Well?' asked Hammond, returning to his office.

'Either Constable Fields is one of the least observant policemen I've ever met or there are question marks over this tramp.'

Hammond shot a look towards the door and lowered his voice as he asked, 'You think Fields may have been involved?'

'I think it's worth looking into. He certainly has no liking for "the Jew", as he terms it.' He stood up. 'I don't necessarily think he did it, but there may be some collusion with whoever did. But that's just my opinion.'

There was a knock at the door and a desk sergeant appeared. 'Sorry to trouble you, sirs,' he said. 'There's a telephone call for DCI Stark.'

Immediately, Stark was alert. The hospital? If so, it could only mean bad news. He felt a surge of relief at the desk sergeant's next words. 'It was Chief Superintendent Benson, sir. He said there was no need to talk to you, but he wants you back at Scotland Yard immediately.'

'Thank you, Sergeant.'

Stark waited till the sergeant had gone and the door was shut, before saying, 'I'm sorry I wasn't able to suggest that everything was all right and Rothstein *did* murder Harry Jukes. It would have been much simpler.'

'Simpler, but not just,' said Hammond. 'And that's what we're about, isn't it, Paul? Justice?'

'That's what you and I are about, Billy. I wish I could be as confident about the rest of them.'

'Thanks for coming. If there are any developments on the case, I'll let you know.'

'That would be good. And if I'm not in the office, you can leave a message with my Sergeant, Robert Danvers.'

'Is he any good?'

Stark nodded. 'Very good.'

FIFTEEN

Danvers sat across the table in the basement canteen from Ted Bell, clerk in the records office and Gallipoli veteran. On the table in front of them were two mugs of strong tea.

'It was hell,' Bell said. The messenger had been right: Bell was only too happy to talk about his experiences. Unlike Stark, Danvers reflected, who barely mentioned his own experiences of the war, and then only if it related to a case.

'We were put ashore at Cape Helles, at the south of the peninsula. The Australians and New Zealanders landed further north at Gaba Tepe, which became known as Anzac Cove because of the Anzac forces being there.'

The Anzacs, thought Danvers. Australian and New Zealand Army Corps.

'We were told it would be easy, that the Turks didn't have the guts for a fight and they'd surrender as soon as we landed.' He shook his head. 'They couldn't have been more wrong. The Turks were there in their thousands, behind strong defences they'd put at the top of the high cliffs overlooking the beaches. They'd dug in and they had all the weapons they needed. Machine guns, everything.

'We found out afterwards they'd had plenty of time to get ready. We went ashore on the twenty-fifth of April, but British and French ships had been in the Dardanelles Straits from as far back as February, so the Turks knew that the invasion was coming and they'd had two months to prepare their defences. And it wasn't just the Turks. The Germans were there as well, building the defences, supplying them with arms.

'When we went ashore, they just cut us to ribbons. All we could do was dig trenches on the beaches to shelter in while our commanders tried to work out what to do. Those of us who didn't get killed in the first few waves, that is.

'The Navy did their best, shelling the Turkish positions from the Straits, but the Turks had dug in well. They just took cover until the shelling stooped, then they opened up with their machine guns at us again.

'A few times our commanders ordered some of us to launch an attack, but it was hopeless – the cliffs were too steep. We couldn't get up those cliffs, not under fire. It was stalemate. We couldn't get up the cliffs. They wouldn't come down. They didn't need to. They had us where they wanted us.

'We were there for nine months before we were evacuated from those beaches. In that time we took over two hundred thousand casualties, including forty-three thousand dead. I was one of the lucky ones.'

'There must have been a lot of anger among the troops over what had happened,' said Danvers.

'It was war,' said Bell with a shrug. 'That's what happens in war.'

'But someone must have been to blame,' persisted Danvers. 'The top brass and politicians who organized the campaign.'

'Organized?' laughed Bell caustically. 'It may have been planned before it happened, but once it kicked off there was no organiza- tion. It was just about trying to survive. The politicians blamed Churchill; he carried the can for it, didn't he? Resigning and all that. But, if you ask me, it wasn't his fault. It was the commanders there who messed it up. They underestimated the Turks. They thought we'd just be able to walk in. They were wrong.'

'What about Lord Fairfax?'

'The bloke who was murdered?'

Danvers nodded. 'It was said he was one of the organizers of the campaign, along with Churchill.'

Bell shook his head. 'He wasn't there, though, was he? Nor was Churchill. No, the only one of that lot who was involved in the action was Kitchener, and he's long dead.'

When he got back to Scotland Yard, Stark considered seeking out Sergeant Danvers first to find out what was so urgent that Chief Superintendent Benson had sent for him, but then decided against it. Politics dictated that he report to the man himself, so Stark headed straight for Benson's office.

The chief superintendent was not in a good mood. As Stark pushed open the door of Benson's office in response to the chief super's growl of 'Come in!', Benson was on the telephone, and scowling heavily. 'I want to know what levels of authority this man has!' he barked into the phone. 'Surely someone at the Home Office has the answer to that simple question?' He listened a bit more, then interrupted curtly, 'I want an answer, and soon.' With that he replaced the receiver and glowered at Stark. 'What were you doing at Finsbury Park, Stark?'

'Giving advice to a senior colleague on a murder case. A factory owner has been arrested for allegedly killing a business associate.'

'Is it connected with the Lord Fairfax and Carl Adams murders?'

'There was a suggestion it may have been, sir. That's why I went. However, it would appear not to be related.'

'I could have told you that, Stark, without going all the way to Finsbury Park!' growled Benson. 'Get your priorities right! We have a murder here where important people are involved. Concentrate on that!'

'Yes, sir.'

'And to that end we've got a visitor here from America who's been waiting to see you. Special Agent Donald Noble of the American Bureau of Investigation. He just arrived from America today. Although, officially, Mr Noble has no territorial powers in this country, the Home Secretary has agreed that Mr Noble can be involved in the investigation as the double killing involved an American citizen.'

Stark frowned. 'The journey from America takes about a week, sir. Do we know why Agent Noble was coming to England?'

'No. I've left that for you to deal with.'

'Where is he? With Sergeant Danvers?'

'Noble is a top official from America, Stark. He wants to talk to the man in charge, not his lackey. I found an empty office for him while I chased around trying to find out where you were. I left him with some newspapers to read, so he could get an English perspective on the case while he waited.'

'DS Danvers knew where I was, sir. I'd left him a note of my whereabouts in case there was an urgent break in the case.'

'Yes, as I discovered. But I wasn't going to leave Agent Noble kicking his heels in your office with Sergeant Danvers. It doesn't create the best impression for someone from America. They're used to efficiency there. Well, you're here now. I'll take you to him.'

'Yes, sir. By the way, before we do, I believe we've uncovered the identity of the person who sent you that anonymous letter naming Lady Amelia Fairfax as the murderer.'

'Oh?'

'Yes, sir. Lady Ambleton.'

Benson stared at Stark, his mouth dropping open. Then his jaws snapped shut and he barked, 'Nonsense! I know Lady Ambleton! This is preposterous!'

'That may be, sir, but I'm basing it on three things: one, the deduction by a handwriting expert at the British Museum, Sir Bernard Wallis; two, I visited Lady Ambleton and saw a note in her handwriting, and it was the same as in that letter; and three, she was informed about the murder soon after seven o'clock on the morning it happened. She was one of only a handful of people who knew Lord Fairfax had been murdered in time to send that letter.'

'But . . . but . . . what would be her motive?'

'Jealousy, sir. We've established that she was in a relationship with Lord Fairfax, but he was still enamoured of Lady Amelia, and his feelings for Lady Amelia had most likely prevented him from marrying Lady Ambleton.'

'No, Stark! I can't believe this.'

'If you like, sir, I can bring in Sir Bernard Wallis to examine both pieces of paper and you can talk to him. And I can bring in Lady Ambleton for questioning.'

'No, Stark! Absolutely not! It's obvious that the anonymous letter has no bearing on this case!'

'But you felt it did, sir. You said—'

'That was before this . . . preposterous suggestion. Which, if true, can only be the result of the deep grief felt by Lady Ambleton, which caused her to strike out at . . . whoever.'

'Lady Amelia Fairfax, sir.'

'It's irrelevant, Stark. This goes no further.'

'Yes, sir.'

Benson headed for the door. 'I'll take you to see Mr Noble.'

Stark followed the chief superintendent along the corridor, then up a flight of stairs to the next level, before finally halting at a door marked *Interview Room 3*. He opened the door and strode in.

A man was sitting at the desk, on which newspapers and magazines were stacked in neat piles.

'Special Agent Noble, allow me to introduce Detective Chief Inspector Stark,' said Benson.

The man put down the newspaper he was reading and got to his feet, his hand outstretched. He was short and stocky, neatly dressed, his hair cut very short, almost cropped, in a military style. 'Chief Inspector,' he greeted.

Stark shook the hand. It was a firm handshake. No smile, Stark noticed; Special Agent Noble was a serious man on a mission.

'Agent Noble,' returned Stark.

'I'll leave you two to get acquainted,' said Benson. 'I'm confident that Inspector Stark will be able to answer all your questions.'

With that, Benson withdrew. Noble looked at the door as it closed, waited a second, then commented wryly, 'I don't think your superintendent likes me. He thinks I'm an interloper trespassing on his territory.'

'I wouldn't take it personally,' commented Stark sagely. 'The chief superintendent doesn't like many people.'

'I don't think he likes you,' observed Noble. 'He seemed pretty annoyed when he found you weren't in the building.'

'My point, exactly.' He gestured at the door. 'Let's go to my office. We can be more comfortable there, and I'll introduce you to my sergeant. Have you been offered any refreshment?'

'The chief superintendent offered me tea, but I asked for coffee.' He grimaced. 'It was lousy.'

'Yes, I'm afraid it is,' agreed Stark ruefully.

He opened the door and Noble followed him out of the interview room and along the corridor.

'When did you arrive?'

'The boat docked about five hours ago. Fortunately, there was a good train service from Southampton. Though, my God, your carriages are small after what we've grown used to in the States!'

'So far it doesn't seem as if your trip to this country has been a roaring success,' said Stark.

'No, it hasn't,' agreed Noble. 'From the moment I docked and got the message from the embassy telling me that Carl had been murdered.'

'Can I ask how you knew him?' asked Stark.

'He was a special agent, like me. We were working together on an operation. I've been looking after the American end. At least, I was until I got a telegram from him last week saying I needed to join him here.'

'What was the operation?'

'What do you know about the Ku Klux Klan' asked Noble.

Stark shook his head. 'Absolutely nothing,' he said.

He saw Sergeant Danvers approaching along the corridor from the opposite direction and halted outside their office.

'My sergeant,' he explained to Noble. Stark did the introductions. 'Sergeant Danvers, Special Agent Noble from the American Bureau of Investigation. He's just arrived from America. He's going to be working with us on the murder investigation.'

'A pleasure to meet you, sir,' greeted Danvers, shaking Noble's hand. He looked towards Stark. 'I've just been talking to Ted Bell in Records about Gallipoli, sir. Getting his story. He was there.'

'Gallipoli!' grunted Noble disapprovingly. 'What an unholy mess!'

'I think there are few people who'd disagree with you, Mr Noble,' said Stark. 'Except, perhaps, the Turks.'

'I don't know about that,' scowled Noble. 'They lost about a quarter of a million there, as I recall.'

'True,' agreed Stark.

He opened the door and the three men entered the office. 'Carl Adams was an agent with the American Bureau,' Stark told Danvers.

'He was working undercover,' said Noble.

Stark gestured Noble to take a chair, then said to Danvers, 'Agent Noble was just asking me what I know about something called the Ku Klux Klan. I admitted it means nothing to me. How about you, Sergeant?'

Danvers shook his head. 'I'm sorry, sir. It means nothing to me, either.'

They both looked questioningly at Noble.

'It's an organization,' explained Noble. 'One promoting white supremacy. The current Klan is the second incarnation. The first was set up by former soldiers of the Confederate army in Tennessee after our civil war, but that sort of died down. This latest confederation sprung up in Georgia about six years ago, and at first most people thought it would go the way of the first and fade away. But this year it's seen a surge in membership, mostly in the Southern states – Alabama, Georgia, Arkansas, Tennessee, Texas, California – and it's been spreading north and gaining in popularity. Detroit, Michigan, even parts of Massachusetts have become Klan strongholds. Right now the strongest Klan base is in Indiana.'

'Which, as I understand, is where Edgar Cavendish is from.'

Noble nodded. 'Correct. Edgar Cavendish is a Klan member, and a very important one. I believe he called on you, Chief Inspector.'

'Yes, he did,' nodded Stark.

'What did he tell you?'

'That he was shocked at Carl Adams' death. That he believed it must have been a tragic accident, a case of Adams being in the wrong place at the wrong time, and that the real target must have been Lord Fairfax.'

'Trying to put you off the scent,' grunted Noble.

'You think that Cavendish was involved in the murder of Mr Adams?' asked Stark.

'I do,' said Noble. 'He may not have carried it out himself – he's too sharp for that and you can bet he'll have had an alibi for when it happened – but I'd bet his fingers are on this somewhere. He must have got wind that Carl was working for us and decided to silence him.'

'He'd only do that if Adams had found out something new, something your people didn't know already,' said Stark. 'Otherwise, all he'd be doing is bringing a more stringent investigation on himself and his organization.'

'Yes, that's what I thought, too,' said Noble grimly. 'So the question is: what did Carl discover that's so dangerous to Cavendish that he had to silence him?' He paced the room in thoughtful silence, then said, 'It has to be something that's connected to the visit here. To England.'

'Involving Lord Fairfax?'

'Who knows? Maybe. Maybe not. The thing is, we suspect that the Klan have ambitions beyond domestic politics in the States. From talk we've heard, we believe they envisage some kind of global connections.'

'World domination?' smiled Stark. 'We've heard that sort of thing before, down the centuries, from the Romans onwards.'

'This is no laughing matter,' said Noble sourly. 'These people are serious. We're pretty sure that's why Cavendish is here in London.'

'Under cover of doing business deals. The motion picture industry.'

Noble gave a harsh laugh. 'Let me guess, he told you about his great triumph. *The Birth of a Nation.*'

'He did indeed,' said Stark.

'Have you seen it?'

'No,' said Stark. 'As I told Mr Cavendish, when it came out in the cinemas here, I was otherwise engaged.'

'It was a pile of white supremacist crap!' snorted Noble. 'All about how noble the Ku Klux Klan is and how all blacks – played by white actors wearing blackface – are mad and dangerous.'

'Thank you,' said Stark drily. 'You've saved me from spending my money if it returns to my local cinema.'

'So Cavendish was telling the truth – he really is involved in the motion picture business?' asked Danvers.

'As a front,' growled Noble. 'Cavendish's main business is Klan business. Like I said, he's trying to set up a world-wide confederation of similar-minded groups.'

'White supremacists?' mused Stark.

'Not just white supremacy,' said Noble. 'They're also opposed to Jews and communists and Catholics.' He scowled. 'Hell, they're against everything that ain't white and Protestant.'

Jews. The word struck Stark. What had Hammond said? There have been attacks on Jews lately.

'Are you saying that Cavendish – or this Ku Klux Klan – is seriously trying to set up some kind of global conspiracy?'

'Absolutely,' nodded Noble. 'It seems that since the war different organizations have sprung up across Europe, as well as in America, that have the same aim. Putting blacks back into slavery to serve the white race, and especially getting rid of Jews.'

'Like the British Union of Patriots?' asked Stark.

Noble shook his head. 'Sorry, the name means nothing to me. But then, I've only just landed here.' His eyes fell on the clock and he got to his feet. 'You'll have to excuse me, Chief Inspector. I need to get to my embassy and update them on what's happening. Perhaps we could meet later – say, at my hotel? To compare notes and put our heads together. I believe we have a common interest here.'

'My pleasure,' nodded Stark. 'Where are you staying?'

'The Claremont in Baker Street. Do you know it?'

'I can find it,' said Stark.

'Shall we say seven?' asked Noble.

'Eight would be better,' said Stark. 'I have a visit to make first.'

'Eight will be fine. You're invited too, Sergeant. If you're free.'

'Thank you, sir, but I'm afraid I have a family engagement this evening.'

'No problem,' said Noble.

'I'll walk you down to reception,' offered Stark.

'No need, I can find my way,' said Noble. 'I had time to explore while I was waiting for you.' He held out his hand, and Stark and Danvers both shook it. 'See you at eight,' said Noble, and left.

After the door had shut on the American, Stark turned to Danvers. 'A family engagement?' he asked.

'If I don't have a heart-to-heart with Lettie soon, I'm never going to hear the end of it from my parents,' said Danvers unhappily. 'I might as well grasp the nettle this evening, rather than later, especially in view of what Agent Noble told us about Cavendish.'

'Yes, it does throw a new light on Mr Cavendish. And I think we can accept what Noble says; his outfit have obviously been keeping tabs on Cavendish and his actions for a long while.'

Stark frowned thoughtfully, watched by Danvers. 'Let's make an assumption, Sergeant. Let's say that Adams discovered something going on here which alarms him enough to send a telegram to Noble asking him to come to England urgently. But it will take Noble a week to get here. So Adams decides he needs help. He's a stranger here, knowing no one except the people he's met through Cavendish. Which means he can't trust just anyone. So he turns to someone he met while in action in France in 1918 – Lord Fairfax. Why choose Lord Fairfax?'

'Because they're fellow warriors. The comradeship of battle.'

'That's not enough. Lord Fairfax might have changed his political views in the last three years. He could be an associate of Cavendish.

'When I tried to get details of Lord Fairfax's actions in France during the war, I assumed the reason I got nowhere was because some jumped-up bureaucrat at the War Office was just being difficult because that's what they do. But think about it. We have an experienced, older soldier, well respected, who is in an administrative role, but now and then is sent to where the action is. And the War Office is reluctant to give out any information about him.'

'Military intelligence!' exclaimed Danvers.

'Exactly,' nodded Stark. 'Adams was in American intelligence. I bet he was already part of the organization in 1918. So when he and Fairfax met in France during the war . . .'

'It was as intelligence officers,' finished Danvers.

'The question is, what did Adams discover here in England that was so important that he urged Noble to come, and about which he felt he had to inform British military intelligence through Lord Fairfax?'

'I'm still puzzled why he had to confide in Lord Fairfax?' frowned Danvers. 'Surely, as an American government agent, he could have gone direct to British intelligence – Special Branch, or someone.'

'Because, as I said, he didn't know whom he could trust. Which suggests that there is top-level involvement here. Certainly threads through the official organizations. People sympathetic to Cavendish's views.'

'This British Union of Patriots you mentioned?'

Stark nodded. 'Their name has come up twice in the last twenty-four hours. Once in relation to Lady Ambleton, who we know sent that anonymous letter naming Lady Amelia. And today, when I went to see Superintendent Hammond at Finsbury Park. According to DS Hammond, there have been quite a few incidents lately where properties owned by Jews have been attacked. And this latest incident he asked me to look into concerns a Jewish factory owner who claims he's been framed for a murder.

'In the light of what Agent Noble said about the Ku Klux Klan trying to set up a European conspiracy, I think this British Union of Patriots is worth a look. And while I'm doing that, I'd like you to check with the stations in areas where there's a sizeable Jewish community and see if there have been any similar attacks lately. Especially any noticeable increase in such attacks.'

'Right, sir. By the way, I did try to find out if the War Office had received any angry letters about Gallipoli.'

'And?'

Danvers gave a rueful shrug. 'Exactly as you said it would be, sir. They refused to give me any information at all.'

'It's not a campaign they remember with pride,' said Stark. 'Although they should. The campaign failed, but it was a failure of the people in charge, not the men who fought in it. Too many brave men died in the Dardanelles.' He was quiet for a moment, then added reflectively, 'Too many brave men died in the whole bloody war.'

'Yes, sir. So Ted Bell said,' nodded Danvers awkwardly. A part of him still felt guilty because he'd never got the chance to fight. 'Where will you be, in case I need to get hold of you?' he asked. 'In case the hospital calls with a message.'

'To begin with, Records, to find out where this BUP is based. And afterwards, their offices. I'll call you from Records when I find their telephone number.'

SIXTEEN

Aⁿccording to Records, the headquarters of the British Union of Patriots was in Warren Street, just a stone's throw from University College Hospital. Stark checked the time. Two thirty. Perfect for three-o'clock visiting, and then the short walk to Warren Street afterwards. Stark telephoned Danvers and gave him the address and phone number of the BUP.

'Just in case you need to get hold of me,' he said. 'But I shall be calling on my father first.'

'I hope he's getting better, sir,' said Danvers.

'So do I,' said Stark.

Stark half expected to find his mother at UCH when he arrived, but there was no sign of her. He expected she was waiting at the school gates to collect Stephen.

She's doing too much. Looking after Stephen, visiting Dad, walking everywhere at her age, and in the winter. She'll be the next one in hospital. I have to get her some help. But would she accept it? She accuses me of being stubborn, but she's the most stubborn of all of us. If we were a titled family, that would be our motto, he reflected. *Stubborn and pig-headed.*

Henry was lying in bed, propped up on a pile of pillows, his eyes closed, his chest rising and falling. His laboured breathing, the painful wheezing, made an ominous rattle. A spittoon was on the bedside table.

Stark sat down beside his father's bed. Henry's face had become skull-like, his eyes sunk into their sockets, his cheeks hollowed, the skin on his face almost transparent.

He's dead, but he refuses to die, realized Stark.

Henry must have become aware of his presence, because his eyelids flickered and then opened, and Stark found himself looking into the black pin-points of his father's angry gaze.

What's he angry about? Is he angry at me? Why? At this stage?

'You look better than you did last night, Dad,' said Stark.

Henry opened his lips to try to say something, but instead erupted into a burst of savage coughing that shook his frail frame violently.

'No need to talk,' said Stark. 'I'll do the talking for both of us.'

His father seemed to sink further into the pillows that supported him. He took deep breaths, which rattled in his throat. Stark saw that Henry was struggling to push himself up, and stood and put his hands beneath his father's armpits, helping him raise himself up, before gently laying him back on the pillows.

Henry's breath rasped painfully as he looked at his son – no, he *glared* at Stark. And then suddenly Henry reached out with a claw-like talon and gripped Stark's hand, tightening his grip as he looked intently at his son, and the realization hit Stark. *He's not angry at me; he's angry because he's dying and he's not ready to go yet. He's telling me he loves me.*

Stark squeezed his father's hand in return, letting him know he understood. At this, Henry's grip eased and he relaxed back on the pillows.

'We're going to do everything we can to get you well, Dad,' Stark promised fervently.

Footsteps approaching made him look up, and he saw his mother appear.

'I popped home to sort Stephen out after school,' she said. 'Mrs Pierce is taking care of him.'

Stark stood up and let his mother sit down in the chair. He noticed that she was out of breath. 'You should have caught a taxi, or a bus,' he admonished her.

'I can't be hanging around waiting for them,' she said. She reached out and took Henry's hand. 'I'm here, Henry.'

'I've got one more call to make and then I'll be home,' Stark told her.

'It'll have to be pie and mash from the shop tonight,' said Sarah. 'I ain't got time for anything else.'

'Don't worry about me,' said Stark. 'I've got to go out to dinner.'

She shot him an inquiring look.

'Strictly business,' he said. 'I've got to meet a policeman who's just arrived from America.' He hesitated, looking around, then added, 'I'll tell you about it when I get home.' He reached out and brushed his hand over his father's forehead. It was wet with sweat. 'I'll call in later, Dad. Hang in there.'

Danvers put down the receiver and added Stamford Hill to his list. Out of the seven police stations he'd contacted, three had reported a recent spate of attacks on properties owned or managed by Jews. Most had been shops, with bricks thrown through windows, but at least one synagogue had been the target of an arson attack.

He was just reaching for the phone to call another of the local stations, when it rang. 'DS Danvers.'

'Robert, have you had a chance to talk to Lettie yet about Mr Cavendish?' demanded his mother's voice.

Damn, damn, damn! he cursed silently. 'Mother, I was just about to telephone her,' he lied. There was no putting it off. He'd have to make arrangements to see her. 'Is she there?' he asked. 'I'll talk to her now.'

'You need to talk to her face to face,' insisted his mother. 'She won't take any notice otherwise.'

'All right,' said Danvers resignedly. 'Get her to come to the phone and I'll fix a time we can meet.'

His mother hesitated, then said in annoyed tones, 'She won't talk to anyone at the moment. She's getting ready to go out. Even though she isn't leaving for hours. It's ridiculous how long that girl takes to decide what to wear.' She hesitated again, then said, 'Cavendish is supposed to be taking her out tonight, to some talk he's giving.'

'On what?'

'I don't know. The moving picture business, I expect. But your father thinks it's a ruse to . . . to trap her. Lettie can be very naïve and unworldly, for all her pretence at sophistication.'

In the background, Danvers heard his father growl, 'The man's a bad lot! But she won't listen to me.'

'All right, I'll go along and keep them company,' sighed Danvers. 'I'll say I'd heard he was giving a talk, and I was interested in the subject.' He picked up a pencil. 'Where's it going to be?'

'At the Mitre Hall in James Street. Apparently, he's giving a talk to the British Union of Patriots.'

The pencil stopped in Danvers' hand. 'The British Union of Patriots?' he repeated.

'Yes. That's what Lettie said. Although it sounds a strange organization for a talk about moving pictures.'

'Yes, it does. I don't suppose you know anyone who's in this organization?'

'Well . . . there's Lord Wickford. And Sir Watkyn Keyes. And Lady Mantle. They're all very respectable people, so I'm sure the organization itself must be above board, but it's just what Mr Cavendish might be thinking of for after the meeting. You know, taking Lettie to a club, and so forth.'

'Yes, I understand,' said Danvers. 'What time is the talk taking place?'

'Eight o'clock. Lettie says Cavendish is picking her up at half past seven.'

'I'll be there,' promised Danvers. 'I'll make sure I talk to her then.'

The British Union of Patriots' headquarters was a small shop on the corner of a nondescript turning off Warren Street. The large shop window had a display of books and publications, most of them following the same theme. Stark noticed one book entitled

The Jew Menace, another *The Chinese Menace*, while a third was called *The Negro Menace*. Another, with a picture of Lenin on the cover, was called *The Murdering Bolsheviks of Russia*. There were photographs and portraits of great British war heroes, including Lord Kitchener, with one of Lord Nelson standing proudly to attention in full dress uniform as Admiral of the Fleet, a telescope to his one good eye. The rest of the window was draped with Union Jack flags.

Stark pushed open the door and stepped in.

A small thin man who was sitting at a table reading a newspaper – the *Daily Target*, noted Stark – got to his feet and regarded Stark with a suspicious glower. 'Yes?' he snapped. 'Can I help you?'

'I'm Detective Chief Inspector Stark from Scotland Yard.'

It was as if a switch had been thrown inside the man. The look of wary suspicion vanished from his face to be replaced by smile of genuine welcome. He strode forward, his hand outstretched.

'The man who saved the life of the King! This is a great honour, sir! Please allow me to shake your hand!'

Stark forced a smile and shook the man's hand. *I shall have to do something about this*, he thought ruefully. Protecting the King from a group of assassins had been a team operation, but for some reason the newspapers had selected him as the main focus.

'Thank you,' acknowledged Stark. 'But we were just doing our job.'

'Doing your duty, sir,' nodded the man. 'As we all did!'

The war again, thought Stark. *It's what links so many of us.*

'Chief Petty Officer Eric Short, Royal Navy, sir,' said the man smartly to the unspoken question, and he snapped to attention and gave Stark a smart salute. 'I was at Gallipoli.'

Gallipoli again, noted Stark. But then, he supposed he shouldn't be surprised; hundreds of thousands had been involved in the Gallipoli campaign.

'How can I help you, sir?'

'I'm investigating the murder of Lord Fairfax . . .'

Short's face darkened. 'An absolute disgrace! Lord Fairfax was a hero. A patriot!'

'Yes, indeed he was,' agreed Stark.

'You'll find the communists were behind it. Or the Jews. Or both.'

'Do you have any evidence of that, Mr Short?'

'It's obvious, isn't it! The Jews are trying to bleed this country white. The communists want to turn Britain into Russia. They oppose anybody who tries to stand in their way. People like us. People like Lord Fairfax.' He gestured at the large window. 'We've had attacks by them on us already. That window's been smashed twice. The door broken. With respect, sir, the police seem helpless against them.'

'Was Lord Fairfax a member of your organization?'

Short hesitated, then said defensively, 'Not officially, perhaps. But he was sympathetic. He knew what we're fighting for! And once the rest of the people know the truth, they'll be joining us!'

'And what truth would that be?' queried Stark.

'That the Jews were responsible for the war,' said Short.

Stark frowned. 'I thought it was the assassination of Archduke Ferdinand.'

'That may have been the trigger, but what was it really about? Money! Building up wealth! And we all know which race are the ones with the grasping claws when it comes to money, sir. Them and the Bolsheviks!'

'I've been told the Bolsheviks are against private money,' said Stark. 'Communism is said to be about taking money from the rich and sharing it out to everyone.'

'Really? Giving it to who?' asked Short, and he winked. 'Karl Marx. He was the man who started it, wasn't he, sir? And what was he? A Jew. Most of the top Russian revolutionaries were Jews. Why did they do it? So they could get their hands on the riches of the Russian royal family. Their lands. Their estates. Their gold and jewels.' He laughed. 'Give it to the poor! Ha! The poor in Russia are as poor as they've always been. Only now the money and power are in different hands. Jewish hands.' He leant in confidentially to Stark. 'They're trying to start another war, sir. So they can get the rest of the money they couldn't lay their hands on last time. Our money. British money. Even German money. That's why we have to be on our guard. That's why we exist, sir. The British Union of Patriots.' Then he frowned, curious. 'But I'm not sure how we can help with the murder of Lord Fairfax?'

'Clutching at straws, to be honest, Mr Short,' said Stark. 'Someone suggested that some of your members might be able to throw some light on a motive for the killings.'

'How?' asked Short, still puzzled.

'Some of them might have had a social acquaintance with Lord Fairfax. Any information they have could help us. If I had a look at your membership list, I might spot some names it might be useful to talk to.'

Short shook his head apologetically. 'I'm sorry, sir. I'd like to help you, but our membership list is confidential.'

'I understand, but this is a murder enquiry. And not just any murder, but – as you said – the truly dreadful killing of a great British patriot and soldier.'

'That may be the case, sir, but I've been given strict instructions not to reveal details of our members to anyone.'

'Including the police?'

Short hesitated, then said, 'The fact is that we have quite a few of your colleagues in our organization. Senior police officers. Very senior. As well as top military figures, and other influential people. Members of Parliament and from the House of Lords.'

Stark studied Short. The man was obviously sincere, and his sense of apology to Stark seemed genuine: he was a man torn between doing what Stark asked and following orders. But, as an ex-Navy CPO, Stark knew Short would obey the orders from his superiors.

Influential people, Short had said. Threats would cut no ice with Short, and if Stark brought in uniformed officers to forcibly remove the information, these influential people would have him thrown off the case. Discreetly, of course. And Stark was determined he wasn't going to let that happen. He was going to stay on this case and find out who'd murdered Amelia's former husband. Until he removed that cloud hanging over her, there was no chance for them to be together.

'Very well, Mr Short,' he said. 'It seems I have to take this up with my superior officers.'

'Thank you, Chief Inspector,' said Short, obviously relieved. 'I'm sure that everyone wants to find out who committed this terrible crime and see them hanged. Everyone except the Jews and Bolsheviks, that is.'

Stark arrived back at Scotland Yard to find Danvers putting on his coat.

'Off home?' he asked.

'Yes, sir,' said Danvers. 'I promised I'd see my sister this evening.' He smiled. 'And it turns out to be fortuitous, sir. She's attending a talk Mr Cavendish is giving to the British Union of Patriots.'

'Well done, Sergeant!' he said. 'How did you manage that?'

'To be honest, sir, I didn't,' admitted Danvers. 'My mother telephoned and told me that Lettie was going to this talk, and when I heard it was the BUP, it seemed a good opportunity to get inside and perhaps find out who they are and what they're up to.'

'Oh, I certainly think we know what they're up to, Sergeant,' said Stark. 'Inciting hatred. But they're also very secretive, from what I can gather. I certainly had no luck today at their head-quarters in finding out who their members were.'

'I've already got the names of a couple, sir. Lord Wickford. Sir Watkyn Keyes. Lady Mantle. According to my mother, that is. I hope I'll be able to find out even more this evening.'

'You're certainly doing much better than me. Perhaps I'll find out something from Special Agent Noble.'

'Yes, sir. How was your father, sir?'

Stark hesitated. The honest answer was that Henry was dying, but he was reluctant to say it out loud. It was as though, as long as he didn't put it into words, his father might pull through.

'He's holding his own, thank you, Sergeant. All we can do is keep our fingers crossed.'

'Yes, sir. They are very good at UCH. A friend of mine had his appendix out there. He spoke very highly of them.'

'Yes. They seem very caring.' And coldly officious, he was tempted to add. But then, that was the same with any organiza-tion, including the police. And the doctor he and his mother had spoken to the previous night had impressed him.

'Oh, I telephoned around different police stations, as you asked, sir, about attacks on Jews,' said Danvers. He went to his desk and picked up his notes. 'I talked to twelve stations, and four reported a number of attacks on Jewish properties in the last month. Normally, they told me, they wouldn't have noticed, but there have been more than the usual number.'

'The usual number?' queried Stark.

'What they meant, sir, was that there are often disturbances in most of the different communities – Jewish, Irish, Chinese and so on – but most of these are fights *within* the community – Irish against Irish, Chinese against Chinese. The Jewish community keeps very much to itself and looks after itself. But lately they've been reporting attacks on their shops and factories, and their synagogues, and by non-Jews.'

'Where did most of the attacks take place?'

Danvers checked his notes. 'Cable Street in the East End. Quite a few attacks there. Stamford Hill. Golders Green. Finsbury Park. Tottenham.'

'Jewish areas,' nodded Stark.

'It wouldn't surprise me if there'd been others in other districts, sir, but I got the impression that at some of the stations the officers aren't bothered. In fact, one officer actually said to me, "Who's interested in a bunch of Yids?"'

What was it Short had told him? *We have quite a few of your colleagues in our organization.*

'Thank you, Sergeant. That's good work,' said Stark.

'You think this is what was behind the murders? This global conspiracy, as Agent Noble called it?'

'I don't know about the global aspect,' said Stark, 'but it certainly seems to be pointing towards something being rotten here in Britain.' He told Danvers about what had happened at Finsbury Park: the killing of Harry Jukes and the apparent evidence implicating Israel Rothstein as the murderer, and his suspicions about PC Fields. 'It follows a surge in attacks on the Jewish community in the area, which seems to be happening in other areas too, with the suggestion that the British Union of Patriots may be behind it. If Carl Adams had uncovered a conspiracy involving the BUP and the Ku Klux Klan, that strikes me as a more likely motive for their murder than any supposed revenge for Gallipoli.' He regarded Danvers with concern. 'In which case, you'll need to be careful this evening. I don't want you putting yourself at risk.'

'I don't think there's any danger of that, sir,' smiled Danvers confidently. 'After all, I'm going as Lettie's brother. And I'm pretty sure I'll know quite a few of them, if what my mother says is right. They'll just see me as one of their own social set rather than an investigating outsider.'

'I hope you're right. But be on your guard, Sergeant. At this stage we still don't know exactly who, or what, we're dealing with. According to a man I met at the offices of the BUP today, the membership of the organization includes quite a few police officers, and many of them very senior officers.' He shot a careful glance at the door. 'The fact is, apart from each other, we don't know whom we can trust.'

SEVENTEEN

S tark was pleased to see Stephen's face light up as Freddy the pie man spooned the food into the pudding bowl and stuck a paper lid on top to keep it hot. Pie and mash, covered with 'liquor', a parsley sauce, had long been one of Stark's favourite treats, and he was delighted that his son shared the same taste. It was only a short walk back from the shop to their house, and Stephen cuddled the warm bowl to him in his gloved hands. Stark doubted that his forthcoming meal with Agent Noble would be as tasty, and wondered if he should have invited the American to join him in the delights of Freddy's Pie Shop.

Sarah Stark served on to two plates, and looked questioningly at Stark. 'You sure you don't want some?' she asked.

'I'd better not,' he said. 'Don't want to ruin my appetite and upset Special Agent Noble.'

'Is that this American?'

'Special Agent?' piped up Stephen. 'Does he carry a gun?'

'He may do when he's in America, but not here in Britain.'

'Why's he here?' asked Sarah.

'This case I'm investigating. Two men were murdered. One of them was an American.'

'Who was the other one?' asked Stephen.

Stark hesitated, then replied, 'A man called Lord Fairfax.'

His mother shot him a sharp glance. 'Lord Fairfax?'

'That's right, Mum. Amelia's ex-husband.'

'And you're investigating it?'

'Someone has to. Sergeant Danvers and I caught the case. The thing is, I'm not meeting Agent Noble until eight o'clock, so I'll drop you off at UCH for visiting on my way there. But you have to promise me you'll catch a taxi home afterwards.'

Sarah hesitated, then nodded. 'If it makes you happy.'

'It does. It'll be cold and dark, and we don't want you catching a cold and going down with something. You won't be able to go and see Dad if that happens. Or look after Stephen.'

'Yes, all right, you've made your point,' she said crossly.

'I'll leave a note of the telephone number of the Claremont Hotel with the hospital. That's where I'll be. But I won't be late back.'

The Mitre Hall was a nondescript building in James Street, a little-used thoroughfare not far from Covent Garden. But tonight James Street was busy. Taxi cabs and private cars pulled up in the narrow road and disgorged men in smart suits and women in fur coats that covered fashionable and expensive dresses. This was certainly a gathering of the elite, decided Danvers as he made his way towards the entrance. He knew some of the faces from social gatherings he'd attended with his parents, and one or two of the men he recognized as people he had been at school with. Chuffy Worthington – or the Honourable Reginald Worthington, to give him his full name and title – had been in the same form as him at Harrow.

Two large men, one tall and one short, both dressed in smart suits that barely fitted their muscular frames, were at the door, checking the invitations and membership cards of the guests as they entered the hall. Both had the battered faces that indicated they were boxers. As Danvers went to walk past them into the hall, the two men moved together to block his path.

'Sorry, sir. This is a private event – members only,' said the short one.

'That's all right, I'm here as a guest of Letitia Danvers. I'm her brother, Robert. She's here with Mr Edgar Cavendish.'

The two men exchanged glances of doubt and concern. Then the short one asked, 'Do you have any proof of who you are, sir?'

Suddenly, Danvers remembered what Stark had said about many police officers being members of the BUP. 'I have my police warrant card,' said Danvers. He reached into his pocket, took it out and showed it to the men. 'There. Detective Sergeant Robert Danvers. And you can check with my sister. She'll vouch for me.'

The two men looked discomforted.

'Is she expecting you this evening?' asked the taller of the two.

'Well, no,' admitted Danvers. 'But I heard she would be here, so I thought I'd surprise her. Look, can't you go and find her and get her say-so?'

The two men hesitated, then the shorter one said, 'You wait here, Bert. I'll go and see the boss.'

The short man slipped into the hall, while Danvers stood on the steps with Bert, watching as other people arrived, showed their invitations or membership cards to Bert and were waved in.

'Dibs!'

Danvers turned and saw another classmate from school. Walter Bagshot had arrived at the door and was holding a printed invitation card.

'Walter!' Danvers greeted him.

'So you're here for this do as well, are you?' smiled Bagshot.

'Providing they let me in,' said Danvers ruefully. 'I'm here to see Lettie. She's with the chap who's giving the talk.'

'Edgar Cavendish, the American,' nodded Bagshot. He smiled. 'The moving picture business, eh!' And he gave Danvers a wink.

Danvers frowned, puzzled. 'Of course,' he said. 'Why?'

The smile vanished from Bagshot's face and he looked uncomfortable. 'Nothing,' he said. Then he gave Danvers another smile, a false one this time, and hurried inside the hall.

Danvers was just about to call after Bagshot when he heard his sister's voice. 'Bobby!'

Danvers saw that Lettie had appeared from the door of the hall, accompanied by the short muscular doorman and a moustached man in an expensively cut evening suit.

'Hello, Lettie,' Danvers greeted his sister cheerily. 'Mother told me Mr Cavendish was giving a talk this evening, and you know how interested I am in moving pictures. So here I am.'

The man in the smart suit standing next to Lettie stepped forward, a smile on his face, his hand outstretched. 'Bobby! What a great pleasure it is to meet you! I'm Edgar Cavendish.'

'Mr Cavendish,' smiled Danvers, shaking Cavendish's hand.

The smile of welcome on Cavendish's face vanished to be replaced by a regretful, apologetic one. 'I'm just so sorry that you won't be able to come in and hear me.' He gestured ruefully at the doors of the Mitre Hall. 'I'm afraid it's not my decision, but this meeting is for members only. I don't know why – I guess that's just the way it is. The management committee, or whatever they are, insist.'

'But surely they'd make an exception in Bobby's case!' pleaded Lettie. 'After all, he's my brother. And he's come all this way. And you are the special guest speaker.'

'I'm the *invited* speaker, Lettie, and it would be rude of me to make demands.' He lowered his voice and added, 'It would also be very bad business. These people represent a lot of money, and it would be a really bad idea to upset them. We're hoping for some good investments.'

'That's all right,' nodded Danvers. 'I quite understand. I should have checked first.' He held out his hand to Cavendish. 'I wish you all the best with your talk.' Then he added brightly, 'Perhaps we could meet up afterwards and you can tell me how it went.'

'What a lovely idea!' squeaked Lettie. She turned to Cavendish. 'Oh, Edgar, do say yes!'

Cavendish smiled at her. 'Of course,' he said. He looked at his watch. 'Give me a couple of hours for the talk and the schmoozing afterwards. Shall we say ten o'clock, at the Savoy?'

'That will be excellent!' nodded Danvers. 'I look forward to seeing you both there.'

As Danvers walked away from the hall, he was aware of the two unsmiling doormen watching him closely.

The restaurant of the Claremont Hotel was busy – mostly businessmen engaged in earnest conversations over their meals, but with one or two couples out for dinner. It was a comfortable room. Stark never felt happy if he was forced to dine at the more luxurious hotels such as the Savoy, where he felt the staff looked down their noses at him. It may have been a result of his acknowledged lower-class inverted snobbery, as Amelia had once pointed out, but the fact that the Savoy's menus were all in French seemed to him unnecessarily pretentious. The Claremont offered good food and friendly service in well-appointed surroundings. He was glad the American Embassy had chosen to lodge Agent Noble here rather than somewhere more grandiose.

At the thought of Amelia, Stark felt that same twinge of sadness he'd felt so often since their last meeting. Was it really over between them? It wasn't for him, but a real relationship meant two people. Was she really saying goodbye to him?

He also felt guilty that he hadn't gone to the hospital to see his father again. He told himself that he did it to give his mother time alone with Henry, but he knew that was a lie. What was there to say? Especially in a public place where every word of every conversation was listened to.

'You look thoughtful, Chief Inspector.' Noble's voice cut into his thoughts.

Stark gave the American a smile of apology. 'Sorry,' he said. 'There's a lot in my head at the moment.' He picked up the menu. 'Food will help. And what do you fancy drinking? Beer? Whisky? I don't know if they have any bourbon here.'

'Not for me,' said Noble. 'I don't. I used to, but when Prohibition came in last year, I thought it would be hypocritical of me, as a government agent, to break the law.'

'I though the laws only applied to alcohol in public places,' said Stark. 'Isn't it legal to drink at home?'

'Depends where you live,' said Noble. 'In some states the law is applied very vigorously. Wine used for religious ceremonies may be exempt, but everything else is illegal.' He shrugged. 'I move around the country a lot, so I decided it was easier just to give it up. I was drinking too much, anyhow. But don't let me stop you.'

Stark shook his head with a smile. 'No, it would do me good to have an evening's abstinence. A lemonade will do me fine.'

Noble laughed. 'If people could see us!' he chuckled. 'Law enforcement people are supposed to have a reputation as hard drinkers.'

The waiter came and they ordered their meals, and two glasses of lemonade – to some eyebrow raising from the waiter – then Stark said, 'It might be useful for me to know what cover you're using while you're here in England. If I have to introduce you to people.'

Noble shook his head. 'No cover. Exactly what I am – a special agent working for the American government. Let's face it, the people who killed Carl must have known who he was working for. If they've got the kind of contacts I think they have, they'll know about me. So why pretend? It's all legit: an American citizen has been killed on British soil. I'm working with the police on the case. Who knows, that might set a few rabbits running. Maybe flush out some of the bad guys.'

'You don't think they might treat you the same way they did Carl Adams. Kill you?'

'They can try, but I'm trusting you to keep me alive.' He

looked quizzically at Stark. 'Look, do you mind if we drop all this chief inspector and special agent stuff while we're off duty? How about just Don and Paul? I've got used to calling people I work with by their first names. At least the ones I like – not the stuffy ones.'

'I'm flattered,' said Stark. 'But you don't really know me yet. I could be just the stuffy kind of person you talk about.'

Noble shook his head. 'Trust me, I know people. I get a hunch about them in the first few minutes. You and your sergeant – Sergeant Danvers – you're both OK guys. Your boss, on the other hand, he's an idiot.'

We're agreed on that, reflected Stark silently. 'He has his uses,' he said noncommittally.

'Name one,' challenged Noble.

It was time to change the subject, decided Stark, before he said something that might come back later to haunt him. Instead, he said, 'If you'll excuse my asking a personal question, when you told us about the Ku Klux Klan earlier, you seemed particularly . . . vehement. Angry.'

'You're asking if I've got a personal axe to grind?' asked Noble.

'Yes,' nodded Stark.

'Is it that obvious?' asked Noble.

'I don't know,' shrugged Stark. 'It was just a feeling I got.'

'Yes, you're right,' nodded Noble. 'I come from a small town in Georgia called Harlem. I don't know whether you know it?'

'The only Harlem I know of is the one in New York City,' replied Stark.

'Same name, very different place.'

'Georgia was one of the Confederate States during your civil war, wasn't it?' asked Stark.

'It was,' nodded Noble. 'Good-old-boy segregationist country.'

'And fertile ground for the Ku Klux Klan?'

'It was. However, my daddy didn't share the KKK's views. Far from it. He was the most decent man I ever knew. He brought me and my brother and two sisters up to treat everyone as equal, regardless of their colour, race or religion. "Take the whole person as they are," he used to say. God made us all equal in his eyes.'

'I bet that made him unpopular in Georgia.'

'No, sir – only with certain segments. Contrary to public

opinion, not everyone in the South is racist. Unfortunately, admittedly, it's a big percentage that are. But my daddy always said that one day things will change.'

'And will they?'

Noble frowned. 'Who knows. After the Civil War, the blacks got given their freedom. But they didn't get the same rights. In many states, they still can't eat in the same restaurants as whites. They can't ride the same buses. They can't even use the same public bathrooms!'

Just then, their meals arrived and he sat silent while the waiter placed their plates in front of them.

After the waiter had left, he gave Stark an apologetic smile. 'You have to excuse me, Paul. I get on my high horse when the KKK comes up.'

'Because of something that happened. To your father?'

Noble shook his head. 'No, to a friend of mine. A black friend. Jeremiah. Like I say, my daddy encouraged us to mix with all types, see everyone as equal, and I was about six years old when I met him playing in the street, and me and Jerry hit it off right away. He was fun and funny. Not a vicious or malicious bone in his body. Which, I have to admit, wouldn't have been the case if I'd had his skin, because he was abused by some just cos he was black. When I asked him about it, about how resentful he had to feel, he just shrugged and said that was the way it was, and he was used to it. But one day, he told me, he'd get away to the north, where his colour wouldn't be a problem, and he could do what he wanted to do, which was to be a doctor and heal people.'

Suddenly, he fell silent and his face darkened as he stared down at his plate. Stark didn't interrupt him, just watched, letting the American be lost in some dark thoughts. Then Noble said, 'I'll cut the long story short. There was a woman in the town who was noted for having a bad reputation. Men. Lots of men. One day her husband came home and found her in bed with a black kid. The black kid ran. The woman said he'd come in the house and raped her. And she named Jerry. Of course, it wasn't him – she did it to protect the boy she was having the affair with. But that didn't count, especially with the local KKK. As far as they were concerned, a black boy had raped a white woman, and that black boy was Jerry.

'So, they took him and stripped him and hung him from a tree and castrated him. He was thirteen, the same age as me.' He looked at Stark and forced a smile. 'That was it for me. As soon as I could, I left Georgia, and I've been hunting the Ku Klux Klan ever since.'

Danvers sat in the bar of the Savoy, sipping at a whisky. He looked at his watch. Nine thirty. Half an hour before Lettie and Cavendish joined him.

He was still puzzled by the wink that Walter Bagshot had given him as he'd said, 'The moving picture business, eh!' So the meeting wasn't about the moving picture business. Or it purported to be, but there was something else going on.

Reaching a decision, he finished his drink and headed out of the Savoy and into the Strand. He already knew some of the people he'd seen going into the hall, but he needed to find out who else was involved. James Street was only a five-minute walk away. He'd wait outside the Mitre Hall and make note of as many people he recognized as he could as the audience left. He was sure that Lettie and Cavendish would be among the last to leave, and as they came out he'd simply walk up to them, smile and say he'd decided to wait for them outside the hall, and then accompany them back to the Savoy.

Danvers made his way to James Street and took up a position in a doorway a short distance from the Mitre Hall, on the other side of the street, from where he had a good view of the entrance. The two muscular men were still on duty on the door.

Danvers took his notebook from his pocket. Although it was dark in the doorway, there was enough light filtering through from a nearby street lamp for him to be able to see to write. He began with names of those he'd recognized from his earlier visit: Walter Bagshot, Reginald Worthington, Lord and Lady Monkton . . .

Suddenly, he was aware of a movement just beside him. He began to turn, but before he could, he found himself grabbed and hauled out from the doorway, powerful arms wrapped around him in a strong grip.

'We don't like spies,' growled a voice in his ear.

A tall, powerfully built man appeared in front of him, and Danvers saw the glint of metal on his fingers: a knuckle-duster. Danvers tried to break free, but the arms holding him, clamping his arms to his sides, were too strong.

The punch hard into his stomach from the metal-covered fist

drove all the air out of his body, and he felt vomit rising in his throat as he doubled over.

The grip on him from behind was released and he crumpled to the pavement, his face smashing into the kerb.

He saw the glint of metal on the toecaps of one of the men, saw that foot lifted and pulled back, and then, before he could dodge out of the way, it smashed into his face and an excruciating pain exploded inside his head and he was falling, falling, falling . . .

EIGHTEEN

'How was your dinner?'

Stark sipped at his cup of cocoa, then said, 'All right. Not as good as pie and mash. Was Stephen all right?'

Sarah nodded. 'He wants to go and see his grandad at the hospital. I said I'd take him for tomorrow evening's visiting.'

Stark looked doubtful. 'You don't think it might frighten him?' he asked. 'He's only eight. Dad didn't look too good when I last saw him.'

'I was working when I was Stephen's age,' said Sarah. 'So was your dad.'

'Yes, but they were different times.'

'People are still the same. And there's always been a strong bond between him and his grandad. It's right that we don't keep Stephen out of the picture; otherwise, he'll only imagine things even worse.'

'Yes, you're right,' sighed Stark. 'We'll all go together.'

'Will you be home tomorrow night? What about this American?'

'I'll be home,' Stark assured her.

The shrill ringing of the telephone made them both jump. Stark looked at the clock. Eleven at night. It could only be bad news.

Sarah watched him anxiously as he ran to the phone. He picked up the receiver and heard the familiar voice of Sergeant Hathaway, one of the desk sergeants at Scotland Yard say, 'I'm sorry to trouble you, Chief Inspector, but there's been an incident involving DS Danvers.'

Immediately, Stark felt a sickness in the pit of his stomach.

'What sort of incident?' he asked, forcing himself to stay calm.

'He was assaulted, sir. He was found unconscious in the street. He's been taken to Charing Cross Hospital. He's still hasn't regained consciousness.'

'What do the doctors say about his condition?'

'I'm afraid I haven't any more information, sir.'

'Please send a car to pick me up and take me to Charing Cross.'

'Yes, sir. I thought you might say that, so I despatched one already. It should be with you within the next twenty minutes.'

'Thank you, Sergeant.'

'Any time, sir. And do give my best wishes to Sergeant Danvers, when he wakes up.'

Sarah appeared beside him. 'What's happened?' she asked, worried. 'Is your dad all right?'

'That wasn't about Dad. Sergeant Danvers has been attacked,' he told her. 'He's been taken to Charing Cross Hospital. I'm going to see him. I don't know when I'll be back.'

As Stark entered the waiting area outside Ward C, he saw Lettie and Cavendish in deep and worried conversation with a distin-guished-looking elderly man. Lettie saw him and immediately rushed towards him. He could see that she'd been crying.

'Oh Chief Inspector!' she burst out, and threw herself at him, burying her face in his shoulder. Instinctively, he hugged her, although it felt distinctly uncomfortable. He wasn't a person giving to hugging people he didn't know well. In fact, he wasn't one for hugging at all. He was relieved when Cavendish walked towards him and he was able to gently disentangle himself from Lettie.

'A terrible business, Chief Inspector,' said the American sombrely.

'How is he?' asked Stark.

'Still unconscious, I'm afraid,' replied Cavendish. 'He took a bad beating. Most of it to the head, from what the medics say.' He turned and indicated the elderly man who'd now joined them. He was short, but ramrod-straight, shoulders thrown back, a tanned face with white hair and a neat white moustache. *A former military man*, deduced Stark. *And a high-ranking one, I'd guess, from his bearing. A man used to issuing orders*. His guess was confirmed when Cavendish introduced him. 'This is General Squires.'

'Good evening, Chief Inspector,' said Squires, shaking Stark's hand. 'Dreadful business! I was chairing this evening's meeting. Felt it my duty to come and make sure the young chap got the right treatment. Lucky we got to the scene before it got any worse.'

'What actually happened?' asked Stark.

Squires looked towards Cavendish, who took up the tale. 'I'd just finished giving my talk, when one of the security people burst in saying there was a terrible assault taking place outside. A man being beaten.'

'Security people?' asked Stark.

'Unfortunately, we've had threats, Chief Inspector,' said Squires. 'Mainly from Jews and communists. They threatened to disrupt our meeting this evening, which is why we restricted it to members only.' He scowled. 'We should have let your brother in, my dear. Then none of this would have happened. The trouble is, if we'd let Bobby in, then other members would have complained that they also had family and friends they would have liked to bring to hear Mr Cavendish's talk. It would have caused bad feeling.'

'I'm sure Lettie appreciates that, don't you, Lettie?' said Cavendish sympathetically.

'Of course,' said Lettie, although the misery of her posture belied her words. 'What I can't understand is why Bobby was waiting outside the Mitre Hall. We'd agreed to see him at ten at the Savoy.'

'Anyway,' continued Squires, 'Mr Cavendish hurried out to see what was happening, along with some others, and there was your poor sergeant lying on the ground while these thugs kicked him.'

'I ran towards them, and they high-tailed it,' said Cavendish.

'You could have been hurt yourself!' said Lettie, horrified.

Cavendish shook his head. 'I don't like to see those kind of odds. And anyway, there were others with me.'

'Did you get a look at any of them?' asked Stark.

'Yes, but I didn't know them. Don't forget, I'm a stranger here.' He turned to General Squires. 'But General Squires here says he knows who they were.'

Stark looked inquisitively at the general.

'They were a gang of Jewish thugs,' scowled Squires. 'One

of my people recognized one of them as someone who turns up at our offices to harass us.'

'Do you know his name?'

Squires shook his head. 'My man said his name is Izzy, but he doesn't know his second name. Just that he's one of a bunch of Jewish thugs who seem determined to make our life a misery.' He gestured towards the ward doors. 'So far it's just taken the form of verbal abuse and things thrown at our office windows, but they've overstepped the mark this time. Trying to kill a police sergeant.' He turned apologetically to Lettie as they heard her stifle a sob. 'I'm sorry, my dear. I didn't mean for it to sound so brutal.'

'Would it be possible to talk to your man? The one who recognized this Izzy character?' asked Stark.

'Of course,' nodded Squires. 'I'll make arrangements for him to call on you at Scotland Yard. Will tomorrow afternoon be all right? I'll need to get hold of him first.'

'Tomorrow afternoon will be fine, thank you, General,' said Stark. 'I would suggest two o'clock. If he's not able to make that time . . .'

'He will,' said Squires, his face grim. 'This issue is too important not to be acted upon with immediacy.'

Cavendish put his arm protectively around Lettie's shoulders. 'We ought to be getting you home, my dear,' he said.

She shook her head. 'I need to stay here. With Bobby.'

'I'll stay with him, Miss Danvers,' Stark assured her. 'Mr Cavendish is right. You need to get some rest. If there's any news, I'll telephone your home immediately.'

'Good man,' said Squires approvingly. He turned to Cavendish. 'Perhaps we could share a taxi. We're all in the same area.'

'Certainly, General,' said Cavendish.

He looked solemnly at Stark. 'If there's anything I can do to help you get the people who did this . . .' he began, his voice concerned.

'Thank you, Mr Cavendish,' acknowledged Stark. 'I will certainly let you know if there is.'

He watched the three leave, feeling the muscles of his fists tighten as he watched them go. *You were part of this, Cavendish,* he said to himself silently, filled with a huge rage. *I don't know how, but I know you were involved. And I'll get you for it if it's the last thing I do*. His immediate concern was to keep Danvers protected, and right now he didn't know who else might be involved.

The British Union of Patriots seemed to be behind the murders of Lord Fairfax and Carl Adams, the murder of Harry Jukes and the attack on Israel Rothstein, and now – despite what General Squires said – this attack on Sergeant Danvers. So far Danvers was safe because he'd been brought to the hospital. For Stark, that indicated that Squires, for all his involvement with the BUP, was not part of the murderous clique. But Cavendish was. And others would be, too. And they would have no qualms about coming to the hospital and finishing Danvers off, to stop him talking about what had really happened at the Mitre Hall.

Normally, Stark would arrange for a police guard on Danvers while he was in the hospital, but that guard could turn out to be someone murderously sympathetic to the BUP, like PC Danny Fields.

No, he'd have to stay here himself, at least until he could arrange for personnel he could trust to take over.

He stepped into the ward, heading for the nurse's station, but a ward sister in a stiff white starched uniform held up a hand to stop him, and shepherded him back out to the waiting area.

Stark held out his warrant card to her and said, 'I'm Detective Chief Inspector Stark from Scotland Yard. My sergeant, Robert Danvers, was brought in here earlier. How is he?'

She frowned. 'Do you mean the Honourable Robert Danvers?'

The Honourable? The title gave Stark a jolt. But why was he surprised? He kept on receiving additional insights into his sergeant's background. 'Yes,' he said.

The ward sister regarded Stark suspiciously, as if she was having difficulty equating a member of the upper classes with the police force, before replying, 'He's still unconscious. At least, he was when I last looked in on him five minutes ago.'

'What's his prognosis?' asked Stark. When he saw her hesitate, he told her in gentle but firm tones, 'I'm not just a chief inspector, I also had a great deal of experience of hospitals during the war and I know about head injuries. Is he expected to survive?'

'We . . . hope so,' she said.

'And if he does, will he be able to function normally? Or will there be brain damage?'

'I'm afraid we won't be able to determine that until he recovers consciousness. *If* he recovers consciousness.'

Stark nodded at the words, his fears realized. *Please, God, don't let him die*, he prayed silently, at the same time telling himself acidly, *So much for not being a believer.*

'I would like to sit with him,' he said.

Stark saw the sister hesitate. Before she could start talking about permitted visiting hours, he added quickly, 'This is, after all, a police matter, which we are treating as attempted murder. If he dies, it will be a murder enquiry.'

She nodded. 'Very well,' she said. 'His sister authorized a private room for him, so you won't be disturbing the other patients.'

She led him back into the ward, then pushed open a door to a small room just inside the ward entrance. The blinds had been pulled and the room was illuminated by one small night light which gave a blueish glow. Danvers lay on his back in the bed, propped up on a bank of pillows. His eyes were closed, his head swathed in thick bandages. Stark noticed an oxygen cylinder by the bed and looked enquiringly at the ward sister.

'In case it was necessary,' she explained. 'His breathing stopped and we thought we might lose him. But then he started breathing again, on his own.'

'Thank you,' said Stark.

There was a chair in the corner of the room and he moved it so that it was next to Danvers' bed, and then settled himself down. It was going to be a long night.

NINETEEN

Stark fixed his eyes on his unconscious sergeant. Two nights, two hospitals. Last night at University College Hospital he had been restricted to the public waiting area. Here, thanks to Danvers' upper-class family and money, they were in a private room, one where visiting hours didn't appear to apply. It might have been due to the power of his warrant card as a detective chief inspector, but that hadn't helped him the previous evening at UCH.

In Danvers' small private room, the smells of disinfectant and ether gas permeating from the main ward took him back to his own experience of being in a field hospital towards the end of the war. Badly injured, stitched up, bandaged, and surrounded by men dying from wounds even worse than his. Then, the overwhelming smell had been of putrefying flesh. Here, in more civilized surroundings, everything seemed under control, but Stark knew it was all just a surface illusion. People were injured or became ill, and sometimes they died and sometimes they recovered, and there seemed to be very little the doctors and nurses could do to affect the outcome. It was like a game of chance. The throw of a dice.

It's my fault, Stark told himself as he looked at the still form of Danvers. *I should never have let you go there on your own. Agent Noble had warned us about the kind of people we're dealing with.* The brutal, almost sadistic way Fairfax and Adams had been killed showed their ruthlessness.

A beating by Jewish thugs, Squires had said. In just the same way that a Jewish factory owner was supposed to have beaten a trade union official to death in Finsbury Park.

Cavendish was a senior figure in the Ku Klux Klan. The KKK had murdered Noble's young friend back home in Georgia. For all his smooth surface condolences, Cavendish was rotten. How had that actor, Noël Coward, described him? Like a snake. Yes, that's what he was. Smooth and charming on the surface, reptilian and viciously dangerous underneath. The whole set-up stank.

He sat, almost motionless, watching Danvers, watching his chest beneath the blankets slowly rise and fall as he breathed. At least he was breathing evenly. He'd been with men on so many occasions during the war, watching them helplessly as their lives were ending, their breathing becoming uneven, ragged, sometimes great desperate gulps for air, other times a painful low humming sound, and he thought of his father, struggling for air.

He should telephone and see how he was. Right now, though, Stark wasn't going to be leaving Danvers unprotected. The vultures were out there, waiting.

Stay alive, Robert, he urged silently. *Don't die.*

Towards one o' clock he felt a drowsiness sweeping over him, and he fought against it to keep his eyes open.

It's because all I'm doing is sitting here in this half-light. My brain thinks I'm asleep so my body's following it. Maybe I should get up and go for a walk, outside, pace the hospital corridors, get some air. Wake me up.

He looked again at the comatose Danvers.

No. He might wake. He'll open his eyes, and there'll be no one here for him. I've been there. I know what that's like.

He dug his fingernails into the skin of his wrist, urging the pain to keep him awake. Then he settled back into his vigil.

It was about half an hour later that he heard a spluttering cough, and he realized with a shock that he must have fallen asleep. He turned towards the bed and saw Danvers stirring, his mouth open, breathing hard.

Danvers' eyes flickered and then opened. 'Where . . . where . . . ?' came the words, the bewilderment. His voice was hoarse and dry.

'It's all right, Robert. You're in hospital.'

'Sir?'

Stark saw that Danvers was struggling to push himself up, and he got up and gently eased him back down on to the pillows. 'Stay down,' he said. 'We don't know what the damage is yet.'

'I was kicked,' said Danvers.

'Yes,' said Stark. 'Don't move. That's an order. I'm going to get a nurse.'

As Stark made for the door, Danvers said weakly, 'It was the men from the hall.'

'Yes, I thought it might be,' said Stark. 'But don't talk now. We'll talk later. Stay where you are.'

Stark stepped out of the small side room just as the sister appeared. *She's been checking on us*, Stark realized. 'He's awake,' he said.

'Thank you,' she said.

As she made for the side room, Stark saw two figures hurry into the ward from the corridor: Danvers' parents.

'Mrs Danvers. Colonel,' nodded Stark.

'Mr Stark, where is he? How is he?' demanded Danvers' mother.

'He's in that side room,' said Stark. 'He's just come round. The ward sister is attending to him.'

Mrs Danvers moved swiftly to the side room and entered, the door closing behind her.

'Can we step outside?' asked Colonel Danvers. He gestured towards the darkened ward. 'Don't want to disturb the other patients by chattering here.'

Stark indicated the door of the side room. 'Perhaps we'd better wait for your wife, sir,' he said. 'The ward sister may ask her to leave.'

'I'd like to see her try!' said the colonel. 'Have you ever seen a mother tiger protecting her cub?'

'No, but I've seen a cow protecting her calf,' said Stark.

The colonel nodded. 'Exactly,' he said.

The two men went through the double doors of the ward into the waiting area.

'You look rough,' commented the colonel. 'I expect you haven't had any sleep.'

'No,' agreed Stark. Curious, he asked, 'When did you hear?'

'Only about half an hour ago. Victoria had got up for something – a premonition, I expect she'd tell you – and she heard Lettie sobbing in her room. She went in and Lettie told her about Robert. Stupid girl. She should have told us as soon as she got in.' He shook his head. 'Didn't want that character Cavendish having to face me, I suppose. Anyway, she told us that you'd volunteered to stay with him, but we decided to come. She said he was badly injured.'

'He's been unconscious since it happened. He only recovered consciousness a moment ago.'

'How did he seem?'

'It's a bit too early to say, but he was aware of what had happened. He tried to tell me about it, but I told him to wait. Thought the medicos ought to look at him first.'

'Good thinking,' nodded the colonel approvingly. 'I don't suppose we know what happened, do we? I got some garbled story from Lettie about some Jewish gangsters.'

'At the moment it's speculation,' cautioned Stark. 'I'm sure we'll get the full story when Robert's well enough to tell us.'

'Yes,' said the colonel. 'Look, Mr Stark, don't think I'm butting in, but we can take over from here. My man, Bridges, is with our car downstairs. He can run you home and then come back for us.'

'That's very kind of you, sir, but—'

'No buts, Chief Inspector. You've done your duty here. More

than done it, and we're very grateful. But we can carry on from here. Family and all that, you know.'

'The mother tiger?' suggested Stark.

The colonel gave a small smile. 'Exactly,' he said.

'The thing is, Colonel, I was staying because I'm concerned there might be another attack on Robert.'

'Another attack?' queried the colonel, puzzled.

Stark hesitated before enlarging on the statement. At the moment it was just a feeling he had, but it was one he didn't want to ignore. 'I may be wrong, but I suspect that there was more to the attack on him than just some thugs. We're working on a case that has . . . implications of something bigger. A conspiracy. I may be wrong, but if I'm not—'

'You're worried they may come here and try something?'

'Yes, sir.'

'In that case, you can rest easy, Mr Stark. We'll take watch from here on in.' He smiled. 'The mother tiger will keep him safe. And you'll need to get some sleep if you're going to be investigating this tomorrow. Need to be on top of your game.' Then he gave an apologetic frown. 'Sorry. You'd know all about that, of course, as an ex-soldier. Sleep when we can – that's the motto.'

'It is indeed, Colonel.'

Stark returned to the small side room to make one last check on Danvers. His sergeant was sleeping again, but more peacefully, his breathing normal. The staff nurse was checking his signs, his pulse and heart rate, and seemed satisfied.

'We cannot thank you enough for looking after Robert the way you did, Mr Stark,' Danvers' mother said earnestly. 'Not just tonight, but ever since he's been assigned to you.'

'Thank you, but there has been very little looking after to do,' murmured Stark.

As he headed down the marble stairs to the exit and the waiting car, he told himself off angrily for being a fraud. *I did not look after him. If I had, he wouldn't be lying in a hospital bed, his head swathed in bandages.*

He found Danvers' father's car parked a few yards from the hospital, as the colonel had described.

'How is Master Robert, sir?' asked Bridges as Stark opened the car door.

He's been expecting me, realized Stark. The colonel's orders.

Stark filled Bridges in on Danvers' condition, then let himself be driven to Camden Town. At this time of night the roads were virtually deserted, just the occasional horse and cart trundling along laden with early-morning deliveries.

Stark let himself into the house as quietly as he could, but even as he closed the front door he heard a sound from the landing. His mother appeared down the stairs, a look of concern on her face.

'How's your sergeant?' she asked.

'He's regained consciousness. He was kicked in the head. I hope he's going to be all right. Any phone calls from the hospital about Dad?'

Sarah shook her head.

'No news is good news,' said Stark. It was a platitude, but he felt at a loss to say anything else.

'Will you take me to the hospital in the morning, like you did yesterday?' she asked.

'Of course,' said Stark.

Sarah was about to return to her room, when she stopped and said, 'Your sergeant had better be careful. Head wounds can be bad. Tell him that from me. He's a good young man. He's got to be careful.'

'I will,' said Stark. 'I'm sorry I woke you, Mum.'

'I wasn't asleep, anyway. I can't sleep properly without your dad.' She headed back up the stairs. 'Goodnight, Paul.'

'Goodnight, Mum.'

TWENTY

Next morning Stark was up at his usual time of seven thirty, shaved and washed and sitting down to breakfast with Stephen and Sarah as the clock neared eight. He was just about to take his first spoonful of porridge when the sound of the telephone shattered the household.

Stark hurried to the phone, apprehensive. Which one was it? His father? Or had Danvers relapsed in the night? Had the injury been worse than they'd thought?

He snatched up the receiver.

'Mr Stark, it's Victoria Danvers.'

'Yes, Mrs Danvers.'

'I'm just letting you know that Robert's home. The hospital said that he's fit enough to be discharged, but they advise he needs to be looked after for a day or two, until we can be sure that everything is all right, so he's staying with us. I just wanted you to know.'

'Thank you. If it's all right with you, I shall call on him later today.'

'I think that is a very good idea. I know he'll be looking forward to it.'

'It's all right; it wasn't about Dad,' he told his anxious mother as he returned to the kitchen. 'It was Sergeant Danvers' mother to tell me he's home from hospital.'

As Stark picked up his spoon once more, he told himself, *And the next thing to do is get the bastards who did it.*

When Stark's driver arrived, it was a repeat of the previous morning: they let Stephen off at the school gates, then on to University College Hospital.

'I won't be a moment,' Stark told his driver.

Stark escorted his mother to the reception area. 'You take a seat, Mum. I want to see if I can have a word with the doctor.'

'I want to know how your dad is.'

'That's what I'm going to ask,' said Stark.

Reluctantly, Sarah allowed him to steer her towards the long bench. Stark went to the desk. A different nurse was on duty, but she had the same severe look about her.

'Good morning,' he said. 'I'm Detective Chief Inspector Stark.'

'Yes, sir,' nodded the nurse, and Stark was surprised to catch a hint of a smile of sympathy. 'I recognized you from your picture in the newspaper. I'm sorry about your father.'

'Yes, well . . .' Stark felt awkward. He'd come to the desk expecting to do battle against the forces of officialdom. 'How is my father this morning?' he asked.

'If you hold on a moment, I'll ring through to the ward.' She picked up a handwritten list of wards and patients.

'Ward ten,' Stark told her.

'Thank you.'

The answer she got to her enquiry was brief. 'Mr Stark had a comfortable night,' she told him.

'Is there any change in his condition?'

'Not according to the ward sister.'

'Is it possible to speak to Doctor Meek?'

She checked her lists again, then told him, 'I'm afraid Doctor Meek is on his rounds at the moment.'

'Is there anyone else I can talk to? Another doctor who's looking after my father?'

'I'm afraid they're all on their rounds. I can take a message. I'll see that Doctor Meek gets it.'

Stark nodded. Ideally, he'd have preferred to talk to Dr Meek – he'd been impressed by the doctor the previous evening – but the nurse seemed sincere when she said his message would get to Meek.

'Thank you, I'll be grateful if you would. Would you tell him that Mr Henry Stark's son, Detective Chief Inspector Stark . . .'

'He knows who you are,' she said gently, writing on a notepad. 'We all do.'

He gave her a grateful smile. 'Would you tell Doctor Meek that Mr Stark's son asks that if anything can be done to help his father's situation – a private room, private treatment, anything – DCI Stark will pay for it. I don't want his treatment to be limited under the Poor Law.'

She finished writing, then looked at him full in the face and said, 'I can assure you, Mr Stark, that is not the case here. Doctor Meek is deeply conscientious and will do everything above and beyond the call of duty to care for your father.'

'I apologize if I offended you,' said Stark. 'It wasn't my intention. I certainly didn't intend to cast aspersions on the staff here. It's just that, as I'm sure you are aware, we are very concerned. It's a very fine line between life and death.'

'I understand,' said the nurse. 'I'll see that Doctor Meek gets your message.'

Stark gestured towards Sarah on the bench. 'In the meantime, that is my mother sitting there.'

'Yes, I saw her yesterday.'

'She knows that visiting doesn't happen until ten o'clock, but she and my father have never been parted in over forty years of marriage. You seem a very kind person. I'd be most grateful if you could keep an eye on her. She won't be any trouble, but . . .'

'Of course.' She gave him that same gentle sympathetic smile. 'We'll do our best, Chief Inspector.'

The attack on Sergeant Danvers was the main topic of conversation when Stark arrived at the Yard. The newspaper headlines he'd seen at the news-stand as he'd left the hospital had made sure of that, with one blaring, 'Copper in coma.' And another: 'Detective at death's door.' They do love their alliterations, reflected Stark.

The desk sergeant, Sergeant Thorpe, was reading the report of the attack in the *Daily Target*.

'That's bad news about your sergeant, sir,' said Thorpe.

'Fortunately, his situation's improved since the press got hold of it,' said Stark. 'He's at home, recovering.'

'That's a relief,' said Thorpe. 'We ought to hang the bastards when we catch 'em.' He pointed upwards. 'The guvnor was in early today. He told me to tell you he needs to see you as soon as you got in.'

'Message received,' said Stark.

It had to be politics, Stark decided as he mounted the stairs to Benson's office. He couldn't think of any police reason why Benson needed to see him so urgently. Some politician must have been on Benson's back.

Benson was sitting at his desk when Stark entered his office. Stark was surprised to see the chief superintendent had a copy of the *Daily Target* open in front of him. A bit beneath Benson's opinion of himself, he thought. He was usually seen with *The Times*, or sometimes the *Telegraph*.

'You wanted to see me, sir,' said Stark.

'Yes,' nodded Benson. He tapped the newspaper. 'Dreadful business about Danvers. Nearly killed. In hospital, life hanging by a thread.'

'Yes, sir. Fortunately, he's been discharged and is at home now.'

'An attack by some Jewish thugs, I understand.'

'We're not sure about that, sir.'

Benson regarded Stark with a frown. 'Well, Lord Glenavon is, and he was at that meeting last night. The place where Danvers was attacked.'

'The BUP meeting at the Mitre Hall.'

'Yes. And so was General Squires. Both very respected men, and they are in no doubt about who was responsible.'

'Yes, General Squires gave me the same information when I saw him last night at the hospital.'

'There you are, then,' said Benson. He shook his head. 'We can't have this sort of thing, Stark. Attacks on police officers. It strikes at the very heart of society. Fortunately, Lord Glenavon has offered his assistance in solving the case and bringing the thugs who did it to justice.'

'His assistance, sir?'

'Lord Glenavon owns one of the most popular daily newspapers, the *Daily Target*. They are offering a reward of a hundred pounds for information leading to the arrest of the people who attacked Sergeant Danvers. What do you think about that?'

'Very generous of them, sir.'

'And in return I've agreed that one of their reporters can be involved in your investigation.'

Stark regarded the Chief Superintendent with stunned incredulity. 'Involved?'

'Yes, Stark.'

'How involved?'

'By accompanying you as you carry out your investigations.'

Stark shook his head. 'No, sir. Absolutely out of the question.'

Benson stared at Stark, equally incredulous. 'You are refusing this generous offer?'

'It is not a generous offer, sir. It is a way of this newspaper attempting to control the investigation and slant any evidence that is turned up to their political agenda. Frankly, sir, I have grave doubts that there were any so-called Jewish thugs involved in the attack on Sergeant Danvers. In fact, it is more likely that the attack was carried out by members of the British Union of Patriots.'

'That is preposterous! We have the word of General Squires! Are you saying he is lying?'

'We have the word of someone who reported that so-called fact to General Squires. I have the word of Sergeant Danvers, who informed me last night that he is fairly sure that one of the men who attacked him was from the BUP meeting at the Mitre Hall last night.'

Benson fell silent, mulling this over, before saying dismissively, 'Sergeant Danvers suffered a serious concussion. He is obviously confusing this man, who came to his aid, with those who attacked him.'

'I don't think so, sir.'

'Whatever the case, we have an excellent opportunity to get vital publicity for your investigation. This is the future, Stark. Working in cooperation with the newspapers! Think of the huge number of readers they have. Getting those readers on side increases the numbers of eyes and ears we have working for us.'

'The *Daily Target* will distort facts to suit its political agenda. We are supposed to be impartial, sir. There will be nothing impartial if we align ourselves with one particular newspaper.'

'Lord Glenavon is an honourable man, Stark. And a patriot. He supports the police, while some of those other so-called newspapers are vitriolic towards us in their editorials, with their allegations of corruption and favouritism.'

'That is why we should not be associated with any particular newspaper, sir.'

'And if I order you to take this reporter under your wing?'

'I shall refuse, sir. And if it becomes a resigning issue, then I shall resign. And I will give the reasons for my resignation in my letter to the Chief Constable, and to the Home Secretary.' He hesitated, then added, 'And, of course, to the newspapers. *All* the newspapers.'

Benson glared at Stark, a red flush of anger rising up from his collar. 'You are treading on very dangerous ground Stark,' he growled.

'Yes, sir. I believe I am. And so was Sergeant Danvers, which is why he was nearly killed.'

Stark felt a sense of rage inside him as he walked to his office. What was it that Short had said? 'We've got a lot of your people among us. Senior officers.' Was Benson part of this conspiracy, or was he just stupid, letting his vanity dominate his decision-making?

As he neared his office, he saw Donald Noble waiting outside. He, too, had a copy of the *Daily Target* clutched in his hand.

'I see in the paper your sergeant got a pretty bad going-over. Nearly killed. Is that right?'

'Yes. He was badly beaten and knocked unconscious. Fortunately, he seems to be recovering well. He's been discharged from the hospital.' *I think it would be a good idea to print a statement I can just hand to people*, he thought. *I'm going to be getting this all day.*

Noble followed him into the office. 'According to this paper, he was beaten up by some Jewish gang,' he said.

'Yes, that's what that particular newspaper would have us believe.'

'You don't buy it?'

'No. Even though a member of the British Union of Patriots claims to have identified one of the thugs as some kind of Jewish gangster called Izzy.'

'A stitch-up?' frowned Noble.

'Yes, I believe it may well be. I think that Danvers was beaten up to stop him noting who was going into the Mitre Hall. And also as a warning.'

'What is this British Union of Patriots?' asked Noble.

'Actually, I was hoping you might be able to help me with that,' said Stark. 'With your knowledge of the Ku Klux Klan, and your theory that Cavendish is over here to form links with right-wing groups in Europe.'

'He is,' said Noble firmly. 'The trouble is, there are so many of these groups springing up we can't keep tabs on them all.'

'Sergeant Danvers mentioned before he went to the meeting that his mother knew some of the people involved. I told her I'd pay the sergeant a visit at home. See how he is, and also get some names. Fancy coming with me?'

'Good idea. The more I can find out about what's going on, the nearer I'll be to nailing Cavendish.'

'You're convinced he's our murderer?'

'He's involved – that I'm sure of. How far is your sergeant's place?'

'His parents' home. Hampstead.'

'In walking distance?'

'If you've got an hour to spare. I suggest we get a car from the motor pool.'

They headed down the stairs and into the main reception. Stark was just leading the way to the door that led to the underground car park when he heard Amelia's voice call out, 'Paul!'

He turned, surprised, and saw her hurrying towards him. Like nearly everyone else he'd met today, she was holding a newspaper, and she thrust it towards him. 'Is this true? About Bobby?'

'It's true that he was badly beaten and hospitalized. As to the culprits, we're still working on that.' He saw that Noble was watching this encounter with interest, and he introduced him. 'This is Special Agent Donald Noble with the American Bureau of Investigation. Agent Noble, this is Lady Amelia Fairfax.'

As Noble took Amelia's hand to shake it, he stopped. 'Lady Amelia? Lord Fairfax's widow?'

'Ex-wife. We were divorced,' said Amelia.

'I am still sorry for your loss,' said Noble.

'Agent Noble is investigating Carl Adams' death,' explained Stark. 'We therefore have a mutual interest that has led to us working together.'

'How is Bobby?' asked Amelia. 'I telephoned the hospital, but they refused to give out any information about his condition except to family. I did think of saying I was a relative, but I thought that might make things unpleasant for Victoria or Lettie if they telephoned.'

'He's been released,' said Stark. 'Agent Noble and I are going to visit him at the family home.'

'Can I come?' asked Amelia. She saw Stark's hesitation, and added hastily, 'No, of course not. Official business.'

'It's not just that,' said Stark. 'He's still recovering. Too many people . . .'

'Of course,' she said quickly. She hesitated, then asked, 'Can we have a private word?'

Noble nodded and moved away a discreet distance, but Stark was aware that he was watching them. A policeman's curiosity aroused? That, and plain nosiness, just like Stark.

'I hear that your father's in hospital,' she said.

'Where did you hear that?'

'A friend.'

'A friend?' he echoed.

'All right, it was at a women's meeting. Last night.'

'Social?'

She glared at him, insulted.

'All right, I apologize,' he said. 'Politics. Equal voting rights.'

'Among many things that are unequal in this society. Property rights. The right to be a doctor.' She stopped and shook her head. 'My turn to apologize. I didn't intend this to be political. Someone I know was at this meeting. She's a staff nurse at UCH, and she was telling me about the famous Chief Inspector Stark coming in.'

'The *famous*?' said Stark, incredulously.

'Don't worry, she said it sarcastically. She's anti-royalist, so although she thinks what you did was brave, she's not sure about saving the monarchy.'

'I'm not sure which is worse, her being sarcastic or—'

'Forget that. The point is, she told me about your father. Pneumonia, pleurisy, bronchitis.'

'I'm sure that's unethical, passing on information like that.'

'She did it because she knows . . . how I feel about you.'

'How does she know that?'

'Because I may have said something when I first met you,' Amelia admitted angrily.

'*May*?'

'Will you stop treating this like an interrogation! The point is, your father is seriously ill!'

'Yes, I am aware of that,' said Stark, wondering where this was leading.

'And you and I both know that there is a division in this country when it comes to medical treatment. The rich get everything they want. The poor . . . struggle through. If they're lucky.'

Stark felt himself tense, felt anger towards her rising within him.

'The thing is,' she continued, 'I'd like to help. If money's needed . . .'

He glared at her. 'What is this? Lady Bountiful helping the deserving poor?'

She stared at him, shocked.

'We're not poor!' he snapped.

'You're always telling me you are. That's why you've got such a big chip on your shoulder. You're almost as bad as I am about social injustice. We both know it happens. That's why I'm involved in politics.'

'So my father's a political cause now, is he?'

She glared at him, and Stark felt that if they hadn't been in a public place, she would have hit him. Immediately, he knew he'd gone too far. 'I'm sorry . . .' he began.

'No, you're not,' she snapped. 'You're too bloody bogged down in your holier-than-thou hair-shirt anger. This was nothing to do with politics. It was to do with how I feel about you. Well, you can forget it. And don't ask me how I feel about you, because you don't want to know!'

With that, she turned and stormed away from him, and out into the street.

Noble approached him. 'I couldn't hear what was said, but I saw the body language. That was pretty fast, the way you turned someone who obviously liked you into someone ready to spit on your grave.'

'It's . . . complicated,' said Stark.

'It certainly is,' agreed Noble. 'Lady Amelia Fairfax. Widow of the victim of the murder we're investigating.'

'Divorced years ago.'

'Do you want to talk about it?' asked Noble.

'No,' said Stark. 'It's not an issue.'

Noble shrugged. 'If you say so.' He regarded Stark quizzically. 'Anything else I should know about?'

'No,' said Stark.

TWENTY-ONE

If Noble was impressed by the Danvers' large house in Hampstead, he didn't show it. But then, Stark reflected, these town houses were small beer by comparison with some of the grand houses in America he'd seen pictures of. America had its own aristocracy, although there it was based on money and political power. True, there were the 'old families', those who had gone to America with the Pilgrim Fathers, and those first plantation owners in the Southern states. But mainly it seemed to Stark that social prestige in America was based on money rather than a bloodline. And *earned* money, rather than inherited because, way back in time long gone, some ancestor had once given a king a particularly sumptuous meal.

Bridges showed Stark and Noble into the drawing room, where they found Sergeant Danvers reading a newspaper, while his mother flicked through the pages of a magazine. Both stood up as Stark and Noble walked in. Stark did the introductions, and then they all took their seats while Bridges departed to the kitchen with orders for coffee and biscuits. Stark observed that, although Danvers still had a bandage wrapped around the top of his head, it was only a light one rather than the bulky turban-like one he'd worn the last time Stark had seen him.

'I'm afraid the colonel's out,' apologized Danvers' mother. 'He's got an appointment with his tailor. He tried to cancel it, but I insisted he keep it.'

'Mother thinks that father dresses like a tramp,' smiled Danvers.

'I do not say that,' his mother reprimanded him. 'I just feel he should wear more than just the same clothes he always does.' She turned back to her guests. 'Letitia is here, but in her room. She's being . . .'

'Odd,' finished Danvers. 'She's acting like the depressed heroine of some romantic novel.'

'I think she's just upset because of what happened to you, Robert.' His mother hesitated, then admitted, 'Although the fact that she hasn't heard from Mr Cavendish this morning may be another factor. I've noticed that every time the telephone rings she rushes to answer it, and seems very disappointed when she discovers it's mostly people asking how Robert is.'

'And how are you?' asked Stark.

'Not too bad, thank you, sir,' said Danvers. 'I've still got a bit of an ache on one side of my head. The doctor said there might be a slight fracture, but he assured me it's nothing to worry about and it will heal.'

'A fractured skull?' said Noble, concerned. 'Nothing to worry about?'

Danvers touched the bandage around his head. 'It's not as bad as it looks. This is mainly to remind me so I don't go banging my head against things.'

The door opened and Mrs Henderson, the housekeeper, came in bearing a tray with coffee and biscuits. Victoria Danvers got up.

'Thank you, Mrs Henderson. I'll take my coffee in the library.'
She turned to the men. 'I know you have business to talk about
with Robert, so I'll leave you to that.'

Mrs Henderson put the tray down on a small table, then she
and Mrs Danvers left.

'Thank you for staying with me, sir,' said Danvers. 'My parents
told me.'

'It was the least I could do,' said Stark. 'You were there because
of me.'

Noble produced the copy of the *Daily Target* he'd brought
with him.

'The paper says you were attacked by a bunch of Jews,' he said.

'That's not how I remember it,' said Danvers. 'I'm fairly sure
that I saw one of the men who attacked me, inside the hall,
showing people in, while I was waiting for Lettie to appear.'

Danvers filled them in on what had happened the night before:
being refused admission into the hall, arranging to meet Lettie
and Cavendish at the Savoy at ten. 'But then I thought it might
be interesting to see how many names I could spot as people
came out. I already had a few from earlier: two I'd been at school
with – Reginald Worthington and Walter Bagshot – and Lord
and Lady Monkton, plus some my mother had mentioned to me
as members of the BUP – Lord Wickford, Sir Watkyn Keyes,
Lady Mantle.'

'A select crowd,' growled Noble. 'The crème de la crème of
society.'

'Unfortunately, I didn't get a chance to get many more, because
I was grabbed by this man and some others.'

'And you're certain the man who attacked you was part of the
meeting?'

'Yes, sir. It was only a fleeting glance, but I saw four men just
inside the entrance acting as ushers when I was there before, in
addition to the two men acting as security outside, and I could
swear that one of the men who attacked me was one of those.'

'It would be interesting to find out what was going on at that
meeting that was so secret they needed to keep people out.'

'I could try talking to Chuffy Worthingon or Walter Bagshot?'
suggested Danvers.

'At the moment, Sergeant, I'd prefer it if you kept a low
profile,' said Stark. 'At least until we know your head is feeling

better.' He hesitated, then said quietly, 'There is one person in this house who was inside the Mitre Hall last night.'

'Lettie?' said Danvers. He thought it over, then nodded. 'But you've seen how protective she is of Cavendish. She may have been told to keep quiet.'

'And she may not have been,' countered Stark. 'There's only one way to find out.'

'I'll go and get her,' said Danvers, getting up.

He returned a short while later with Lettie. She looked nervous.

'This is all so terrible!' she said. 'What's going on? Why did those Jews attack Bobby?'

'That's what we're trying to find out,' said Stark gently. 'It would help us if we could work out why they, or anyone else, would want to mess up the meeting. What sort of meeting was it?'

'It was a talk,' said Lettie. Her face lit up as she added, 'Edgar was giving it.'

'A talk about what?'

'About the moving picture business.'

'About the stars? Charlie Chaplin, Tom Mix?'

'Well, I *thought* it was going to be about the stars, and things like that, but it was mainly about how it was run. I'm sure if you ask Edgar himself, he'd be happy to tell you all about what he said.'

'I'm sure,' nodded Stark, 'but we're trying to go as fast as we can to get to the people who attacked your brother.'

'Oh, I see!' said Lettie. 'The Jews.'

Stark saw that Noble was about to say something, so he cut in quickly and gently added, 'Yes. Did Mr Cavendish – Edgar – mention anything about Jews in his talk? Anything that might make them want to turn up and interrupt it, as General Squires said?'

Lettie nodded. 'Yes. He was worried about what they were doing. He said that the Jews were infiltrating the moving picture business to try to undermine our way of life. The American and British way, that is. He said they were set on making films that sold Bolshevik and Jewish propaganda. He said there were a lot of Jews from Russia who'd come to America to make pictures to upset things without people realizing what was going on. He even mentioned the names of the people who were behind it.'

'What were they?' asked Stark. 'Can you remember?'

'They were funny names,' said Lettie. 'Jewish names. There was someone called Goldfish. Samuel Goldfish. Edgar said he's changed his name to Samuel Goldwyn so no one would know he was a Jew. And another one called Mayer something.'

'Louis B. Mayer?' asked Noble.

'Yes, that's him!' said Lettie. 'Edgar said he had a different name in Russia, but he changed it when he came to America. Edgar said that's what they all did to hide who they really were, and what they were after.'

'And what are they after?' asked Stark.

'To take over,' said Lettie. 'He said that's what the Jews are doing. Bit by bit, they're taking over everything. All the factories. The banks. And now the moving picture business.' She looked at Danvers. 'Is that why they beat you up, Bobby? Part of their plan to try to break up the meeting. That's what Edgar said they were trying to do.'

'I don't think it was Jews who beat me up, Lettie,' said Danvers. 'I think it was people hired by the BUP. The British Union of Patriots.'

Lettie stared at him, stunned. 'But . . . why would they do that?'

'I think they thought I was spying on the meeting.'

'But that's nonsense! You were waiting for us!'

Stark looked questioningly at Danvers, who hesitated, then admitted awkwardly, 'Yes, I was waiting for you, Lettie. But I also wanted to find out what was going on at the meeting, and who was there.'

'But all you had to do was ask!'

'I did ask if I could come in, but Edgar said I couldn't, if you remember.'

'Because he had no say in the matter.' She looked at Danvers, then at Stark and Noble with sudden suspicion. 'What's going on?' she demanded accusingly. She turned on her brother. 'What were you actually doing at the hall last night? Were you spying?'

'Yes,' admitted Danvers.

'Why?'

'Because, Miss Danvers, we don't think that Edgar Cavendish is what he says he is,' said Noble.

'Who's we?' she demanded curtly.

'The American Bureau of Investigation,' said Noble. 'Carl

Adams was an undercover agent for the Bureau. He came to England to keep an eye on your friend Cavendish.'

'But Edgar *is* a film producer!' protested Lettie angrily. 'He made *The Birth of a Nation!*'

'He was a distributor,' corrected Noble. 'And I'm not saying he isn't connected with the moving picture business. I'm saying he has a bigger and hidden agenda.'

'Politics,' added Stark. 'Anti-Jewish politics.'

'He's a leading member of the Ku Klux Klan,' said Noble.

Lettie leapt to her feet, her face white with anger. 'I don't know who or what this Ku Klux . . . thing . . . is!' she snapped. 'And I know what this is about! You've been asked by Mummy and Daddy to turn me against Edgar! Well, I won't!'

With that, she stormed across the room and out, slamming the door behind her.

Stark looked ruefully at his sergeant. 'I don't think we've helped the atmosphere in this house,' he said.

The door opened and Victoria Danvers came in, worried. 'What's going on?' she demanded. 'Letitia has just snatched her coat and stormed out of the house.'

'I'm afraid I finally had that heart-to-heart talk with her about Cavendish,' said Danvers. 'I told her some home truths about him, which she didn't like.'

'*We* told her some facts about him that upset her,' corrected Stark apologetically.

'What sort of facts?'

'The stuff you and Father wanted me to tell her about him,' said Danvers, his manner slightly defensive. 'That he's a person who can't be trusted.'

'He's here to stir up trouble against Jews under the pretence of getting money for film production,' said Noble. 'Your daughter unwittingly confirmed that, although we were pretty sure of it beforehand.'

Victoria Danvers looked at them, bewildered, helpless. 'But . . . what are we to do?' she asked.

'Be there for her,' advised Stark.

TWENTY-TWO

As Stark and Noble headed back towards Scotland Yard, Noble said, 'So, what's our next move? Pick up Cavendish?'

'On what grounds?' asked Stark. 'Yes, he's promoting anti-Semitic views, but that's not against the law in this country.'

'For murder,' said Noble. 'You and I both know he was involved in the murders of Carl and Lord Fairfax.'

'We *suspect* it,' clarified Stark. 'He's an American citizen, and a prominent one at that. We can't pull him in without evidence.'

'He did it!' burst out Noble.

'I agree that he either did it himself, with others, or he organized it. But without firm evidence we can't move against him.'

'What sort of evidence?'

'For one thing, finding out what Carl Adams was meeting Lord Fairfax about. That's the key to this. Cavendish and his accomplices had to stop them talking, and stop Lord Fairfax from passing on whatever Adams told him.'

'How do we find that out?'

'We keep asking questions,' replied Stark.

'OK, I'll start at the embassy,' said Noble. 'There are people there I knew back in the States. Cavendish would have used the embassy, that's for sure. What about you?'

'I have to meet a man who's going to lie to me,' said Stark.

Even without being told, Stark was fairly sure the very large man sitting on one of the benches in the reception area of Scotland Yard, and wearing a tight-fitting blue suit, was Herbert Jolly. For one thing, he didn't look happy. It wasn't just the fact that his clothes were too small for him for comfort; it showed in the beads of sweat on his forehead, and the way he kept his head down, bringing it up now and then to dart suspicious glances at everyone. A man who definitely doesn't want to be here and is only here under great pressure, but is worried that he might say something that will incriminate him, or others. Then there was the broken nose, one ear flattened, thickened skin around his eyes. A fighter. A tough doorman. However, it was worth checking. Stark didn't want to be embarrassed by approaching someone who might turn out to be something completely different: a solicitor's clerk rather than a client.

'Is anyone waiting for me?' he asked at the desk.

The sergeant checked the register, then announced, 'There's a Mr Herbert Jolly. Says he's been sent by a General Squires.' He gestured towards the man in the blue suit. 'He's over there.'

Stark strode over to the man. 'Mr Jolly?' he asked.

The man looked up at Stark warily.

'I'm Detective Chief Inspector Stark. Thank you so much for coming in.'

'The General said for me to come,' grunted Jolly, getting to his feet.

'Indeed, he did,' nodded Stark. 'We'll talk in my office. More private.'

Stark led the way as Jolly lumbered along unwillingly beside him. Not light on his feet. Not agile. So, not a real boxer. A street fighter. Or more likely just another lump of muscle who gets put into a ring and beaten to a pulp to make the next up-and-coming championship contender look good.

Stark wondered if it had been Jolly who'd beaten Danvers? There was one way to find out: call the sergeant in and let him take a look at the man, see if he recognized him. But would Squires or Cavendish take that much of a chance, to send the attacker to the Yard to spin the spurious story? Jolly didn't look as if he had the kind of brain that could handle awkward questioning. It was more likely that Jolly was just a stooge sent to feed Stark a lie. But there was always a chance that Squires had overreached himself.

They got to Stark's office and Stark said, 'Would you mind waiting here, outside, just for a moment, Mr Jolly? There's a telephone call I need to make.'

Jolly didn't look happy about being anywhere here in the heart of Scotland Yard, but he nodded. Stark pointed at a chair a few paces along the corridor. 'There, take a seat. I won't be long.'

Stark went into the office, picked up the phone and asked to be connected to Danvers' parents' house. Bridges, the valet, answered, and soon afterwards Stark was talking to Sergeant Danvers.

'If you're up to it, I want you to come in and sit in reception at the Yard.'

'I'm up to it, sir. I'm going mad sitting around here, kicking my heels. What's the job?'

'A case of identifying someone. When you get here, ask the desk sergeant to ring our office to let me know you've arrived. I'll come down with a man in a blue suit. I want you to see if you recognize him.'

'Will do, sir.'

That done, Stark opened the door and ushered Jolly into the office.

'My apologies for that. Just some business. Do come in, Mr Jolly. Take a seat.' As the large man settled himself down in the chair on the other side of the desk, Stark began, 'General Squires said you saw who attacked my sergeant last night outside the Mitre Hall.'

'Yus,' said Jolly. 'That's right.'

'What exactly were your duties last night?'

The big man frowned. 'What?'

'What had the general asked you to do?'

'To guard the door. Not let people in if they didn't have the proper stuff.'

'And what was the proper stuff?'

'An invitation or a membership card.'

'What sort of membership card?'

'One of these.' And the man took out a card from his inside pocket and slid it across the desk to Stark. It had the words *British Union of Patriots* in bold type across the top, with a Union Jack at one side and a cross on the other. Below, where it said *Member's Name*, someone had written in a neat hand *Herbert Jolly*. Beneath that, where it said *Member's Signature*, there was an indecipherable squiggle. Lastly, the membership number at the bottom proclaimed that Herbert Jolly was Member Number 459.

'Thank you,' said Stark, returning the card. 'How long have you been a member?'

'About two months,' said Jolly. Even this answer he gave with a suspicious look at Stark, as if it was some kind of trap.

'The general said that you recognized one of the attackers.'

'Yus,' nodded Jolly. 'Izzy.'

'Izzy?'

'Yus.'

'Do you happen to know his second name?'

Jolly shook his head.

'How do you know he's called Izzy?'

'Cos that's what I heard one of the others call him.'

'When? Last night?'

Jolly shook his head. 'About a week ago. I was at the shop.'

'The shop?'

'The headquarters, in Warren Street.'

'Yes, I know it,' nodded Stark. 'I was in there only recently, talking to Eric Short.'

At this, the tension in Jolly eased a little. 'Eric!' he beamed. 'Good bloke!'

'Yes, indeed, so he seemed to me,' agreed Stark. 'So, what happened at the shop?'

'This bunch of Jews came in and started throwing their weight about. Calling us names. Then one of 'em started taking books out of the case and chucking 'em on the floor. That's when I had to take some action. Defending our property, it was.'

'Indeed,' nodded Stark sympathetically. 'What action did you take?'

'I 'it one of 'em. Straight out the shop door he went. Landed on 'is arse on the pavement. That's when one of the others shouted out, "Leg it, Izzy!" And this one with a bald head ran out. And so did the others.'

'So this one with the bald head was Izzy?'

Jolly nodded firmly. 'Yus. On account of 'im doin' a runner when they called that name.'

'You didn't hear any other names called?'

Jolly shook his head. 'No. Just that one.'

'And you recognized this same man, the bald-headed one, as one of the men attacking Sergeant Danvers last night?'

A firm nod of the head again. 'Yes. It was 'im. No mistake. Izzy. The Jew.'

'And what about the other men?'

'They all ran off as they saw us coming. It was dark there at that point in the street.'

'But you saw enough to identify Izzy.'

Jolly hesitated momentarily, then nodded. 'It was the bald head.' Then his face lit up with a grin. 'And the street lamp.'

'The street lamp?'

'Across the street. It ain't very strong, but there was enough for me to see the bloke's face.' He nodded. 'It was Izzy.'

There was a click as the door opened, and Jolly swung round, suddenly on his guard, but then he visibly relaxed as he saw Chief Superintendent Benson. Stark shot a look at Benson, and was sure he saw a tremor of alarm in the chief superintendent's face. *They know one other*, he realized.

'Stark,' said Benson tautly, 'I need to talk to you.'

'Yes, sir. Now?'

By way of answer, Benson retreated to the corridor, Stark following. As soon as the door was shut, Benson demanded, 'Who is that man?'

'A Herbert Jolly, sir.'

'What's he doing here?'

'He's helping us with our enquiries.'

Benson hesitated, then demanded, 'Which particular enquiries?'

'The murders of Lord Fairfax and the American, Carl Adams, and the attack on Sergeant Danvers.'

Stark was sure he saw Benson swallow nervously before asking, 'Are you saying he's a suspect?'

'I'm just saying that he's helping us with our enquiries. Why, sir? Do you know him in some way?'

Benson shook his head. 'No,' he said curtly. 'Keep me informed. Take no action without first consulting me.'

As Benson turned and began to walk away, Stark called after him, 'Yes, sir. Was there anything in particular you wanted to see me about?'

'It can wait,' snapped back Benson. 'It's not important.'

Interesting, thought Stark. He went back into the office.

'I'm sorry about that, Mr Jolly,' he smiled apologetically. 'Just one or two more quick questions?'

This made Jolly look apprehensive again, and Stark hurried to reassure him. 'Nothing about the attack. Just routine for the records.' He drew a sheet of paper towards him, took out his pen and said, 'Your address, just in case we need to get in touch with you again.'

'Why might you do that?' demanded Jolly suspiciously. 'I've told you everything.'

'Yes, but say we are able to lay our hands on this Izzy, you're the one who can identify him,' said Stark.

'I don't know about that,' said Jolly doubtfully.

'Oh, come, Mr Jolly, I'm sure you're as eager as us to bring this thug to justice. After all, he attacked a policeman. And he tried to smash up the BUP shop.'

'Well . . . yeah,' agreed Jolly, but with reluctance.

Just then the telephone rang.

'Excuse me,' apologized Stark, and he picked up the receiver.

'This is the main desk, sir,' said a voice. 'DS Danvers is in reception.'

'Thank you, Sergeant,' said Stark. 'Please tell him I'll be down shortly.'

He replaced the receiver, then smiled at Jolly. 'You were about to tell me your address.'

'Yus,' nodded Jolly. 'It's Red Tops. Near Parliament Hill Fields. Lord Glenavon's place.'

'Lord Glenavon?'

Again, Jolly nodded. 'Yus. I work for him. General handyman. I live in.'

'Thank you,' said Stark, writing the address down. He stood up. 'That's all for the moment. I'll walk you down to reception.'

As they walked down the stairs, Stark added, 'We do appreciate your coming in, Mr Jolly. If only every person was as responsible a citizen, our job would be a whole lot easier. As I'm sure you'll have heard already from Chief Superintendent Benson.'

Jolly stopped on the stairs. 'Who?' he demanded, his voice flat, looking at Stark with that same look of suspicion.

'My boss,' said Stark. 'The one who came into the room. I got the impression he recognized you.'

'No,' said Jolly. 'Never see 'im before.'

'My mistake,' murmured Stark.

They continued down to the ground floor, then Stark walked the big man across the reception area to the double doors to the street. He shook him by the hand, then walked over to where Danvers was sitting.

'Well?' he asked.

Danvers shook his head. 'I recognize him, but not as one of those who attacked me. He was one of the men on duty at the door when I first turned up.'

'Any chance he could have been one of those who beat you up?'

'It's possible. He was certainly part of the security detail for the evening. But I can't swear to it. I'm sorry, sir.'

'No problem, Sergeant. It was worth a try. One good thing, though, I think we may be disturbing this particular hornet's nest. All we have to do is see what flies out. And make sure we don't get stung.'

'There is one positive thing, sir,' said Danvers. 'The doctor says there isn't a fracture or serious damage, and I can return to work. So I'll be back tomorrow morning.'

TWENTY-THREE

Noble showed his pass to the uniformed sentry guarding the entrance to the American Embassy and was waved in. He was thinking about the scene between Stark and Lady Amelia Fairfax. The widow of the murder victim, for Chrissake! Yes, there was definitely something going on there. Noble just hoped it wouldn't compromise the investigation. He liked Stark. The chief inspector came over as a straight-arrow kind of guy. Maybe whatever was happening between the pair of them was separate from this case, but it sure added another dimension.

But then, it was an easy thing to fall into. It had happened to him with that dame in Wyoming. How was he to know she was the sister of the guy he was tailing? That had been a difficult one, especially when she had tried to stab him. She'd come at him with a knife when he was lying in bed, after they'd had sex. Maybe that had been a good move on her part, maybe a bad one. If she tried it before they'd had sex, he might have been more alert, on edge, so maybe she was thinking he'd be relaxed, almost sleepy. What saved him was needing to pee; he was just about to get out of bed and go to the bathroom when she ran in from the kitchen, knife clenched in her hand. He still had the scar.

He'd try to find out more about this Lady Amelia Fairfax. That was a strange coupling: the lady and the copper. Two worlds colliding.

Like Carl and Lord Fairfax. Two strangers meet, and something weird happens. But Carl and Fairfax weren't strangers. Carl had sought out this Lord Fairfax, so they knew one another. Buddies from the war, he guessed. But why kill them?

It was Cavendish, of course. Had to be. Somehow he'd spotted that Carl was on to him. But hell, everyone knew about Cavendish's connection with the KKK. Back in the States, it was even something he boasted about. No, something had happened here that Carl had discovered, that Cavendish desperately needed to be kept quiet. So desperately that he'd had Carl killed, along with that English lord.

Why the weed killer? Why not just stab them, or shoot them, or strangle them?

Because Cavendish and whoever he was working with needed to know what they knew. Who else had Adams talked to? So they'd killed Lord Fairfax first to show Carl how bad this way of dying was. But Carl hadn't been able to tell them anything else, because there was nothing else. The only person he'd been in touch with had been Noble, and by wire.

So, whatever it was that Adams had discovered, it had happened around the time he sent the wire. And, ever after, he'd been on borrowed time.

How had Cavendish found out about Carl's wire to Noble? The leak had to be inside the embassy.

Once again Noble felt the rage welling up in him. Carl and him. The boy from Georgia and the kid from Chicago. They'd met up on the Bureau of Investigation training course in Washington. Carl had been a former patrolman. Noble had got into covert investigations as he hunted down the KKK, and had been headhunted by the honchos at the Bureau. He and Carl had found they were like peas in the pod: the same tastes – well, apart from the football and baseball teams they supported – and the same politics. Democrats in a world where almost everyone else seemed to be Republicans.

They worked cases together, and they brought the bad guys to book. They had a style: Carl played the cool one, laid-back, almost horizontal, whereas Noble was Mr Angry. Good cop, bad cop. The bad guys preferred being grabbed by Carl, Mr Nice

Guy. What they didn't realize was that, beneath that cool cover, Carl was harder than Noble. He'd smile lazily while working out how to kill you.

When the order came to keep a close watch on Edgar Cavendish while he was in England and find out what he was doing, it was obvious that it had to be Carl who moved in and became close to him. In KKK circles, Noble was too well known as the enemy.

So Carl had arranged an introduction to Cavendish with prettied-up credentials saying he was some hotshot backroom financier in the moving picture business. The Bureau of Investigation had even arranged letters of introduction for Carl from some movie big names. Non-Jewish, of course. But people who were patriots. Republicans, mostly. And with Carl saying his company would pay his expenses because it was a great opportunity for them to break into the European market, plus a bit of flattery from Carl to Cavendish about what a genius he was and how Carl hoped to learn from him, the deal was done.

So what had gone wrong?

Maybe they'd underestimated Cavendish. He came across as some sort of slick snake-oil salesman, a smooth-talking charmer who tried to dress and look like Douglas Fairbanks – something that worked with the women, for sure. Mr Smooth, a respectable front for the KKK. But not dangerous. There was nothing in the file on him to indicate that he'd ever engaged in violence. He'd instigated it and encouraged it by others, sure. And the Bureau said that in England he wouldn't have his KKK bully boys around him, so Carl would be safe, even if he was discovered. Carl could handle himself against a pussy like Cavendish.

But Carl hadn't been able to handle himself, and now he was dead.

Noble found the person he was looking for in the press office: Jerry O'Keeffe. Originally from Boston – of course he was, with a name like O'Keeffe – and now a senior press officer with the embassy, part of the US government's propaganda machine putting out the government line to the British press. Noble and O'Keeffe had first met at a Democratic Party convention two years before. At first Noble had been suspicious of him: was he here as a Republican to trash the Democrats?

'A Republican?' O'Keeffe had laughed. 'Hell, I got this job

because of the work I did to get Woodrow Wilson elected for his second term.'

The victory for Republican Warren G. Harding over the Democrats earlier in the year had changed things in Washington, and O'Keeffe had found himself being offered the posting to the American Embassy in London.

'Sure, it's a demotion being pushed out of Washington,' O'Keeffe had told Noble with a shrug after he'd been told the news, 'but so what? It's a job, and doing something I enjoy and I'm good at. In these hard times, that's great. Plus it means Eileen and I will be nearer to the old families back in County Cork. We'll be able to catch up. Big Irish wakes. You can't beat 'em!'

Noble rapped at the door of the press room and saw O'Keeffe looking up quizzically from his desk as he pushed open the door. O'Keeffe's face split into a grin as he saw it was Noble, and he got up and hurried towards him, his hand outstretched.

'Don, you son of a gun! When did you land?'

'The day before yesterday. When I heard about Carl.'

O'Keeffe's face clouded over. 'How on earth did that happen? Who'd do a thing like that? And why?'

'We've got our suspicions,' said Noble.

'Do you think he was the target? Or was it that other fella? Lord Fairfax?'

Noble gave a rueful sigh. Even though he counted O'Keeffe as a friend, he was first and foremost a press officer looking for a story.

'We're not sure, but I promise you, Jerry, as soon as we find out, you'll be the first to know. One of the reasons I'm here is to see if you can throw any light on what may have been going on with Carl here in England.'

O'Keeffe shrugged. 'On the surface, he was just a businessman trying to drum up a connection for Stateside picture makers.'

'On the surface?' queried Noble.

'Oh, come on, Don! How long have I been in this game? All those years in Washington? And, let's face it, Cavendish has hardly been shy about his KKK credentials. He's a big shot back in Indiana because of it. He's built a career out of it. So it was obvious to me that Carl had been sent to keep an eye on Cavendish.'

Noble looked around him, uncomfortable. 'Anyone else here work that out?'

O'Keeffe shrugged. 'If they did, no one said anything to me. But there's only a few of us home-grown Yanks here. Most of the workers are British who know zilch about things American, except what they read in the magazines.'

'What about the people from back home?'

O'Keeffe shook his head. 'To be frank, I doubt it. Most of them have been here so long they've almost become English. They still wait for the baseball results as eagerly as ever, but mostly they've settled here. They pay attention to whatever's happening in politics back home, but only really when there's a presidential election. And that's because they're wondering how they'll be affected.'

'Did Carl ever call in here?'

'He came in a couple of times with Cavendish to see the ambassador.'

'And how is the Honourable George Brinton McClellan Harvey?' asked Noble acidly.

'Hey, don't knock him,' protested O'Keeffe. 'He's not a bad guy. He's a good front man for America.' He smiled. 'And I'm not betraying any confidences when I tell you he doesn't like it here. He's hoping that Harding will bring him back to Washington, where he wants to be, among the real action.'

'Did Carl ever come here on his own? Without Cavendish?'

O'Keeffe frowned thoughtfully. 'He did, now you come to mention it. Not that he was here for long. He just popped in. The thing was, when Cavendish was in the house, everyone knew about it. You know what I mean? That moving-picture style of slick: noisy, brash. Greeting everyone. Patting them on the back. Smiling. God, that man can smile for America. Carl was different. He could slip in and out of a room and you'd hardly have noticed he'd been there.'

'Was Cavendish here a lot? I mean, without Carl.'

'Was he ever!' nodded O'Keeffe. 'The embassy should have charged the guy rent! He was always poking around, listening, at the same time as he was glad-handing everyone. And everyone loved it because he kept using that moving-picture hooey to get in and out of rooms he shouldn't have been allowed into. I had a word with Security about it, but they just cold-shouldered me: said he was doing good for America.' He scowled. 'A few of 'em are KKK supporters, if you want my opinion, and Cavendish used that.'

'Which rooms?' asked Noble.

'Pardon me?'

'The ones you said he wormed his way into when he shouldn't.'

'Well, the ambassador's private office, for one. But the most dangerous was the wire room.'

Where the telegrams were sent from.

'I put a stop to that, though,' said O'Keeffe. 'I had a word with the communications chief, and he had a discreet word with Cavendish.'

'When was he in there?'

'I first spotted him coming out of there about two days after he arrived in England. I was going in to send a wire as he was coming out. I asked the girl in there what he'd been doing, and she said he was just talking to her about the motion picture business. She was all excited. Said he'd offered her a screen test.' He shook his head. 'Some people are so gullible.'

'Who is this girl?'

'Name's Myrtle Evans. British.'

'Been here long?'

'As long as I have.'

'Jerry, can you do me a favour? Can I use your office for a few moments? I'd like to talk to this Myrtle Evans.'

'Think she can help you find out what happened to Carl?'

'Maybe. But I won't know till I talk to her.'

O'Keeffe hesitated. 'This is unofficial, right?'

'You lending me your office, yes. For the rest, though, I'm an agent of the American government investigating the murder of another American agent. And here in this embassy is American territory.'

'So why not use an official office? The deputy ambassador's?'

'Because I don't know whom I can trust, except you.'

O'Keeffe smiled. 'I don't know whether to be flattered or worried for my job.'

'Trust me, Jerry, you won't be brought in to it. You go out for a bit, and if anything comes back, I'll say I hijacked your office without you knowing.'

'You could always talk to her in the wire room?'

'Too open to interruptions. And I need somewhere that looks official.'

O'Keeffe hesitated, then shrugged. 'OK,' he said. He went to the coat stand and took down his coat. 'I said I'd meet a friend of mine at the National Gallery. I'll be gone for a couple of hours. As far as I was concerned, you left this office at the same time as I did.' He winked. 'See you, Don.'

'One moment, before you go, do you know anything about a Lady Amelia Fairfax?'

'The commie broad!' O'Keeffe chuckled. 'Hell, every press man in England knows about her.'

'What do you mean, the commie broad?'

'For all her title, she's some kind of social revolutionary. Works part-time volunteering at the offices of the Communist Party at some dump of a building out in East London. Also part of the campaign for votes for women.'

'I thought women had the vote here?'

'Yes and no. Some do, some don't. Then there's property rights. Women aren't allowed to own property in their own right – everything has to be done through a man. Then there's . . .'

'Yeah, OK. I get it,' said Noble, putting up a hand to stop O'Keeffe. 'She's some kind of radical.'

'And how,' nodded O'Keeffe.

'How radical?' asked Noble. 'Radical enough to bump someone off?'

O'Keeffe looked quizzically at Noble. 'You thinking of her late husband? If so, in my opinion you're barking up the wrong tree there. Apart from the fact that she's some kind of Bolshevik, I've only heard good things about her. Decent. A straight shooter.' He grinned. 'Then again, she's a redhead. Who knows what redheads can do if you rub 'em up the wrong way.'

TWENTY-FOUR

As Stark walked into the house, he was startled to see Sarah on the telephone.

'Thank you. We'll be there,' she said.

She rushed to grab her coat. 'The hospital just telephoned. Your dad's taken a turn for the worse. They think we ought to be there.'

Stark snatched up the telephone.

'You take Stephen next door. I'll get us a taxi.'

'Can't I come with you?' asked Stephen.

'Not today,' said Stark.

Myrtle Evans was Welsh, in her twenties and attractive – and she knew it, although at this moment she looked very uneasy. The man sitting opposite her across the desk wasn't smiling at her, as most men did. In fact, he was looking at her with outright hostility, something she wasn't used to. Especially not here at the American Embassy. Yes, sometimes she got cold looks from some of the other women, but she knew that was because they were jealous of her. But the men were always nice to her. It was because she was nice to them. Flattery always works with men – that's what her mum had told her. And she was hoping it would work here at the embassy for her. Land a nice American man who'd marry her and take her to America with him. Because that's where she wanted to be: America, the Land of Opportunity. She'd seen the picture in the magazines. Great fashions. Wonderful outfits. Fantastic cities. She could be something there. But this man sitting opposite her, with his grim, almost hate-filled eyes, unsettled her. Had she done something wrong? His manner been very curt when he opened the door of this office to her and just pointed at the chair, not even invited her to sit down politely like a gentleman should.

'My name is Special Agent Noble, with the American Bureau of Investigation,' he said as he sat down. No 'Thank you for coming' or any other pleasantries. Instead, he looked at her with that unfriendly glare and demanded, 'Edgar Cavendish. You know him?'

Myrtle wondered if this was a test. 'Yes,' she nodded. And she gave the man a smile to try to soften him. 'He's a film producer and really nice.'

'In what way?'

'Kind.' She hesitated, and added almost nervously, 'He said I'd got the perfect face for moving pictures.'

'Did he?' snapped Noble, his voice harsh, unimpressed, his face still unsmiling.

'Yes. In fact, he said he'd arrange a screen test for me.' *There*, she thought. *That ought to soften him up, when he realizes he's talking to someone who's going to be a star!*

'A screen test,' repeated Noble.

'Yes,' she nodded, smiling more now, eager to impress on him how important she was going to be. 'First here in London, at some studio, and then in America!'

'So, because of that, you told him about the wire you sent?'

She looked at him, stunned, then tried to look blank. 'What wire?' she asked.

'Edgar Cavendish asked you about a telegraphic wire that Carl Adams sent to Washington. And you told him what it contained.'

'No . . .'

'Yes!' snarled Noble, and he crashed his fist on to the surface of the desk, making her jump. 'You told him!'

'It . . . it wasn't a secret . . .'

'It *was* a secret,' Noble corrected her firmly. 'All wire communications in and out of this embassy are secret.'

'But Mr Cavendish worked here. He was an American.'

'He did not work here,' snapped Noble. 'He visited. That's all. And when it was discovered that he had made unauthorized visits to the wire room, he was barred from doing it. So he asked you to keep him informed of any wires that Carl Adams sent. And you did. That is treason, which is a capital offence, punishable by death.'

'But I'm not an American!' burst out Evans, obviously close to tears.

'This embassy is American territory. Anything happening here that is reckoned to be against the interests of the United States of America is treason. I can have you extradited to the States and put on trial there, and hanged.'

'No!' she moaned.

'Yes,' said Noble curtly.

'But Edgar . . .'

'Despite what he appears to be, Edgar Cavendish is a person of interest to the Bureau of Investigation,' interrupted Noble.

'I didn't know!' Evans appealed. 'He was *nice*! And he was American!'

She sat there, then her head dropped down and she began to cry. Noble sat and watched her. *You hard-hearted bastard*, he told himself. *She was just a dupe.*

But a dupe that got Carl killed.

He let her cry for a few more minutes, then he said, 'Miss Evans. There might be a way out of this.'

She sat upright, her make-up streaked with tears, her mouth open. 'How?' she asked in a strangled whisper.

'You told Cavendish about the wire that Carl Adams sent to me in Washington,' he said. He didn't say it as a question. 'By then he'd been barred from the wire room. So how did he know it had been sent? Did you tell him?'

Evans' head dropped again, and her hands went to her face.

'Miss Evans, listen to me. This is your chance to get out of this. How did you tell him?'

She mumbled something in a voice too low for Noble to hear.

'I can't hear you,' snapped Noble.

'He . . . gave me a telephone number.' She looked appealingly at Noble again. 'I didn't know I was doing anything wrong! He told me it was about business!'

'Business?'

'He said that there were lots of rival companies trying to muscle in the film business. He said they were dangerous, so he needed to know what they were up to. He said . . . he said he suspected that the other man with him, Mr Adams, was trying to undercut him for a rival. Mr Adams was in the same business, moving pictures. So he asked me to let him know if Mr Adams sent any telegraphic wires to anyone.'

'So when Mr Adams sent a wire, you telephoned Cavendish and told him who the wire was to, and what it said.'

'Yes,' she admitted in a low and tear-stained voice.

'How many wires did Mr Adams send?'

'Just the one.'

'To me. In Washington.'

'Yes.'

'OK. Then this is how we get you out of what you've done. I'm going to draft a wire for you to send to the Bureau of Investigation. Once you've sent it, I want you to telephone Mr Cavendish and tell him about my wire, and what it said.'

'But . . . but won't that still be treason?' she asked nervously.

'No,' said Noble. 'Because you're doing it on the direct orders of an agent with the Bureau. You will not – and I repeat *not* – tell Mr Cavendish about this meeting. If he asks why you're telling him about this wire, you can tell him you noticed it was going to the same telegraphic address as the one that Mr Adams sent. You got that?'

She nodded. 'Yes,' she said.

'OK,' said Noble. 'This is the message. "Scot Yard arrest of EC for murder imminent. Signed, Donald Noble." Send it to Hal Peters, Bureau of Investigation in Washington.'

When they arrived at UCH, Stark and Sarah headed for the lift, but were stopped by an orderly.

'I'm sorry, sir. Public visiting hours aren't until seven.'

'We've been called in by the medical staff treating my father.'

'Then you'll have to report to reception,' said the orderly.

'No,' grated Stark, doing his best to control his temper. '*You* check with reception. We are going up. And if you try to stop us' – he produced his warrant card – 'I will arrest you for obstructing the police.'

With that, Stark led Sarah past the stunned orderly to the lifts.

'There was no need for that,' complained his mother. 'He was only doing his job.'

'No, he was enjoying using petty power against people he thought wouldn't kick back,' grunted Stark.

They headed out of the lift to Ward 10, and found Dr Meek waiting for them. One look at the doctor's face told Stark it was too late.

'I'm so sorry,' said Dr Meek.

Stark felt his mother sag beside him and almost fall, but he caught her. Sarah recovered her balance, but leant against Stark for support.

'When did it happen?' she asked.

'Five minutes ago.'

He couldn't hang on for another five minutes, Stark raged angrily to himself.

'Can I see him?'

'The nurses are just . . . organizing him,' said Meek. 'If we can give them a few minutes. Please, come to my office.'

They followed him along the corridor to an office, where the doctor sat them down. Stark looked in concern at his mother. She was still dry-eyed, but he could tell by the tightness of her clenched jaw that she was only just holding herself together.

Dr Meek opened a desk drawer and took out a bottle. 'I don't normally do this, but if a brandy would help . . .'

Sarah shook her head, and Stark also gently declined. The doctor put the bottle back.

'I'm afraid the strain his body had been under was too much for his heart,' said Meek. He talked them through the complications that occurred when bronchitis was worsened by the addition of pleurisy and pneumonia.

'Could anything else have been done, Doctor?' asked Stark.

'No,' said Meek. 'I got your message, Mr Stark, about private treatment. But with the best will in the world, we don't yet have a way to deal effectively with these of ailments. I believe there are science laboratories, predominantly in France, working to try to come up with some way of combating viruses and bacteria, but so far nothing that works.'

There was a tap at the door, and a nurse appeared. 'He's ready, Doctor,' she said.

'Thank you, Nurse.' Meek got to his feet. 'Please, if you'd come with me. And, once again, I'm so sorry.'

The curtains had been pulled around the bed, giving some privacy. Henry lay on his back on freshly laundered sheets and pillows, the blankets pulled up almost to his chin, his arms and hands lying crossed on his chest on top of the covers. His eyes were closed and he could have been sleeping peacefully. The nursing staff had done a good job of making him presentable. Having seen his father struggling for life on the blood-soaked bedding at home, Stark was almost glad that they'd just missed the moment of death, which would surely have been as gory and painful. At least, for Sarah's sake. But he was being unfair to her. She'd seen Henry in all states of health, from his best to his worst. And she'd had the chance to say goodbye to him, sitting beside his bed these last few days.

I should have come back and seen him this afternoon, Stark told himself angrily. It had been Henry's last day on earth. No police investigation was worth missing that. And what had he learned today that he hadn't already known? Nothing. The interview with Herbert Jolly had just reinforced his suspicions about the BUP's involvement in the murder case and the attack on Danvers.

Sarah sat down and reached out to touch Henry's hands. Then her head sank forward on to the blankets and she began to cry.

TWENTY-FIVE

As their taxi pulled up, Stark was surprised to find a car parked outside their house. A smartly dressed man got out, expensive overcoat and bow tie, a smile of welcome on his face and a notebook in his hand. A reporter, guessed Stark.

'Chief Inspector! Harry Turner from the *Daily Target*. I hope you don't mind my calling on you at home . . .'

'Yes I do,' snapped Stark. 'I mind it very much. Please leave.'

'I only want a minute of your time—'

'I don't want to talk to him,' said his mother.

'You don't have to,' said Stark. 'Go in. I'll be there in a moment.'

'I've got to pick up Stephen.'

'We'll get him in a minute.'

Stark guided Sarah to the door, followed by Turner.

'Is this a bad time?' asked Turner, his expression one of earnest sympathy. 'I was talking to your neighbour while I waited, and she said your dad's in hospital . . .'

Stark waited until the door had closed on Sarah before turning to face Turner. 'You will leave now,' he snapped. 'You have no business here.'

'That's not strictly true, Inspector. I'm only doing my job, and it's a free country.' He put on his hopeful, appealing smile again. 'Your sergeant was attacked and badly injured, nearly killed, last night. We want to get those who were responsible for the attack. Don't you care enough about your own colleague to want to put those who did it behind bars?'

'That is a police matter, and we are dealing with it.'

'We can help. The power of the press. People talk to us.'

'*I* don't. Now go.'

Turner shook his head, his smile now replaced by an expression of baffled concern. Another act, Stark felt angrily. 'I don't see what your problem is, Mr Stark.'

'My problem is with the *Daily Target*.'

'We're a patriotic paper. I'd have thought you'd have shared those views. You fought in the war. Decorated. Promoted in the field. And not so long ago you put your life on the line to stop the King from being assassinated. In my book, it doesn't come more patriotic than that.'

'Yes, Mr Turner, I am a patriot. But that doesn't mean I hate everyone who isn't British or may have different political views to me.'

'Can I quote you on that?' asked Turner, switching his smile back on, but this time it was insolent and challenging.

'You can tell your employer that if anyone else is sent to harass my family, I will arrest them.'

Turner gave a rueful sigh. 'Very well, Chief Inspector. I'll pass those comments back to my editor. But you're passing up a great opportunity.'

'Go,' snapped Stark.

Turner looked as if he was going to make another attempt to involve Stark, but then he shrugged and got back into his car. Stark waited until he was sure Turner had left before entering the house.

His mother was in the kitchen, putting the kettle on. Having cried her eyes dry at the hospital, she seemed to have herself under control again. Doing routine actions – making a cup of tea, preparing meals, tending to Stephen – would help her keep that control. It would be in the hours of the night, alone in bed, without the familiar figure of Henry beside her, that she would be at her lowest.

Time helps heal the pain, Stark had been told when Susan had died. No it doesn't. The pain is always there; it just becomes less raw as time passes.

'You ought to go next door and get Stephen,' she said.

'Are you sure?' asked Stark. 'Are you ready for him?'

'He'll be wondering what happened. He needs to know.'

Stark nodded and went next door. One look at Stark's face and Mrs Pierce understood. 'I'm sorry,' she whispered.

Stephen appeared. 'How's grandad?' he asked.

'It's not good news, I'm afraid,' said Stark.

'But he's going to get better?'

'Let's talk at home.'

Stephen frowned, but gathered his coat and followed his father home. Once they were inside and the door was shut, Stark stopped Stephen and knelt down so that he was at his son's eye level.

'I'm afraid your grandad died,' he said.

Stephen stared at him, then his lips trembled and he suddenly burst into tears. Stark pulled him close to him.

'We have to be strong for your grandma's sake,' he said quietly. 'It's what your grandad would have wanted from us. It's going to be hard for her.'

He stood up, still keeping his arms around his sobbing son, and led him into the kitchen. Sarah was by the stove, busying herself, and when she saw Stephen, she said, 'You told him, then.'

'Yes,' said Stark.

Stephen suddenly broke away from his father and ran to Sarah, throwing himself into her arms, and as Sarah enfolded him, she began to cry again, this time great sobs that shook her whole body.

'I've got some phone calls to make,' said Stark. 'Things to sort out for tomorrow.'

He left them and went to the phone. Like his mother, he needed to be busy, push what had happened away until he was able to deal with it.

He telephoned Danvers at his flat, but there was no answer, so he tried the family home. Bridges answered.

'Is Master Robert there?' Stark asked.

'Yes, sir,' said Bridges. 'If you'll wait one moment, I'll fetch him.'

Soon after, Danvers was on the phone. 'Yes, sir?'

'Sergeant, I'll need you to look after things first thing in the morning.'

'Yes, sir.' There was a hesitant pause, then Danvers asked, 'Is there anything I should know about?'

'Yes. I'm afraid my father has just passed away. I'll need to make arrangements.'

'I'm so sorry, sir.'

'Thank you. Tell Chief Superintendent Benson, and anyone else who needs to know. I'll be in as soon as I can.'

'I'm sure no one will be expecting you in tomorrow, under the circumstances, sir.'

No, but I need to be busy, thought Stark. 'I'll be there,' said Stark.

TWENTY-SIX

That evening, Stark made lists of things he needed to do.
Contact the funeral directors. Write a letter to Stephen's
school explaining that Stephen would be off the next day.
All the paraphernalia we use to try to keep our mind from dwelling
on what's just happened.

He telephoned Scotland Yard and cancelled his transport for
the morning.

He waited until ten o'clock, after his mother and Stephen had
both gone to bed, before pouring himself a whisky and settling
down. He was just raising the glass in a silent toast to his father
when the telephone rang.

He hurried to pick it up before the shrill sound of the bell
disturbed Sarah, and heard Amelia's voice.

'Paul. I'm sorry to ring so late, but I've just heard about your
father.'

Her anti-royalist nurse friend from the women's meeting. The
bush telegraph works fast.

'I am so sorry, Paul.'

'Thank you, Amelia.'

'If there's anything I can do . . .'

'No. Thank you. But . . . it helps that you called.'

'I'm sorry we parted on bad terms. I really was trying to help.'

'I know. It was just . . . bad timing.'

There was a pause, then she said, 'I do love you. And I do
miss you.'

'I miss you, too. Very much. And when this is over . . .'

'Yes,' she said. 'When will that be?'

'Soon, I hope.'

'You know who killed Johnny and the American?'

'We know one of them for certain, and we think we know
who else may be involved. We're just trying to connect the dots.
Mainly, to do with why.'

'I'll be here when you're ready,' she said. 'Call me if I can help.'

* * *

Next morning, after Stark had delivered the letter to Stephen's school explaining his absence, he called at Levertons, the local funeral directors. He could have carried out his business on the telephone, but he preferred to deal with people face to face. If he had telephoned, he would also have been aware of his mother listening, suffering as details were thrashed out. He knew what was wanted because death was a subject they'd talked about. Cremation, which meant Golders Green crematorium, where most North London cremations traditionally took place. Golders Green was a mainly Jewish area, and once again Stark was reminded of the recent spate of attacks on the Jewish community. Was it just outbreaks of racist hooliganism? No, it was much more organized than that. There was something rotten at the heart of it.

With everything to be organized handed over to Levertons, Stark returned home. He telephoned Scotland Yard for a car to collect him, and then settled down with Sarah and Stephen. His mother had made a stew for their lunch, but Stark noticed that she hardly ate any of hers. They talked of Henry, made small talk and discussed the arrangements for the funeral. Stark was relieved when his car arrived to take him to work.

His driver was someone he'd known for years, Tom Watson, so he'd be spared the trouble of making polite conversation. Stark acknowledged Tom's condolences as he got into the back of the car. He saw that a newspaper had been left on the seat.

'I don't know if you've seen today's paper, sir. The *Target*,' said Tom as the car moved off.

'No.'

'You're on the front page.'

Stark picked the paper up and felt a rush of anger as he saw his photograph next to a banner headline that blared out: *Are the Jews controlling Scotland Yard?*

His anger was replaced by a cold rage as he read the story by the *Daily Target*'s 'special reporter', Harry Turner:

> The *Daily Target* offered a reward of one hundred pounds
> to bring the attackers of Detective Sergeant Robert Danvers
> – the son of Colonel Deverill CBE and Mrs Danvers – to
> justice.
>
> We also supplied the evidence of eye witnesses which

identified the men who attacked Sergeant Danvers as belonging to an extreme group of Jewish thugs who have already carried out similar vicious attacks on British people across London.

The same man refused both of these offers of our assistance: Detective Chief Inspector Paul Stark at Scotland Yard, who is supposed to be investigating this case, and also the double murder of Lord Fairfax and American businessman, Carl Adams. There have been suggestions that anti-British Jewish conspirators were involved in this double murder. Yet Detective Chief Inspector Stark refuses to look at the evidence we have offered him to solve these cases.

Why?

Could it be that DCI Stark has an unhealthy association with these Jewish subversives and is deliberately turning a blind eye to their activities?

We have had reports from a reliable inside source that DCI Stark recently intervened in a case in North London, outside his area of operation, when – as this newspaper reported – a Jew called Israel Rothstein beat a working man to death. DCI Stark took time out of his important investigation into the horrific double murder and made a personal visit to Finsbury Park police station to urge that the charges against Rothstein be dropped.

Why?

What is the link between Detective Chief Inspector Stark and the Jewish conspirators that he can be summoned to their help at a click of their fingers? What is their hold over him?

'A bit rough, sir,' said the driver.

'That's one way of looking at it,' said Stark acidly. He stuffed the newspaper in the pocket of his overcoat and said, 'Change of destination, Tom. Take me to Whitehall.'

TWENTY-SEVEN

S tark sat on the hard wooden bench in the large ornate marbled hall that was the waiting area of the Foreign and Colonial Office. He'd been here for over an hour, but then that was understandable: you didn't just walk off the street and ask to see someone as important as Winston Churchill and expect to be shown to him immediately. He was lucky that Churchill was even in the building; he seemed to spend much of his time chairing different committees, attending government functions or travelling abroad on official missions.

The entrance hall presented a resplendent aspect, with the flags of the different nations of the colonies displayed: Canada, South Africa, Australia and New Zealand alongside those of India and the countries of Africa, Asia and the Americas. He knew them all. He'd fought alongside their soldiers during the Great War. Brave soldiers all, regardless of their race or religion. Which is why he loathed the *Daily Target*'s campaign of racial hatred. There'd been troops from Jewish Syria fighting alongside the Allies at Gallipoli, as well as Russians. Brave allies then, hated traitors now, according to the newspaper in his hand.

I'm getting too close to the truth; that's why this front page is trying to destabilize the investigation. The trouble is, I no longer know whom I can trust. Someone at Finsbury Park had given the paper that story – most likely PC Fields. Conspiracy seemed to be everywhere. He felt like a fox, hunted from all sides, desperate for an earth to seek shelter in, but knowing that he had to stay out in the open.

If he was going to survive this and bring his own prey to justice, like a fox, he had to keep his wits about him.

A messenger in the formal and ancient attire of knee breeches and frock coat came up to him. 'Mr Churchill will see you now, sir.'

'Thank you,' said Stark, folding the newspaper into the pocket of his overcoat.

He followed the messenger across the marbled floor of the large hall and then along a gloomy corridor until they came to a door on which was a sign stating *Secretary of State for the Colonies.*

The messenger tapped at the door, then opened it at the gruff sound of Churchill's 'Enter!'

'Detective Chief Inspector Stark, Mr Secretary,' said the messenger.

Stark entered. Churchill was sitting behind his desk, surrounded by bundles of papers of different colours and sizes, and wreathed in smoke from a large cigar.

'Thank you for seeing me, Minister. I know your time is at a premium.'

'I will always have time for the man who helped me save the life of the King,' said Churchill. 'Sit down, Stark. What is it? Do you have news on Johnny Fairfax's murder? Gallipoli?'

'We're still working on the Gallipoli angle, sir,' said Stark, taking the chair opposite Churchill's. 'But another possible motive has been put forward by Special Agent Noble from America.'

'Ah yes, the Home Secretary mentioned to me that the Americans had their own investigator on the case. Because of this poor chap Adams, of course.'

'Yes, sir,' said Stark. 'The reason I've come to see you is because the suggestion he's made is that there might be a political connection to this case. In particular to an organization called the Ku Klux Klan.'

'Oh?'

'Yes, sir. He seems to feel they are involved in a conspiracy with right-wing organizations in this country. The American who was murdered, Carl Adams, was also an agent with the Bureau of Investigation, working undercover to keep an eye on Mr Edgar Cavendish.'

'The film producer who's over here,' nodded Churchill. 'Yes, I met him. A charming man. Possibly a bit too charming for my taste, but then I assume that is what works in the moving picture business.' He frowned. 'Why was this Carl Adams keeping an eye on him?'

'Because it seems that Mr Cavendish is a key member of the Ku Klux Klan, and is actually here in England to make political connections with like-minded people. According to Agent Noble, the Ku Klux Klan have the aim of some kind of global domination, in which blacks are once again slaves and Jews are . . .

Well, I'm not sure what their plans are for Jews, except that they want to strip them of their money and power.'

Churchill smiled. 'My tailor is Jewish, and he would love to have some power and money to be stripped of. The dominance of the Jewish race as financiers is greatly exaggerated.'

'I know, sir. But there are those who propagate the idea. This Ku Klux Klan is one such organization, according to Agent Noble, and there are powerful people sympathetic to their views in this country.' He hesitated, then added carefully, 'I'm trying to find some leads that might help me with the political dimensions of this case, and I'm on difficult ground because I don't know who might be . . . sympathetic to them.'

He produced the copy of the *Daily Target* from his pocket and pushed it across the desk to Churchill.

Churchill read the front page thoughtfully. 'Someone inside the force is leaking stories to the press,' he announced.

'Yes, sir,' agreed Stark. 'My problem is that my investigations may be uncovering facts that some people don't want revealed.'

Churchill regarded Stark carefully. 'You're suggesting that this anti-Jewishness might extend to your own colleagues in the police force?'

'Yes, sir. I'm certain of it.'

'So you came to me.'

'Because, sir, I know you are not of that mind.'

'Thank you, Chief Inspector. That opinion means a great deal to me.'

Churchill fell silent, momentarily lost in thought. Then he said quietly, 'My mother, Jennie, was American, you know. She was born in Brooklyn. She died just five months ago. She broke her leg coming down some stairs in some new high-heeled shoes. Haemorrhage. She was only sixty-seven. No age.' He looked inward. 'She was a wonderful woman.'

'I'm very sorry, sir.'

'Thank you, Stark. The point is, I have an affinity with Americans. My maternal grandparents are Americans, so I'm part American. They are a powerful and thrusting nation, a power-house, and I would always listen to any opinion the Americans have. But in this case, Agent Noble is wrong.'

'So you don't think there is a conspiracy against the Jews in this country?'

'Johnny Fairfax wasn't Jewish, and neither was this Carl Adams, to judge by his name.'

'No, sir, but Adams was investigating such a conspiracy. He may have been silenced because of what he'd uncovered.'

Churchill hesitated, then he said, 'There may be something in that. But I think Agent Noble's wrong in his assumption that any such conspiracy is driven by the Ku Klux Klan. In my opinion, the Klan is a throwback to segregationist times before the American Civil War. Are they dangerous? Yes. But to *America*. Not to Europe.'

'But the Americans were involved in the war that was fought in Europe. With respect, sir, without the entry of the Americans into the war, we might have lost.'

'That is true. And I believe that should there ever be such a war again, we would need the Americans on our side even more.'

Stark shook his head. 'Surely, after the carnage of the Great War, no country would be prepared to endure that again.'

'That is what we all like to think, Stark. But I believe there are forces who would envisage waging such a war again. And they are in Europe, not America.' He stood up and began to pace around the room. 'It is true that the majority of politicians in Britain and elsewhere seem determined to avoid another war of the same terrible scale at any cost. But I believe that such a policy leaves them open to almost immediate surrender if such a threat materializes.'

'And you believe there is such a threat?' asked Stark.

'I do,' nodded Churchill. 'Although most of my political colleagues seem to disagree with me.' He snorted. 'Appeasement at any price! Anything to avoid another war.'

'The last war was a catastrophe, sir,' said Stark guardedly. 'Millions dead and wounded. The economy in ruins. A whole generation lost. And not just in this country.'

'I know, I know,' growled Churchill. 'But what other option is there if we're faced with domination by a foreign power?'

'With respect, sir, I cannot think of any foreign power involved in the recent war that would risk further losses to its population by engaging another war.'

'The present *government* of a foreign power – yes, Stark. That's right. But what about a political movement inside that country?'

'Are we back to the Ku Klux Klan, sir?'

Churchill waved his hand dismissively. 'Forget the Ku Klux Klan, Stark! I'm talking on our own doorstep! Europe! What do you know of the NSDAP in Germany?'

'Absolutely nothing, Minister. But then I have difficulty enough with the vagaries of British politics.'

'The NSDAP is the National Socialist German Workers Party. Despite their name – the Workers Party – they are opposed to all forms of Bolshevism. They're also known as the Nazi Party, and they share many of the aims of the Ku Klux Klan that Agent Noble mentioned, in particular with relation to the Jews. Until five months ago their leader was a man called Anton Drexler, but in July he was replaced by a former soldier in the German army, a veteran of the trenches in the Great War, called Adolf Hitler.' Churchill's face darkened as he added, 'For my money, this is where the real danger to this country comes from. If Hitler starts forming political alliances with right-wing parties in this country, and elsewhere in Europe, the danger is that we fall victim to foreign control, the control of this Hitler, and without a shot being fired.

'If that happens, then every Jew in Europe is at risk. And not just the Jews. Every person who opposes them. I have no time for the Bolsheviks, but I am proud that we live in a democratic society where the voices of dissent can be aired. As you know, I, too, have been a dissenting voice in the past.'

Oh God, please don't let this turn into a political speech, begged Stark silently. *I really don't have the time.* 'I know, Minister . . .' began Stark, doing his best to interrupt as politely as he could. Churchill was famous for having a temper and could be a formidable opponent when baulked, and Stark needed him on his side.

To Stark's surprise, Churchill stopped and gave the chief inspector a rueful smile. 'Getting on my high horse again.' His tone grew serious again as he said, 'But that's because I care about this country! Our society has been forged over a thousand years to get to where it is now, and I'm not going to let some upstart ruin it!'

'These other organizations that Hitler might form pacts with, might they include the British Union of Patriots?' asked Stark.

Churchill hesitated, then nodded. 'Sadly, it might. I say "sadly" because the Union contains some very good people. People concerned about Britain who have joined the BUP with this country's best interest at heart. Unfortunately, there are those within that organization who are more concerned with another agenda.'

'Anti-Jewish?'

'Anti all foreigners,' said Churchill. 'Anti trade unions. Interestingly, the Nazis claim they are also anti-capitalist, but my understanding is they are funded by some very serious German industrialists.' He shot a steady look at Stark. 'Are you suggesting that the BUP was behind Johnny Fairfax's death?'

'I don't know, sir. There have been other instances of attacks on Jewish property that might be connected with them. And my sergeant, Sergeant Danvers . . .'

'I remember Sergeant Danvers,' nodded Churchill. 'Good man. Brave.' He looked at Stark again. 'I read in the papers that he was attacked. Almost killed. Jewish thugs.'

'Yes, sir; that was what one particular paper said, sir.'

'The *Target* again,' said Churchill. 'Owned by Lord Glenavon. A leading member of the BUP.' He frowned thoughtfully. 'Do I get the impression that you don't think he was attacked by Jews?'

'Sergeant Danvers is fairly sure he was attacked by men associated with the BUP.'

'And then Glenavon blames the Jews for it in his rag,' mused Churchill. 'I have no time for Glenavon. And he has no time for me. Have you read some of the things he's said about me in that so-called newspaper of his?'

'No, sir,' said Stark. 'Until the attack on Sergeant Danvers, I'd never read the *Target*.'

'Scurrilous lies and propaganda!' snorted Churchill. 'I often thought of suing, but then I thought, "Why give the bugger publicity? He'll just sell more papers!"' He snorted. 'If I had my way, I'd close that rag down!'

'But that would be against the idea of a democratic society where all voices and opinions can be aired,' said Stark tactfully.

Churchill smiled. 'Touché, Chief Inspector!' He shook his head. 'Lord Glenavon and the BUP. It's an interesting thought, but my money's still on Gallipoli as the underlying cause of these murders. Revenge, pure and simple. Don't lose sight of that.'

'I won't, sir,' promised Stark.

TWENTY-EIGHT

Danvers sat at the desk, going through the files, seeing what had been added during the short time he'd been off. There were DCI Stark's notes of his interview with Herbert Jolly, but the boss had been careful not to include anything about possible police involvement. It was a delicate balancing act: putting down an accurate record of evidence and clues, but aware that these files could be seen by anybody in authority.

Who guards against the guards? It was a phrase Danvers remembered from his school days, a lesson about democracy in Roman times. Or was it Greek? It didn't matter; the issue was about trusting those who policed a society, its protectors. What if those protectors had their own agenda, one against the interests of society? Danvers hadn't taken much notice at the time; it was all just ancient history. But now, with what was happening with the BUP, the phrase took on a different dimension.

The telephone ringing jerked him back into the present. 'DCI Stark's office. DS Danvers speaking.'

'Is DCI Stark there? It's Superintendent Hammond from Finsbury Park.'

'I'm afraid he's not available, sir.'

'When will he be?'

Danvers hesitated, then said, 'I'm not sure. Sadly, his father passed away last night. He said he would be in later.'

There was a pause, then Hammond said, 'I understand. I'd like to leave a message for him.'

'Certainly, sir.'

'Would you tell him that Mr Israel Rothstein is dead.'

'Mr Rothstein?'

'He'll know what it means. He can call me about it later, when he gets in. And do pass on my condolences to him.'

'I will. Thank you, Superintendent.'

Danvers hung up. Israel Rothstein. The man accused of a killing – an accusation that, according to the boss, had been dubious. Now Rothstein was dead. Danvers had wanted to ask about the circumstances – murder, accident, natural causes? – but he wasn't sure if DCI Stark had promised Superintendent Hammond not to tell anyone about the case, and he didn't want to put the chief inspector in a difficult situation.

He was about to return to the files and notes when there was a rap at the door and Agent Noble appeared.

'Morning, Sergeant. Where's DCI Stark?'

'I'm afraid he may be in rather late today, sir. His father died last night.'

Noble stared at Danvers, stunned. 'Died? How?'

'Pneumonia, pleurisy and bronchitis.'

'So he'd been ill for a while?'

'Just a few days, I believe. It happened very quickly.'

'But I had dinner with him the night before last and he didn't say anything about his father being seriously ill.'

'The DCI is a very private man, sir. He doesn't confide in many people.'

'But you knew?'

'Only in case the hospital telephoned and DCI Stark wasn't here.'

'Damn! I usually spot when someone's got a problem worrying them!'

'As I said, sir, the DCI is a very private man. He keeps his emotions tightly wrapped.'

'He sure does! How about you, Sergeant? How are you now, after the attack? Any after-effects?'

'Not that I've noticed, sir, thank you.'

'Good. Anyway, I've come in because—'

He was interrupted by the door opening and Stark coming in.

'Good morning, Sergeant. Agent Noble.' He looked at the clock which showed almost twelve. 'Well, it is still morning, just.'

'Paul!' Noble strode towards Stark, his hand outstretched. 'My condolences on your father's passing.'

'Thank you,' said Stark, shaking Noble's hand.

Stark felt uncomfortable. He disliked shows of emotions in public. Too often they were what a superintendent of his had called 'crocodile tears'. 'Politicians do it all the time to try to show the voters they've got a heart,' the super had said. 'It's fake.'

But he knew that Noble was being genuine. It was just that he found it hard to express his emotions openly. He guessed that was the result of his four years in the trenches. At first, there had been dreadful shock when a friend had been killed, especially when it happened right before his eyes. Then, as more and more died, it became something to shrug off. In the end, you just thanked God or Fate that it wasn't you. If you didn't, the grief would drive you insane.

He turned to Danvers. 'Any messages?'

'Superintendent Hammond at Finsbury Park just telephoned. He told me to tell you that Mr Rothstein had died. He said you'd know what that meant.'

'Yes, I do,' Stark scowled. He looked at Noble. 'I'll deal with this first, if that's all right?'

'Go ahead,' said Noble.

Stark got through to Billy Hammond, and after receiving Hammond's sympathies about Henry, heard what had happened to Israel Rothstein.

'You saw what that rag, the *Target*, said about you?'

'Yes,' grunted Stark. 'I have my suspicions about the source.'

'So do I, and I'm looking into them,' said Hammond. 'After you came, I decided to release Rothstein on bail. Like you, I had my doubts about his guilt, and I didn't think he'd do a runner while we carried on investigating the case.'

'How did he die?'

'He was stabbed early this morning in the street outside his factory. The word on the street is it was revenge for Harry Jukes. If so, Harry Jukes' family had nothing to do with it. I've talked to them.'

'You believe them?'

'I do. I've known Harry and his family for years. He's a local character. Everyone knew him, and liked him.'

'All right, Billy. I get the picture.'

'Like I said, what worries me now is this thing could explode. Riots. Vigilante attacks.' He paused. 'I can't say too much now . . .'

'I understand,' said Stark. 'Once I get a handle on what's happening here, I'll come and see you again. I think our two cases might be connected.'

'How?'

'It's better we talk later.'

'Understood,' said Hammond. 'Give me a ring and we'll meet up somewhere.'

Stark hung up and filled in the enquiring Danvers and Noble on events at Finsbury Park, the killing of Harry Jukes and now the death of Israel Rothstein, and the suggestion that an anti-Semitic organization such as the BUP might have been involved.

'Which brings us back to Cavendish and the Ku Klux Klan,' he finished.

'And that is where I come in,' said Noble.

He reported on his encounter with Myrtle Evans at the American Embassy the previous day. 'It's another thing that points to Cavendish being involved in the murders,' he finished.

'But not enough evidence to bring him in,' commented Stark.

'No, which is why I've set a hare running.' Noble told them about his ruse with his telegram to Hal Peters. 'Myrtle will tip Cavendish off about it. I'm hoping it will spook Cavendish enough for him to do something rash.'

'Like leave the country?' suggested Stark.

'Maybe,' admitted Noble. 'If he tries, maybe we can pick him up before he gets on the ship.'

'On what evidence?' asked Stark. 'It's still all just hearsay.'

'It'll be an admission of guilt.'

'Not with a clever lawyer working for him. By the way, does the name Adolf Hitler mean anything to you?'

Noble frowned. 'No. Should it? Who is he?'

'He's the leader of a political party in Germany called the NSDAP. Anti-Bolshevik, anti-Jewish. I wondered if the Bureau had anything on him.'

'I wouldn't know,' said Noble. 'They might have, but it's not in my area.'

'I thought one of the reasons Carl Adams was here was to look into Cavendish's associations with right-wing political parties in Europe?'

'Yes, but only in so far as it affects America,' said Noble. 'To be frank, it's only lately we've started to take an interest in what's happening in Europe. After the Great War, the American public, and certainly our politicians, have preferred a policy of isolationism. There's no appetite for us getting dragged into another European war like the last one. That's one of the reasons we're keeping tabs on Cavendish, to make sure he doesn't pull us into whatever's going on in Europe.'

'What about you, Sergeant? Have you heard the name Adolf

Hitler being mentioned by any of your social circle? Those associated with the BUP?'

Danvers shook his head. 'The name means nothing to me, sir.'

'Then I'll go down to Records and see if they've got anything on him.'

'You think he might be important?'

'Winston Churchill seems to think so,' said Stark. 'Although he's still of the opinion this case is about Gallipoli.'

'While you check up on this Hitler guy, I'm off back to the embassy to see if there's been any reaction from Cavendish to my wire. I'll keep you informed.'

As the door closed on Noble, Danvers asked, 'What do you want me to do, sir?'

'Just hold the fort, Sergeant. And keep ploughing through what we've got to see if there's any hard evidence we can use against Mr Cavendish if he does try to make an early return to the States.'

'Yes, sir.'

'Oh, there is one thing.'

'Yes, sir?'

'Just curiosity really. At the hospital they told me that you have a title. The Honourable Robert Danvers. But you never mentioned it on your application to join the police.'

Danvers looked uncomfortable. 'It's not really a title as such.'

'It impressed the staff at Charing Cross Hospital.'

'That was Lettie's doing,' said Danvers. 'I think she told them in the hope I'd get better treatment.'

'It worked,' said Stark. 'A private room. Visits outside of visiting hours.'

'I don't feel good about it, sir,' said Danvers.

'Why not?' asked Stark.

'As I said, sir, it's not a proper title. It's not earned, or anything. I'm the Honourable because my father was the second son of an Earl, so he's the Honourable Deverill Robert Danvers, but he never uses it. He prefers Colonel. He says he earned that rank, whereas the Honourable bit was just handed to him. I feel the same. I worked hard to get the rank of detective sergeant. A title that's just handed to you doesn't have the same value as one you worked for.'

Stark smiled. 'Careful, Sergeant, you're starting to sound like one of Lady Amelia's Bolsheviks.'

TWENTY-NINE

Records did have a file on Adolf Hitler, although it took the clerk in the basement office some time before he put the file on the counter in front of Stark. Stark was about to take the file back to his office, but the clerk put his hand firmly on it to prevent Stark removing it.

'I'm sorry, sir,' he said, 'but there's a yellow sticker on it.'

'Which means?'

'A yellow sticker means it has to stay here in the department to be examined.'

'Why?'

The clerk shrugged. 'I don't know, sir. I just know those are the orders.'

'And who determines whether a file has a yellow sticker?'

'MI5, sir. The Directorate of Military Intelligence.'

More spies, thought Stark ruefully.

'A yellow sticker also means there's a limit to who can have access to it. Only DCIs and above.'

'Then it's lucky I didn't send my sergeant down for it,' observed Stark. 'Thank you.' He gestured to a chair at the other side of the room. 'I shall be just there.'

'Begging your pardon, sir, but a file with a yellow sticker means it has to be signed for if it's taken away from the counter.'

More red tape, thought Stark. 'Very well. Give me the form.'

Stark wrote his name on the form the clerk gave him, then signed it. *Let's hope it's worth all this palaver*, he reflected as he took the file to the chair.

A grainy photograph of a man in his early thirties looked up at him, thin-faced with a small dark moustache. The military cap he wore and the insignia on his collar showed it was an army photograph.

Adolf Hitler. Born 20th April 1889 in Braunau am Inn in Austria-Hungary.

During the Great War: Volunteered for Bavarian Army.

Served as despatch runner on the Western Front. Served at the First Battle of Ypres, and also at the Somme, Arras and Passchendaele. Received Iron Cross, Second Class, for bravery in 1914. Wounded at Somme in 1916. Received Iron Cross, First Class, in August 1918 on recommendation of his superior officer, Hugo Guttman.

Someone had added in a small handwritten note after this: 'Hugo Guttman was Jewish.' The file added that Hitler had been temporarily blinded in October 1918 in a mustard gas attack, before going on to detail his activities once the war ended.

1919: appointed intelligence agent of the Reichswehr to infiltrate and investigate the German Workers Party (DAP). Became influenced by the views of the DAP leader, Anton Drexler: nationalist, anti-Semitic, anti-Marxist, anti-capitalist. In 1920 the DAP changed its name to Nationalsozialistische Deutsche Arbeiterpartei (National Socialist German Workers Party – NSDAP). In July 1921, Hitler replaced Drexler as leader of the NSDAP.

Hitler is at present banned from entering Britain by order of HM Government.

So Hitler and I were both at Passchendaele, on opposite sides, reflected Stark. The business about Hugo Guttman puzzled him. Guttman had recommended Hitler for the Iron Cross, First Class. Yet Guttman had been a Jew. When and why did Hitler become anti-Semitic? Was it purely because he came under the influence of this Anton Drexler?

Stark returned the file to the counter and asked the clerk if he had a file on Drexler. Once again, they went through the same procedure concerning yellow stickers, and a few moments later he was opening a much thinner manila folder with Drexler's name on the cover. There was just one sheet of typed paper inside, with the barest of details.

Anton Drexler. Politician. Born June 1884. Founded German Workers Party DAP (later known as National Socialist German Workers Party – NSDAP). After Adolf Hitler

replaced him as leader in 1921, Drexler became Honorary
President of NSDAP.

Stark returned the file to the clerk, then returned to his office
and Danvers.

'Well, I've learned a little more about this Adolf Hitler, but
not much more than I'd already discovered from Mr Churchill.'

'Does it help us in this case, sir?' asked Danvers.

'To be honest, I don't see how it does,' admitted Stark. 'Herr
Hitler is banned from entering Britain, so the only possible
link between him and Cavendish is if Cavendish goes to
Germany. And, as far as we know, that's not on his agenda.'
He sighed. 'Another dead end in a whole lot of dead ends.
Suspicions, we have plenty of. And likely culprits. But no hard
evidence.'

Stark and Danvers spent the next hour going over everything
in the files – witness statements, pathology reports, double- and
triple-checking for something they might have missed – but they
came up with nothing to indicate why Carl Adams and Lord
Fairfax had been killed. Finally, Stark told Danvers to go home.

'It's your first day back. You don't want to overdo it.'

'With respect, sir, you might consider heading off yourself.
There'll be . . . arrangements to be made.'

'Thank you, Sergeant. The funeral is fixed for next week. The
undertakers are doing most of the arrangements.' Then he nodded.
'But you're right. I should go home and check how my family
are.'

After Danvers had gone, Stark took one last look through the
papers, then reached for his coat. He was heading for the door
when his telephone rang. 'DCI Stark.'

'Chief Inspector, I'm terribly sorry to bother you. It's Mrs
Walker at Lady Amelia's. I wonder if I can trouble you to call
here.'

The worried tone in Mrs Walker's voice alarmed Stark. 'Is
Lady Amelia all right?' he asked.

'To be honest, sir, I'd rather not talk about it over the
telephone.'

Something was very wrong.

'I'll be there straight away.'

THIRTY

Amelia's housekeeper was obviously in distress from the way she paced about her kitchen, nervously clenching and unclenching her hands.

'I'm sure you'll think I'm being very silly, sir . . .'

'Let me be the judge of that,' Stark reassured her. 'Just tell me what's concerned you. Where is Lady Amelia?'

'Well, that's the thing, sir: I'm not really sure. I had the strangest phone call from Mrs Johnson, Lady Ambleton's housekeeper. Said she was informing me that Lady Amelia is staying for a few days with Lady Ambleton.'

'Lady Ambleton?' echoed Stark. 'I never got the impression they were friends.'

'The exact opposite, sir, though I'm not sure if it's my place to say it.'

'When was this phone call?'

'Just before I telephoned you, sir.'

'There must have been something else besides the telephone call to make you suspicious. Otherwise, surely you'd wait and see what happens.'

Mrs Walker nodded. 'Exactly, sir. That's the thing. I went out late this morning to order some provisions – groceries and the like – as I always do. Lady Amelia was here when I left, but when I came home she was gone. And there was no note. Now that's not like her, sir. She always lets me know if she's going to be anywhere, in case there's a message for her. She'll say, "I shall be at the Party offices all afternoon" or "I'm meeting Lady Francome at Claridges" or whatever.'

'Yes, I get the picture,' nodded Stark.

'Also, I could swear there'd been a disturbance.'

'A disturbance? Where?'

'In the hall by the front door. The hall table looked like it had been moved. And some of the coats were on the wrong hooks. It was as if things had been knocked about and then put back, but not in the right places.' She looked apologetically at Stark. 'I'm sorry if this all sounds a bit hysterical, sir . . .'

'Not at all,' said Stark. He knew Mrs Walker enough to be sure that she was level-headed and exceedingly efficient and organized. If she said there had been a disturbance, then there had been. And the mention of Amelia staying at Lady Ambleton's merely added suspicion.

He dialled the number he had for Lady Ambleton, and recognized the voice of the housekeeper, Mrs Johnson, when it answered.

'May I speak to Lady Amelia Fairfax, please?'

'Who, sir?'

'Lady Amelia Fairfax. I understand she's staying there for a few days with Lady Ambleton.'

'I'm sorry, sir, you must be mistaken. There's no Lady Amelia Fairfax here.'

Stark hesitated, then said, 'Would you hold, on for one moment.' He put his hand over the receiver and said to Mrs Walker, 'Have a word with her, and listen to her voice.'

Mrs Walker took the receiver and Stark bent his head forward to eavesdrop as Mrs Walker said, 'Hello. Is that Mrs Johnson?'

'Yes. Who am I speaking to?'

'This is Mrs Walker, Lady Amelia Fairfax's housekeeper. I'm calling because I had a telephone call informing me that Lady Amelia Fairfax was staying with Lady Ambleton.'

'I'm sorry, but as I said to the gentleman just now, I'm afraid you've been misinformed. Lady Amelia Fairfax isn't here. And, as far as I know, there are no arrangements for her to stay here.'

Stark nodded for Mrs Walker to end the call, and as the receiver was replaced on the cradle, asked, 'Was that the person who telephoned you?'

'No, sir,' said Mrs Walker firmly. 'The woman who telephoned before had a Scottish accent.'

'She could have been putting it on.'

'But if so, why would she deny it now? And her voice was very different.' She looked appealingly at Stark. 'I'm not imagining it, am I, sir? Something has happened to her.'

'It does look . . . suspicious,' said Stark carefully. 'Did she say anything before you went out to suggest she was worried about anything?'

'No, sir.'

'Any unusual telephone calls? Strangers calling?'

'No, sir. Nothing.'

'Leave it to me, Mrs Walker. I'll deal with it at once. You can rest assured, I'll get to the bottom of this.'

If some bastard has done anything to Amelia, I'll kill them, he vowed.

He left the house and was surprised to see that his car was gone. In its place, parked outside Amelia's home, was a large crimson Rolls-Royce. The door of the car opened and two men got out. Both wore long overcoats, and as they approached Stark, one flicked his coat back so that Stark could see the revolver concealed beneath it.

Instinctively, Stark looked around for cover, but there was none. There was no one else in the street. No place to hide.

'Rest easy, Inspector,' said one of the men, stopping a short distance away from Stark, the other man also staying at a safe distance. 'We've got orders to take you to meet someone. Nice and quiet and there'll be no trouble.'

'Where's my car?' demanded Stark.

'Gone back to the Yard,' said the man. He gestured towards the Rolls-Royce.

Stark weighed up his options. If he tried to run, he'd be shot down. If he got into the car, what then? Would someone really send a Rolls-Royce on an errand that could end up with a fight inside it, with the upholstery – the car itself – being wrecked? Unlikely: the owners of Rolls-Royces were notoriously proud of their cars.

There was always the possibility that, at the end of the journey, they would take him to some secluded spot and shoot him. But the journey would give him time to work out his strategy of attack.

He climbed into the back of the car. There was one man already there, holding a revolver which he pointed at Stark. Stark was joined by another of the men from the pavement, while the other took his place in the passenger seat next to the driver.

The doors closed, and the car moved off.

THIRTY-ONE

S tark studied the men. Unlike Herbert Jolly, they showed no obvious stress or discomfort. The confidence with which they handled their revolvers showed they were familiar with the weapons and not afraid to use them.

The car headed further into the built-up areas of town, towards the City. Stark wondered about the river. The Thames was a notorious repository for bodies, weighed down and made to vanish. But it still seemed strange to use a very noticeable car like a crimson Rolls-Royce for such a purpose. If a body was discovered and witnesses questioned, someone would surely remember it.

So where was he being taken? And why?

The answer dawned as the car drove along Fleet Street and then, as it reached the offices of the *Daily Target*, turned off the main street into a narrow lane, and then down a ramp that led beneath the building into an underground car park.

So, Lord Glenavon wasn't taking Stark's refusal to talk to his newspaper lightly.

The car pulled up, and the two men in the back with Stark gestured with their guns for him to get out. He did so, and came face to face with the man from the front passenger seat. Flanked tightly on either side, Stark was marched towards a lift door, the third man following. So far nothing offered any chance of escape.

The lift door was opened, and Stark and the three men crammed into the tight space. Buttons were pressed, hidden levers clanked, and the lift rode upwards. When it stopped, Stark was pushed out and marched across a short hallway into a large room. A window with a panoramic view over London ran the whole length of one wall. Two men were standing by the window and they turned as Stark was pushed towards them. One was Edgar Cavendish; the other Stark recognized from photographs as Lord Glenavon.

'Welcome, Chief Inspector,' said Glenavon. 'I'm glad you could join us. Please accept my condolences on the death of your late father.'

'I'll be missed,' said Stark curtly.

'No, you won't,' said Cavendish. 'A note has gone to your home saying you've had to go out on a case.'

'Please, sit down,' said Glenavon. 'There's no reason we shouldn't be comfortable while we talk.'

'That depends on your definition of comfort,' said Stark. 'Personally, I find having a gun pointed at me takes the edge off it.'

'I'd have thought you'd have been used to it after four years in the trenches,' said Glenavon. 'I'm Lord Glenavon, by the way. We haven't been formally introduced.'

'I think I deduced that,' said Stark. 'Certain clues, such as this being the executive office of the *Daily Target*, rather gave the game away.'

Glenavon looked at the three men who were standing with Stark and said, 'Ted, Walter, you can go. Brian, please take a seat in the corner.' As two of the men left and the man with the revolver walked to a chair in the corner of the room, Glenavon added, 'I'm sure you understand the need for some protection here, in case you decide to cut up rough.'

Stark selected a wooden chair pushed back against a wall as a precaution against anyone attacking him from behind.

'Are you sure you're comfortable there?' asked Glenavon. He gestured towards the expensive-looking armchairs.

'I'm fine here,' said Stark. The wooden chair would make a handy weapon, if it came to it.

'Suit yourself,' said Glenavon. 'I expect you're wondering why we've gone to all this trouble?'

'At first I thought it was to kill me, but then I realized if that was your intention, your men would have done it in your underground motor bay, once we were out of the car. Where is Lady Amelia?'

Glenavon nodded. 'You worked that out, did you?'

'It wasn't difficult,' said Stark.

'She's safe,' said Glenavon.

He looked towards Cavendish, who added, 'I can assure you that no harm will come to her if this discussion between us reaches an amicable agreement.'

'In the same way that no harm came to Sergeant Danvers, or Lord Fairfax, or Carl Adams?' asked Stark.

'What happened to Sergeant Danvers was . . . unfortunate,'

said Glenavon. 'It was not intended. Unfortunately, some of our people overreacted.'

'And Lord Fairfax and Carl Adams?'

'Collateral damage,' said Cavendish.

'So, a confession,' said Stark.

'Hardly necessary, I'd have thought, Chief Inspector. You've been on my tail even before our friend, Agent Noble, started to poke his interfering nose in. Why are you so interested in Adolf Hitler?'

'Who says I am?' asked Stark.

'We understand you got a file about him from your records department,' said Cavendish.

So, they really do have their tentacles everywhere, thought Stark. The clerk in the records department.

'We would strongly advise you to forget all about Herr Hitler,' said Glenavon. 'Also, slow down your investigations into the murders of Lord Fairfax and Carl Adams.'

'Which also means pulling Agent Noble off my tail,' snapped Cavendish.

'Three days,' said Glenavon. 'That's all we ask. At the end of that time, we'll provide you with the person who killed Lord Fairfax and the American. Sadly, they'll be dead. They will have committed suicide, but they'll leave a signed confession.'

'A convenient scapegoat,' responded Stark sourly.

'It will keep the top brass at Scotland Yard happy. And the public. You may even get a commendation. Perhaps a promotion for your brilliant work in bringing the guilty party to justice. And, provided you've done as we've asked, Lady Amelia will be released, unharmed.'

'And what happens if I come after you with a warrant once she's free?'

Cavendish smirked. 'You can try, but I'll be safely back home in Indiana by then, where I've got powerful political protection. You won't be able to touch me.'

'And I don't need to tell you how well protected I am,' said Glenavon. 'The judiciary. The ruling elite. Government ministers. And, of course, many inside your own police force.'

'I could still find enough honest officers and judges to ensure a prosecution,' said Stark.

'I wouldn't advise it,' said Glenavon. 'For one thing, I had nothing to do with the deaths of Lord Fairfax and the American,

Carl Adams. Your case will be unsupported supposition and will be thrown out with damages awarded to me. You would also be putting the lives of you, your family and Lady Amelia at risk.'

Cavendish chuckled. 'I can see the newspaper headlines now: "Tragic accident kills family. A young boy and his grandmother died today when their house in Camden Town caught fire. The boy's father, Detective Chief Inspector Stark, and Lady Amelia Fairfax – rumoured to be Inspector Stark's mistress – also died as they battled to save them.'''

At these threats to the people he loved so deeply, Stark had to fight to stop himself getting out of the chair and launching himself at Cavendish. At all costs, he had to protect them. Instead, he replied as coolly and calmly as he could. 'A bit wordy for the *Daily Target*. And no mention of Jews being responsible? Or blacks, or Chinese?'

Stung, Glenavon snapped back, 'I'm disappointed in you, Stark. I'd have thought, with your history, your distinguished war record, the man who saved the life of the King, that you would see what we're doing. We are defending this country against the enemy within. The mongrels. The people who seek to destroy everything this country stands for. The proud and strong traditions built up over the centuries!'

'A country made up of immigrants,' said Stark. 'Saxons. Vikings. Romans. Normans.'

'They are the stock we come from!' thundered Glenavon, rising to his feet.

'And don't forget the Irish, without whom Britain would have no canals and no railways, because they built them,' continued Stark. 'The French, who gave us much of our language. Russian Jewish émigrés. The Chinese, who—'

'Enough!' shouted Glenavon. He was trembling with rage now.

'Easy, Hector,' murmured Cavendish. 'He's only doing it to get to you.'

Stark sat calmly and looked at Glenavon, holding his stare. 'I assume our business here is concluded?' he said.

'If you're going to say, "You won't get away with this!"' smirked Cavendish, 'I'd better remind you that we have, and we will. You're too small to take on what's happening here, Stark. You, Danvers and Noble may think you're the Three Musketeers, but we can swat you like flies any time we want.'

'Our business will be concluded if you do your part,' hissed Glenavon. 'Do nothing for three days. And make sure that your Sergeant Danvers and Special Agent Noble also stay away from this case during that time. If you don't, you and Lady Amelia, and the others you care for so deeply, will die.'

THIRTY-TWO

As Stark walked into his home, Stephen ran to him from the living room, his face flushed with excitement. 'Wow, Dad! Was that really a Rolls-Royce you came home in?'

'It was,' smiled Stark.

'How?'

'Someone at work. They offered to run me home.'

'What's it like?'

'It's every bit as good as people say it is. Comfortable. Roomy. Engine as quiet as anything.'

Sarah appeared from the kitchen, looking suspiciously at Stark. 'What's this about a Rolls-Royce bringing you home?'

'Just something to do with work, Mum.' He gave her an apologetic smile. 'Unfortunately, I've got to go out straight away again. More work.'

'What about your dinner?'

'I'll have it when I get in.'

'I wanted to hear about the car,' complained Stephen.

'I promise I'll tell you all about it when I get in.'

'He might be in bed by then,' said Sarah.

'I'll be as quick as I can,' Stark said. 'And if you are asleep, I'll come and wake you up and tell you.'

'You promise?' asked Stephen.

'I promise,' said Stark. 'I'm sorry. I'll explain when I get back.'

He could feel Sarah's suspicious stare on his back as he pulled the front door shut. She knows something's wrong. All of this on top of Dad dying, it's too much for her. Somehow I'm going to have to make it up to her.

He walked to the taxi rank outside Mornington Crescent underground station and caught a cab to Finsbury Park. No one seemed to follow him, but he kept careful watch the whole journey.

His knock at the door of the terraced house in Hilldrop Crescent was answered by a surprised Billy Hammond. 'Paul!'

'I'm sorry to call unexpectedly like this, Billy, but I've got a problem.'

Hammond ushered him in and showed him into the front room, calling through to the kitchen, 'It's a friend from work!'

He gestured Stark to an armchair. 'If you're calling on me at home, rather than at the station, it suggests you're definitely suspicious of things there,' he said. 'PC Fields?'

'He's just one,' said Stark. 'There are others at Scotland Yard, and more elsewhere.'

'Is this about Israel Rothstein?'

'In part, but it's much bigger than that. I've been warned off, Billy, by some powerful people.'

'The *Daily Target*?'

Stark nodded.

'So what can I do?'

'I need a private investigator and I'm hoping you'll be able to recommend a good one.'

Hammond frowned. 'Surely you've got your own contacts.'

'Maybe, but lately I'm not sure whom I can trust. I'm guessing you're more in touch with private detectives than I am. Being part of Scotland Yard shields you from a lot of the day-to-day stuff.'

'Investigating what?'

'I can't tell you.'

Hammond looked at Stark with obvious disappointment. 'You don't trust me?'

'It's not that. It's politics, Billy. Deep politics. If this goes wrong, things will get bad. At the moment I'm the one in the firing line. I don't want to bring anyone else down with me.'

'That's not fair, Paul,' said Hammond. 'We've always looked out for each other.'

'I know, and that's why I've come to you. After it's all over, I promise I'll tell you the whole thing. But right now, I can't.'

Hammond thought it over, then nodded. 'All right,' he said. 'There's only one guy I'd recommend. He's a former copper. Smart. Intelligent. Honest. And very loyal.' He gave a rueful smile. 'Things that didn't go down well with some of the top brass.'

'Sounds the sort of bloke I'm looking for. Where can I find him?'

Hammond wrote a name, address and phone number on a sheet of paper and passed it to Stark. 'He's local, which is how I know him,' he said. 'His name's Charlie Peters. You can say I sent you.'

'Thanks,' said Stark. 'And this is between us, Billy. You never gave me this.'

'Gave you what?' asked Hammond. He looked quizzically at Stark. 'Is there anyone else I should watch out for at my station, apart from Fields?'

'I don't know,' admitted Stark unhappily. 'That's the trouble, Billy. I just don't know.'

Charlie Peters lived in rooms four streets away from Billy Hammond's house. Where Billy Hammond's place had been so obviously a family home, with all the smells of laundry and cooking and kids that went with it, this house had an air of defeated loneliness about it.

Stark introduced himself at the door, and Peters responded with a wary look. 'I know who you are, Chief Inspector. I read the papers. What can I do for the Yard?'

'It's a private matter. Billy Hammond gave me your name.'

'You'd better come in, then.'

Stark followed Peters to his living room. The smell was of stale tobacco and cheap alcohol. The floral patterned wallpaper was faded and stained, the furniture rickety and old. Peters himself also looked shabby, his shirt dirty, his flannel trousers sprinkled with tobacco ash.

I hope this guy's as good as Billy says, because he certainly doesn't seem to be successful, thought Stark, wondering if he'd done the right thing in pinning all his hopes on Peters.

'Let me guess? Divorce?' asked Peters.

Stark shook his head. 'No. Not that private.' He gestured at a chair. 'Can I sit down?'

'Be my guest,' said Peters.

Stark sat down on the uncomfortable chair with broken springs and said, 'I'll lay my cards on the table, Mr Peters. I've come to you because something is going on and I suspect there could be collusion within the police force. I don't know who I can trust. I can trust Billy Hammond, but I don't want to put him in a spot if things go wrong. It'll be the end of his career.'

'Whereas, me, I don't have a career anymore,' grinned Peters. 'How far does this "collusion", as you call it, go?'

'I don't know. I suspect up to chief superintendent level. Maybe higher. It certainly goes through the ranks, and lots of stations. Including the Yard.'

Charlie Peters stopped grinning. 'It sounds dangerous.'

'It is,' agreed Stark.

'Why are you taking it on?' asked Peters. 'Why not just walk away from it and let it go?'

'Because a friend of mine is in trouble. And because I don't like bullies walking all over me.'

'In that case, you're in the wrong job,' said Peters.

'No, I'm in the right job. It's just that some wrong people are also in the same job, and I want to flush them out and get rid of them.'

'Impossible!' snorted Peters. 'It goes too deep, and they're too powerful.'

'In that case, I'll just do that part I can do. Get my friend out of a tight spot.'

'And who is this friend?'

Stark hesitated, studying Peters. Either he had to level with Peters and put everything at risk, or he had to walk out of this room before he said anything more.

'Billy Hammond says you can be trusted,' he said.

'Billy Hammond's a very trusting man,' answered Peters.

'I need to know you're the right man,' insisted Stark doggedly.

'I'm not sure I am,' said Peters. 'I think there's only one man you really trust, and that's you. You don't know me. You only know what Billy said. I could be fooling him.'

Stark studied the detective, taking in his face, his manner, trying to read what went on behind his eyes. Finally, he said, 'All right. But if I find you sold me out, I'll kill you.'

Peters smiled broadly. 'That's what I like to hear. A bit of honesty. OK, DCI Stark, I think we can do business. Now, who's this friend, and what tight spot are they in?'

'Lady Amelia Fairfax,' said Stark.

Peters' eyebrows went up. 'Lady Communism?' he said. 'Well, well. And what tight spot is she in?'

'She's been kidnapped and is being held hostage.'

'Who by? Or haven't they told you?'

'I've been told all right. Lord Glenavon.'

Peters scowled. 'That bastard! It was him and that paper of his that got me kicked off the force. I was getting close to nailing some top gangster, and the *Target* ran a story about me being in the pocket of his rival. There was no proof, of course, so they made it up. Fitted up the evidence. And that was me out the door.' He shook his head. 'The bastard!' He looked enquiringly at Stark. 'Why's he holding her hostage?'

'To try to stop me making enquiries into what he's up to.'

'And what is he up to?'

'I don't know. That's why I'm making enquiries. So I'm doing it one stage at a time.'

'First, rescue the damsel in distress,' nodded Peters.

A damsel in distress hardly fitted Stark's view of Amelia, but in this case it was apt. 'Yes,' he said.

'I don't do that sort of action stuff anymore,' said Peters.

'I don't need you to,' said Stark. 'Just find out where she is. I'll take it from there.'

'Have you any idea where they might be keeping her?'

'My gut tells me at Lord Glenavon's place, Red Tops at Parliament Hill. Do you know it?'

Peters nodded grimly. 'After I got kicked off the force I went down there to look at his place. I was after some sort of revenge. I fancied breaking in and smashing the place up. But in the end, I just sort of stood there, looking at the place, and thinking that one day I'd get my own back.' He grinned. 'Perhaps this could be that chance.'

'I'm not a hundred per cent sure that's where they're keeping her,' said Stark. 'Like I said, it's just my gut feeling.'

'Nine times out of ten, a copper's stomach is right,' said Peters sagely. 'Any other tips you can give me? Anyone else who might be involved and be worth me keeping an eye on?'

'An American called Edgar Cavendish. He's over here under the cover of setting up moving picture deals. And a woman called Lady Ambleton.'

'All the titled people,' observed Peters.

'You're not writing their names down,' Stark pointed out.

Peters tapped his forehead. 'I don't need to,' he said. 'Instant recall. Lord Glenavon. Red Tops. Edgar Cavendish. Lady Ambleton. Lady Amelia Fairfax. You could reel off a hundred names and I'd remember them all.'

'Very useful,' complimented Stark.

'And very safe,' added Peters. 'No bits of paper with incriminating names on them for people to find.' He regarded Stark thoughtfully. 'If she's being held hostage, as you say, then there's usually a time limit involved.'

'They've told me three days,' said Stark. 'So, if I'm going to do anything about it, I need to make my move inside the next two. In which case, I'll need you to get me a report by tomorrow night, as early as possible.'

'It's tight,' said Peters doubtfully.

'Can you do it?'

'I'll do the best I can. But if she's *not* at Red Tops . . .'

'I know,' nodded Stark. That was his worst fear. If she wasn't at Red Tops, then he'd lost. He pulled out his wallet. 'We haven't discussed your fee. How much do you want in advance?'

'Put it away,' said Peters. 'We'll talk money afterwards.'

'I need to know how much I'm letting myself in for,' said Stark.

Peters reached into a drawer and took out a printed sheet of paper.

'These are my charges,' he said, giving it to Stark. 'So much a day and expenses. It won't be much more than a day.' He smiled again. 'But if this gives me a chance to nail that bastard Lord Glenavon, there'll be a big discount.'

THIRTY-THREE

Stark arrived home to find his mother in the scullery, plunging her hands into a sink filled with washing. *She needs to keep busy to stop thinking about Dad*, he told himself. *The same as me.*

'Where's Stephen?' he asked.

'He's gone to bed. Just a minute or so ago, though.'

Stark headed upstairs. He pushed open the door of his son's

room and heard a sniffling sound coming from the bed, and as
he sat down on the edge of the bed, he realized that Stephen was
crying.

'I'm back, son,' he said.

There was a pause, then Stephen pushed himself up, wiping
his eyes. 'I try not to cry downstairs,' he said. 'For Grandma's
sake. I don't want to upset her.'

Stark reached out and pulled Stephen towards him, enveloping
his son in his arms. 'I know, Stephen,' he said.

'I'm never going to see Grandad again. Mrs Pierce said I'd
see Grandad in heaven, but I don't know where it is. She said
it's in the sky, but I looked up and I couldn't see anything.'

'Mrs Pierce means well, but . . .' Stark stopped. What could
he say? That there was no such place as heaven? That Henry
was gone for ever. That nothing of him existed anymore. But
even some very intelligent people he'd met had talked about
an afterlife. About reincarnation. Souls coming back, being
reborn.

'Stephen, the sad truth is that we all die. The good thing for
your grandad was that he lived to a good age, so he spent time
with you. Lots of people die very young.'

'Like my mum?'

'Yes, like your mum. Some even younger.'

'Will I die?' asked Stephen fearfully. 'Soon, I mean?'

I've said the wrong thing. Stark mentally kicked himself. 'No,'
he said. 'I didn't mean that. That happens sometimes when young
people get very ill. Or an accident happens. A car knocks them
down when they're crossing the road. That's why your grandma
and grandad and me have always been careful about making sure
you eat properly and are kept warm, and you keep safe when
you're going to school and places. And now Grandad's gone, me
and your grandma will keep making sure that you're safe and
looked after.'

'Grandad was looked after, but he got ill.'

'Grandad was old. And he always got ill in the winter with
his lungs. It may have been because of the way he lived when
he was a child. When he was growing up, he worked at the
forge with your great-grandad, who was a blacksmith, and I
think the smoke got into his lungs. And when he was a
carpenter, he worked a lot outside in all weathers, and that

didn't help his lungs. But he was a strong man, your grandad, and he didn't let it stop him doing things. Especially doing things with you.'

'We were going to make a model car, now we've finished the Sopwith Camel,' said Stephen.

'You can still make one. I'll help,' offered Stark.

'You're always busy with work,' pointed out Stephen.

Yes, I am, thought Stark bitterly. 'Once this case I'm working on is over, I'm going to spend less time on work,' he said. *But that's what I always promised, and it never happens*, he admitted to himself. *I have to change things.* To ease the sombre mood, he asked, 'What car were you and Grandad going to make?'

'A Rolls-Royce Silver Ghost,' said Stephen. 'Like the one you came home in today.'

Stark smiled. 'Well, that's perfect! I've been in one, so I know what it's like from the inside. I'll certainly know how it should be when we start making it.'

'Can I get a ride in it?' asked Stephen.

'Possibly,' said Stark. 'I'll see what I can arrange. What colour were you thinking of painting it?'

'Well, me and Grandad talked about crimson, like the one you were in, but I like the silver colour.'

And for the next ten minutes or so, Stark listened as Stephen talked about the Rolls-Royce Silver Ghost, and other cars and aeroplanes, until, as he saw his son's eyes begin to droop, he said quietly, 'I think it's time for sleep now, Stephen. Snuggle down.'

Stephen snuggled down into the bedclothes. 'Thanks, Dad,' he said.

'I'm sorry I haven't been here more often, son,' said Stark. 'But I will be.'

When he got downstairs, he found Sarah sitting in the kitchen by the range.

'What's going on?' she demanded.

'Mum, I want you to go away for a day or two. And take Stephen with you.'

'Why?'

'Because there's danger out there.'

Sarah studied him questioningly. He gave a deep sigh. He was going to have to tell her the truth, or she wouldn't go.

'This investigation I'm doing. These murders. I've uncovered something rotten. Some top people are involved.'

'What sort of top people?'

'Lords and ladies. Members of Parliament. Top army people. Even some top police.'

She stared at him, her mouth dropping open in shock. Then she clamped it shut again, and her eyes took on a suspicious angry look. 'They're trying to shut you up?'

'Yes.'

'That big car you came home in?'

He nodded. 'Yes. The man who owns that is part of it.'

'Who is he?'

'His name's not important, Mum.'

'It is to me. And to Stephen if he comes round here threatening us. That's why you want us to go away, isn't it?'

'Yes,' said Stark.

'Being driven out of our own home,' she said angrily. 'We were never driven out, not even when the Zeppelins were coming over, dropping bombs on us.'

'This is worse than Zeppelins,' said Stark. 'These people look like they're on our side. Ordinary people. Workers. Coppers. Lords and ladies. Toffs who'll charm you.'

'They won't charm me,' snapped Sarah. 'What do they want?'

'They want me to leave off the investigation for three days.'

She looked at him, puzzled. 'Well, what's wrong with that? Three days is nothing. Some murder investigations take years.'

'Because they've also got Amelia. They've threatened to kill her. And I think they'll do it anyway. I've got to try to save her.'

Sarah fell silent. She stood up and paced around, thinking. Finally, she turned to Stark and said, 'Your Aunt Mabel in Finchley.'

'Thanks, Mum.' Then he added quickly, 'But don't tell anyone where you're going. Not even Mrs Pierce. These people might ask her where you've gone.'

'I've got to tell her something,' Sarah said defensively. 'I'll tell her we've gone to your Uncle Walter in Canvey Island.'

'Good.'

'What about Stephen's school?' asked Sarah.

'I'll write a note saying that you've taken him away to help him get over his grandad passing away. They'll understand.'

She nodded. 'You going to get Amelia back safely?'

'I am,' said Stark.

'And afterwards, we'll be safe?'

'I'll make sure of it,' Stark promised.

THIRTY-FOUR

That evening he telephoned Danvers, then Noble at his hotel, and arranged to see them both the next morning.

'Eleven o'clock by the fountains in Trafalgar Square,' he told them.

That done, he walked through to the kitchen where Sarah was sitting by the range, staring into the flickering flames that wrapped around the coals. Stark sat down and watched her. What could he say? Nothing.

It was Sarah who broke the silence. 'He wasn't always miserable, like he was at the end,' she said. 'He was fun when he was younger. You must remember him playing with you in the park.'

'I do,' said Stark, although the truth was his childhood was such a distant memory that he barely remembered it. All he could remember of his father was the way he'd been these last three years: angry and bitter.

'It was the war that really did it,' said Sarah. 'You going off. He spent the whole time in a panic, worried. He took to reading the newspaper every day, studying every word of every battle, in case you were mentioned as killed or missing.'

'They didn't put the names of the dead and injured in the papers,' said Stark. 'Bad for morale back home.'

'He couldn't get to sleep at night for worrying about you. The whole four years. But he had to be strong for Susan and Stephen.' She fell silent, lost in her memories. Finally, she said, 'When we came to see you in the army hospital, when they brought you back, I thought he was going to break down and collapse. You were a mess. Shrapnel. Bullet wounds. The doctor said by rights you ought to be dead; he didn't know how you survived.' She looked at her son. 'It was that same stubbornness that your dad had that kept you alive – same as it did him at the end. The only difference was, his body was worn out by then. He must have coughed his life away every winter these last ten years.'

'I could hear his cough getting worse before I went off to war,' said Stark. 'He said it was bronchitis.'

'It was, but some winters it would get worse. Especially while you were away. Like I said, it was the worry about you. He didn't sleep and his body started to pack up. And then he had the pain of watching you try to recover when you came out of hospital.'

'It wasn't just Dad,' Stark pointed out. 'You had the same worry about me.'

'Yes, but I was always stronger than your dad.' She gave a deep sigh. 'And then Susan died. Your dad really cared for Susan. I did, as well. She was lovely. But your dad . . . he was always soft.' She gave another deep sigh. 'Look at the way he was with Stephen.'

They talked some more about their memories of Henry, mainly Sarah's memories of her younger days with Henry when he was struggling to make ends meet as a carpenter.

'It was never easy for him,' she said.

Finally, she stood up, kissed Stark goodnight and went to bed. Stark soon followed, checking on the sleeping Stephen before going to his own room. His mind was too full for him to sleep. He picked a book which he hoped might lull him to drowsiness, but as he sat up in bed, he couldn't concentrate on the open pages before him. His mother's words about Henry hung over him.

All that pain and worry over me while I was in France, but he never showed it to me once I was back. Why?

He remembered his own awkwardness when Noble had offered his condolences over Henry's death. *God, I'm just as bad as my father was for not showing my emotions! I didn't know how much he cared for me because he never said it, never showed it. And I'm the same!*

In his mind, he went back to when he was Stephen's age – Henry taking him to the park where they flew kites and kicked a ball about. He remembered Henry laughing at himself the time he slipped while trying to kick a ball and fell over. Then there had been the time the kite he was flying got caught in a tree, and Henry had lost his temper and kicked the tree and a load of conkers fell down on him, and again Henry had laughed so much he had fallen over, and the young Stark had fallen to the grass with laughing at the sight.

Such times! Such happy times! The sun always seemed warmer and the winter snow cleaner and deeper. And after, when the day was done, he remembered his father tucking him into his bed and then telling him a story – one Henry had made up. It usually involved blacksmiths, Stark remembered. And a dragon and a princess.

Suddenly, he realized he was crying. Crying for the days that were gone and would never be again. Those wonderful days that had disappeared so painfully these last few years.

Next morning, he told Stephen that he and Sarah would be going away for a few days. 'Your grandma will feel better if she's not here, constantly being reminded of Grandad. It's just for a couple of days.'

'Where are we going?' asked Stephen.

'It's a surprise,' Stark told him.

Stark's hardest task was persuading Sarah to accept a taxi to Finchley.

'It'll cost too much!' she protested. 'We can do it by underground train. Or bus.'

'You're taking a taxi and that's it,' Stark told her firmly.

Finally, still complaining, she and Stephen got into a taxi and headed off.

By five to eleven, Stark was walking into Trafalgar Square. Danvers and Noble were already there. At this time of year there were few others, although the women sitting on upturned wooden crates, surrounded by the paper bags of bird food they sold, were doing a good trade with the few people there.

'So, what's all this cloak-and-dagger stuff?' asked Noble. 'Why here?'

'Less chance of being overheard,' Stark told him. 'Here, we can see everyone. Inside, you never know who's listening at doors.'

He told them of his experiences the previous afternoon: being called to Amelia's house, then being taken at gunpoint to meet Glenavon and Cavendish.

'Then we've got them!' burst out Noble triumphantly. 'I knew my wire would make them move! That's all the evidence we need!'

'Unfortunately, we can't use it while they've got Lady Amelia,' said Stark. 'If we try, they'll kill her.' He then told them about the further threats to his own family, and to Danvers.

'So what do we do?' demanded Noble angrily. 'Let them get away with whatever they're planning? You know they'll kill her anyway!'

'Yes,' agreed Stark. 'Which is why I'm going to rescue her tonight.'

'From where?' demanded Noble. 'We don't even know where they're holding her.'

'I've got someone working on that,' said Stark. 'I hope to get it confirmed later today.'

'Where?' asked Danvers.

'Red Tops.'

'Lord Glenavon's place,' nodded Danvers.

'Do you know it? Have you been there?'

'Sorry, no,' said Danvers. 'My family and Lord Glenavon don't exactly see eye to eye. Well, my parents, that is. It wouldn't surprise me to find that Lettie's been there with Cavendish for some do or other.'

'Maybe you could ask her?' asked Noble.

Danvers gave a regretful sigh. 'I'm afraid my sister isn't talking to me at the moment, not after we had that scene when we asked her about Cavendish.'

'I may have something,' said Noble. 'I went to the embassy to do some nosing around about Cavendish and Glenavon, and I found out they'd both been guests recently at some dinner to promote Anglo-American relations. It sounds like a big-hitting affair – plenty of lords and ladies and dukes and earls. And a member of the royal family. The heir to the throne, the Prince of Wales himself. Prince Edward Albert Christian George Andrew Patrick David Windsor.' He shook his head. 'How does anyone get so many names?'

'By having lots of very important relatives and revered ancestors who have to be taken into consideration,' said Stark.

'I also found out that the Prince was very taken with Cavendish, especially this whole moving picture business. I get the impression the Prince quite fancies himself as some kind of moving picture star.'

'The Palace would never allow it,' said Stark.

'You and I know that, but does the Prince?' asked Noble.

'Of course,' said Stark. 'He's the heir to the throne. His duties would have been made very clear to him almost from birth.'

'My pal in the embassy says he gets the impression that the Prince is not the kind of guy to follow rules so easily. He says he's got his own mind. His own way of doing things.'

'Then he's going to come up against some fierce opposition, both inside his own family and the government,' said Stark.

'Even once he's King?'

'Especially once he's King,' said Stark. 'To outsiders it may look as if the King is some powerful figure, but in reality he's a figurehead. An important one, but the real power is in Parliament. That's why we had a civil war.'

'Yeah, Oliver Cromwell,' nodded Noble. 'We did it in school. Mainly to teach us that kings were a bad thing, and especially British kings. Hence our Declaration of Independence.'

'And here we are, after all these years, making up with a dinner to celebrate Anglo-American relations and a future King who wants to be in moving pictures,' observed Stark.

'Anyway, the thing is, I hear from the same source that the Prince has accepted an invitation to have dinner with Cavendish at Lord Glenavon's place the evening after tomorrow.'

'The evening after tomorrow!' exclaimed Stark.

'That's within the time frame they gave you, sir,' said Danvers.

'Exactly,' nodded Stark grimly. 'Logic says it's connected with whatever it is they're trying to keep secret.'

'If so, Cavendish isn't doing a very good job of hiding it,' observed Noble. 'It's supposed to be hush-hush, and my pal said Cavendish swore him to secrecy. But telling a press officer that is like telling a hooker to give up sex.'

'The Prince of Wales,' mused Stark.

'Exactly! My pal said Cavendish was so puffed up with the Prince having a private dinner with him that he just had to tell someone.'

Stark nodded thoughtfully. 'What would Glenavon and Cavendish want with the Prince? It's obviously nothing to do with the moving pictures, whatever they've told him.'

'Maybe they want to hook him up to their organization?' suggested Noble. 'This BUP outfit?'

'I can't see it,' said Stark doubtfully. 'Members of the royal family don't get involved in politics.'

'Getting back to Lady Amelia,' said Danvers. 'How do we go about rescuing her?'

Stark shook his head. 'I appreciate the offer from both of you, but I can't ask you to put your lives on the line in this way.'

'Hell, you don't have to ask!' snorted Noble. 'We three are in this together!'

'Agreed,' said Danvers.

'This is not an official mission,' Stark pointed out. 'What I'll be doing is strictly illegal.'

'And you can't do it on your own,' said Noble. 'So, the question is: who else can we count on?'

'And that is the problem,' admitted Stark unhappily. He reminded them about the clerk at the records department, PC Fields at Finsbury Park, and Glenavon's boast about his organization having fingers everywhere inside the police. 'They even had my car moved! We can't trust anyone in the police, which is why we're standing here in the cold in Trafalgar Square!'

'What about the officers who helped us when we protected the King?' asked Danvers. He reeled off the names. Sergeant Alder from Maida Vale, along with Constables Forsythe, Smith, Adams, Rushmore and Whittaker. 'And there's Superintendent Hammond from Finsbury Park!'

'All very good men whom I'd trust completely,' agreed Stark. 'But this is not official. I'd be asking them to break the law and put their careers at risk, not to mention their lives and liberty. And we'd never be able to keep it secret. Somehow, someone at Maida Vale or at Finsbury Park would find out what was going on.'

'So it's just us three,' said Danvers.

'Unless I can make contact with some old army comrades who might agree to join in,' said Stark.

'If we were in the States, I'd have a whole heap of guys clamouring to come with us,' said Noble. He gave a rueful grin. 'Unfortunately, we're not in the States.'

'When will we know if Red Tops is the place they're holding Lady Amelia?' asked Danvers.

'Later this afternoon, I hope. In the meantime, I thought we might spend the time spreading disinformation, as I believe the intelligence agencies call it.'

'Not us,' said Noble. 'We call it bullshit.'

'Yes, well, I think it's time to spread some to try to take some of the heat off us from our enemies. Don, you mentioned a telegraph clerk at the American Embassy you used to send a false wire to spook Cavendish.'

'Yeah, and it looked like I succeeded a bit too well. If I hadn't, we wouldn't have been in this spot,' he said ruefully.

'Don't blame yourself,' said Stark. 'I think my asking about Adolf Hitler may have been the final straw for them. But back to this woman . . .'

'Myrtle Evans,' nodded Noble.

'Yes. I think it might be useful for you to send another wire that she can report back to Cavendish. This one should be along the lines of "Re last wire. Been told to hold off from EC by Scotland Yard". That should let Cavendish know that I've passed on their instructions about keeping our hands off the case for three days.

'To the same end, Sergeant, I'd like you to go and see Chief Superintendent Benson and say you're concerned because I've ordered you to hold off from further investigations into the case for the next two days, until I get back.'

'Get back from where?'

'From compassionate leave while I sort out things relating to the recent death of my father.'

'You think that Benson is involved?' asked Noble.

'I don't know,' admitted Stark. 'I may be misjudging him, but there have been certain indications lately. If I'm wrong, there's no harm done. If I'm right, it will give us space from being watched.'

Noble looked around. 'You think they're watching us now?'

'I think it highly likely. This way, they'll think they know what we were talking about: that I was telling you chaps to stand down, just as they ordered me.' He looked at his watch. 'I'm now going to check on my investigator. After that, I'm going to see what I can do about getting us some reinforcements we can trust.'

'Where can we get hold of you?' asked Noble.

'At home. And say nothing incriminating on the telephone. It wouldn't surprise me to find that they've got a few telephone operators feeding them information as well.'

THIRTY-FIVE

As Stark walked into his house, his heart jumped at the sight of the folded piece of paper on his doormat. Another warning from Glenavon or Cavendish? Had they traced Sarah and Stephen?

The note was from Peters. *Got what you wanted. Call me.*

Stark headed for the nearest telephone box and dialled Peters' number.

'Charles Peters.'

'I'm on my way,' Stark told him.

Half an hour later, Stark was once again sitting in Charlie Peters' room, with its overpowering smell of stale tobacco.

Peters rolled himself a cigarette as he talked. 'She's in there.'

'You're certain?'

Peters nodded. 'I did all the usual: talked to locals, the postman, the postmistress, the delivery people, and I got reports of a woman fitting Lady Amelia Fairfax's description being seen looking out of an upstairs room.'

'How sure are they it's her? It could be Lady Glenavon? Or a mistress?'

'For one thing, Lady Glenavon doesn't live at Red Tops. She's been banished to some castle in Scottish Highlands. For another, if what I hear is true, Lord Glenavon doesn't exactly go for mistresses. Or women of any sort. Stable boys and rough trade are more his thing.

'Just to confirm, I managed to get a peek at this particular window. Most times lately it seems the curtains are kept closed, but I managed to get a look when the curtains opened.'

'You're sure it was her?'

'I recognized her from her pictures in the papers. It was only fleeting, because then someone came in and pulled the curtains shut again. But it was her, no question.' He then added, 'They've got another house guest there as well, at the moment. A foreign bloke. The locals think he's German.'

Immediately, Stark was alert. 'Did you get his name?'

Peters shook his head. 'No. It seems it's all very hush-hush. He arrived by car with the windows blacked out. And he hasn't been seen outside since he arrived. I got all this from the post-mistress, who really does know everything that goes on.

'I'll tell you another thing. Since he arrived, security there has been increased. More blokes, with guns.'

'How many?'

'From what I hear, there are ten: five on the day shift, five at night. It ain't going to be easy getting in.' Peters got up and went to a cupboard, from which he took a rolled-up piece of paper. 'I've done a plan of the place. It's only rough, but it shows where the wall is that runs all round the house, the grounds, the outbuild-ings, the doors, and where her room is.'

'Thank you,' said Stark.

He unrolled the paper and studied the drawing. It was better than many he'd seen during the war; drawings showing the supposed enemy lines. He'd done Charlie Peters a disservice. He may appear untidy and dishevelled, but his mind and his detec-tive skills were razor-sharp.

As before, he reached for his wallet, but Peters stopped him. 'Wait till the job's over,' he said. 'Then we can settle up.'

'But I might get killed doing this,' pointed out Stark. 'Then you won't get paid.'

Peters shrugged. 'Then it shows I've been a mug,' he said with a slight grin.

As Stark headed back to town, he reflected that he had all the information he needed. The question now was how to rescue Amelia and make sure they all got out alive. And, at the same time, stop Cavendish and Glenavon taking their revenge.

THIRTY-SIX

Churchill wasn't at the Ministry.

'He's at the House,' Stark was informed by Churchill's private secretary. 'There's a debate on the Colonies Bill.'

The lobby at the Houses of Parliament was filled with people, mostly men – a mixture of political lobbyists, assistants and private secretaries, and journalists. Stark wondered if there was anyone from the *Daily Target*. He couldn't see Harry Turner, but then politics wasn't really Turner's area – at least, not serious politics. Muck-raking politics and gossip and innuendo, certainly, but the root for Turner's kind of stories was usually to be found elsewhere: servants, bar owners, shopkeepers. The same sort of people Charlie Peters used to get his information.

Stark took his place among the throng and waited, his eyes on the door to the Commons. It was another hour before Churchill appeared. Fortunately, he was alone, and he looked angry. He must have lost a vote, decided Stark. If he'd won, he'd have a smile of triumph and be surrounded by sycophants. Stark moved to intercept him. 'Mr Churchill.'

Churchill scowled. 'Sorry, Stark, I'm busy right now. Another time.'

He went to brush past, but Stark leaned in and whispered, 'Hitler's here.'

Churchill stopped and stared at Stark, stunned. 'What do you mean? Here? Where?' He began to look around, as if expecting to see Hitler in the lobby. Then he grabbed Stark by the sleeve and pulled him urgently towards a door. Stark saw that it was the door to the gentlemen's toilets.

Churchill pushed Stark in, then turned on him. 'If this is a joke . . .' he said angrily.

'It's no joke,' said Stark. 'And may I suggest that we talk in a more secure place?'

Churchill grabbed a wooden chair from near the door, obviously for the attendant, and jammed it under the door handle. 'There!' he said. He went to the cubicles and checked them all, pushing at the doors. They were all empty.

Churchill returned to Stark and demanded, 'Where is he? Are you sure it's Hitler?'

'Very,' Stark told him. 'He's being kept under wraps at Lord Glenavon's house, Red Tops.'

'How do you know?'

Stark told him the whole story – the kidnapping of Amelia, and the threats from Glenavon and Cavendish.

'Now I know why he warned me off for three days,' finished Stark. 'Because tomorrow evening Glenavon's hosting a private dinner at Red Tops, with Hitler and the Prince of Wales as his guests. Officially, the Prince thinks he's going there to talk about films . . .'

'An alliance! That's what they're after!' burst out Churchill. 'Setting up some kind of Anglo-German alliance between Hitler and our future King. Well, we'll scupper that! I'll send in police to arrest Hitler. You can take charge of that, Stark.'

'I can't, sir. That's the problem.'

'What do you mean, you can't! The man's barred from entering this country! He's here illegally! What better chance to get him and put him away!'

Stark explained again the problems with supporters of Glenavon within the police. 'They'll alert him as soon as there's any kind of action drawn up. By the time the police arrive, Hitler will be long gone and Lady Amelia will be dead.'

Churchill stared at Stark. 'But this is ridiculous! We have this man within our grasp!'

'And I will get him, sir. But we can't do it officially. We can't trust the police.'

Churchill sank down heavily on to a chair. 'David is being used, of course.'

At first, Stark wondered who this David was, and then remembered that the Prince was known by that name in the royal family's inner circle, which would include Churchill.

'We have to stop this meeting taking place. David is a good man, Stark, but he's naïve. There's no doubt he's quite taken with the idea of this moving picture business – hence his eagerness to accept the invitation.' He shook his head. 'Like a moth to a flame. Even the wisest can be duped by the bright lights. The danger is what might come from any meeting with Hitler. Even getting them talking together in a friendly way . . .' He looked at Stark. 'Tomorrow evening, you say?'

'Yes, sir.'

'I shall see the King today and suggest that he discourages David from going to this dinner at Glenavon's. A little sickness or something.'

'It won't solve the issue of the threat to Lady Amelia, sir. Nor the fact that the Prince might defy his father and go to the dinner anyway.'

'So what do you suggest?'

'I intend to break into Red Tops tonight and rescue Lady Amelia, and at the same time arrest Cavendish and Hitler. The trouble is, to gain entry I'll be operating outside the law.'

'Do you have support?'

'Sergeant Danvers and Special Agent Noble from the American Bureau.'

'And that's it? Just three of you?'

'Yes, sir. They're the only ones I can trust.'

Churchill shook his head. 'You won't stand a chance. I know about Glenavon and his security. You'd be amateurs against professionals, and you'd be dead even before you'd got into the house.' He sat for a moment in thought, then said, 'I may have an answer. There is a group of soldiers who undertake' – he hesitated momentarily – 'certain missions on behalf of the government. Unofficially, of course. I can alert them.'

'Will they be able to act at such short notice?'

'They are always standing by.'

A wave of relief swept over Stark. 'Thank you, sir.'

'Let's leave the thanks until we've got that bastard Hitler in custody and Lady Amelia to safety.'

They became aware of a rattling of the door handle, followed by a fist knocking urgently at the door. 'Who's in there?' demanded an angry Welsh voice. 'Open this bloody door!'

Churchill took the chair from beneath the door handle. The door swung open and the stocky figure of David Lloyd George stumbled in.

'Small problem with the lock, Prime Minister,' said Churchill.

He left, followed by Stark. Lloyd George glared after them before hurrying to one of the cubicles.

Churchill chuckled. 'I bet that'll set some tongues wagging!'

THIRTY-SEVEN

Stark telephoned Danvers and Noble.

'Nelson. One hour,' he said.

As codes went, it wasn't the most brilliant, but he hoped the disinformation Sergeant Danvers and Agent Noble had spread would have meant their enemies were less bothered about keeping a close watch on them.

They met at the foot of Nelson's Column in Trafalgar Square

and walked the short distance to the Colonial Office. 'Safest place, since we don't know whom we can trust,' Churchill had told Stark.

Five men were waiting for them in a small basement room. Handshakes were exchanged and introductions made: Fred, Barney, Joe, Pete and Eric. No surnames were offered. No uniforms were in evidence; the five men were dressed casually: jacket, trousers and pullovers against the winter weather.

The five men, along with Danvers and Noble, took their seats. Stark pinned Charlie Peters' rough plan of Red Tops on a blackboard.

'Just in case the situation hasn't been explained to you, Lady Amelia Fairfax has been kidnapped and is being held prisoner in Red Tops, the home of Lord Glenavon. Also currently at the house is an American called Edgar Cavendish and a German known as Adolf Hitler.'

He looked towards the five men for any sign of interest or curiosity, but they remained impassive, although he caught a couple of them shooting inquisitive looks towards Fred. *So, Fred is their leader*, realized Stark.

'Adolf Hitler is here illegally. Cavendish was involved in the double murder of Lord Fairfax and a special agent with the American Bureau of Investigation, Carl Adams. We suspect that Lord Glenavon and this man, Cavendish, along with Hitler, are involved in a treasonable conspiracy against this country. The problem is, while they are holding Lady Amelia hostage, we can't move against them in an official capacity. This is therefore an unofficial action which offers no protection to any of us if we are caught. I think it's only fair to let you know that.'

Again, he waited, but the five men remained as impassive as ever. *They've been briefed by Churchill. They know what they've let themselves in for.*

'Our task is to get into Red Tops tonight, under cover of darkness, rescue Lady Amelia and arrest Cavendish and Hitler.'

He turned to the plan of Red Tops he'd pinned to the blackboard. 'It seems that Lord Glenavon has turned his house into a fortress. There's a high brick wall that runs all the way around the perimeter, with open ground from that wall to the house and outbuildings. There are two double gates: one at the front for visitors, one at the back for trade deliveries, both at the ends of long drives. Although both these entrances are usually accessible, at this moment they are kept securely shut and only opened by a guard on duty if the people coming in have been authorized. There is a smaller side gate into the grounds that leads into a walled orchard, which is kept locked.'

'How high is the wall that runs round the place?' asked Barney.

'Ten feet,' said Stark. 'Another issue is that there are four armed guards who patrol the grounds at night. They'd spot anyone coming over the wall.'

'OK. As you say, it's a fortress,' grunted Joe.

'We could blow the gates and storm in all guns blazing,' suggested Barney.

'A full-frontal attack could get us shot down before we get to the house, and put the hostage at risk,' said Fred, speaking for the first time.

'So, how do we get in?' asked Pete.

'A Trojan horse,' said Stark. 'There's a grand dinner taking place at the house tomorrow night and deliveries are being made for it today and tomorrow. Fresh food, table linen – all that sort of stuff. My contact has found a coalman who's not fond of Lord Glenavon – apparently, Glenavon cheated him over a bill. He's scheduled to make a delivery to Red Tops early this evening. I've arranged for him to take me and Sergeant Danvers in.'

'And he's doing this just because Glenavon cheated him?' queried Joe suspiciously.

'Plus payment for services rendered,' added Stark. 'There's a storage loft above the coal shed. We'll hide ourselves in there until it gets dark, and then make our way through the orchard to the side gate and let the rest of you in. The orchard should give us the cover we need to get back to the house. Lady Amelia is being kept prisoner in a bedroom on the first floor, here.' Stark marked a cross on the plan of the house. 'We don't know where the men will be. My suggestion would be to make our assault at dinner time, when they should be together in the dining room – here.' Again, he marked an X on a downstairs room in the plan.

He turned to look at the men. 'Any questions?'

Fred raised his hand. 'Excuse me, sir. Could you and I have a private word?'

Here it comes, thought Stark, *the old soldier with his objec-*

tions. From the lack of surprise or curiosity on the faces of the other men, they were expecting this.

'Of course,' said Stark. 'Please excuse us for a moment, gentlemen.'

He and Fred left the room.

'You don't like the plan,' said Stark.

'I think it's a good plan,' said Fred.

'But?' queried Stark.

'But . . . it should be two of our lot who go in with the coal lorry.'

'I understand your concerns, but let me reassure you that I have had military experience.'

'I know, sir. Mr Churchill told us. Four years in the trenches. Made captain. The DSM. But with respect, sir, the war ended three years ago. Since then, you've been a civilian. And your sergeant's definitely a civilian.'

'Sergeant Danvers—'

'Is very brave. I know, sir. As are you. I'm not questioning your courage or your ability. Mr Churchill told us about that business with the King. But it doesn't alter the fact that the men guarding this house are no respecters of the law. If you're caught, it won't be a matter of "Put your hands up"; it'll be shoot first and ask questions afterwards. The fact is, sir, this is what me and the boys do as our regular job. If you and your sergeant get clobbered before you can let us in, the whole thing falls apart.'

'I respect your opinion, but I will make sure that doesn't happen.'

'Good intentions are all very well, sir, but you know from your experience during the war that they're not a guarantee. There's more chance of this working if the right people are doing the jobs they were trained for. And the bottom line is, Mr Churchill has tasked me with keeping you alive during this operation. I can't do that if you're locked inside and we're stuck outside.'

Stark weighed up Fred's words. Everything he said made sense, but with Amelia in danger, *he* wanted to be in the house rescuing her, not coming in later as a glorified observer.

'Would a compromise be acceptable?' he asked. 'I will go in with one of your men.' Before Fred could object, he added quickly, 'Lady Amelia knows me. If we get a chance to get to her before the action starts, which we need to do if she's to be safe, I can get her out without long explanations. That won't be the case with one of your men.'

Fred thought about it, then nodded. 'That makes sense.'

'In that case, shall we return and tell the rest?'

'In a moment, sir.' Fred opened the briefcase he was carrying and handed a sheaf of papers to Stark. They included architect's plans of Red Tops, and photographs of Amelia, Hitler, Glenavon and Cavendish.

'The plans you showed us are useful, but Mr Churchill thought these might help.'

Stark looked at him, concerned. 'That depends on who else knows he's got them,' he said. 'Our enemies have contacts everywhere.'

'You don't want to worry about that, sir. I've known Mr Churchill a long time. He's shrewd. The pictures are from newspapers.'

'The plans?'

'From the planning office. But he didn't just ask for these. He asked for the plans for every house in the area, and a few other areas as well.' He grinned. 'Like I said, he's a clever operator.'

'Who'll be going in with me? You?' asked Stark.

'I was thinking of Eric, sir. He's the best at sneaking through the grounds of houses.'

Stark studied the plans a bit longer, then said, 'According to these, there's an internal door between the coal store and the kitchen.'

'Save the cook from having to go outside in bad weather to get coal for the stove,' nodded Fred.

'If so, it's the perfect way into the house. And it might help us get Lady Amelia away from any shooting. At the same time as Eric goes to open the gate, I'll go through that door into the house. As I said before, if we make it when they're having dinner, I should be able to get to the room where she's being held without bumping into any of them. And by then the cook should have finished in the kitchen.' He frowned. 'Of course, that depends if that door's unlocked.'

'Don't worry about that, sir. Eric will deal with it. That's one of his specialities.'

'Let me guess – a former burglar?' asked Stark, amused.

'He has a talent.'

Stark rolled up the plans. 'We'll share these, and the revised plan, with the others. Thank you, Fred.'

As he headed for the other room, Fred stopped him, wary. 'One thing, sir. Being from North London, you're not an Arsenal fan, are you?'

Stark looked at him, surprised by the question. 'No, I'm not a follower of any particular football club. Why?'

'Well, Eric's a devoted fan of Spurs. Tottenham Hotspur. And like many Spurs fans, he's never forgiven Arsenal from moving to Highbury from Woolwich. Invading Spurs' home territory, he says. It's something he feels very strongly about.'

THIRTY-EIGHT

They travelled from the Ministry in two cars: Stark, Danvers and Noble in one with Fred at the wheel.

'I assume you're all armed,' said Fred.

Noble produced a revolver. 'The Colt 45. Still the most reliable ever made.'

'I borrowed one from my father's collection,' said Danvers, patting his inside pocket.

Noble looked enquiringly at Stark, who shook his head. 'I had enough of guns during the four years of the war to last me a lifetime,' he said.

'That's all very well, sir, but the people we're up against will be armed to the teeth,' Fred pointed out.

'He's right,' said Noble. 'What are you gonna do? Throw rocks at them?'

'I'll manage,' said Stark.

Noble shrugged. 'Suit yourself,' he said. 'So long as I don't have to depend on you to cover my back.'

Stark wanted to say, *We're not going in there to kill them, we're going to arrest them.* But then he'd end up in a long debate about guns, and why British police didn't carry them, whereas the American police force did. From his experiences during the war, many had died from what some joker had called 'friendly fire', accidentally shot by their own side. But he also admitted to himself that Noble was right: a man without a gun was at an unfair disadvantage when faced with a man holding one. And when it was life and death . . .

He shrugged the clash of thoughts aside. His job was to get to Amelia while the others took care of the armed guards.

It was turning dusk when they arrived at the coal merchant's at Parliament Hill Fields.

'Four o'clock,' said Fred. 'You gonna be all right sitting in the coal hole for four hours?'

'I sat for a lot longer than that in my time in the trenches,' said Stark.

Fred nodded. 'Yes, of course, sir. Anyway, you'll have Eric for company.'

The coal merchant, Walter Bird, was a sour-looking man. He looked at Stark and Eric as they entered his office, then shot a glance at the two cars parked in his yard.

'Charlie says you're a copper,' he said. 'So it's proper.'

'It's proper, but undercover,' said Stark.

'I hope you take that bastard Glenavon down!' Bird spat. 'He done me! I did a delivery he claimed was short. I've never done a short delivery in my life! He offered to pay me a quarter of it! A quarter! Ha!' He spat again. 'It's made me sick to my stomach every time I've had to make a delivery to him ever since. I wanted to sue him, but I wouldn't have won. And he'd have put me out of business. He had me over a barrel!' He scowled. 'Bastard!'

Stark and Eric followed Bird out the back, where he gave them each a pair of overalls. 'You'll need these on,' he said. 'They check who's in my cab when I go in and out of the gates, so you'll be hiding in sacks. These'll keep you a bit clean.'

But our shoes will be covered in coal dust, Stark reflected. *We'll be making a mess of Glenavon's carpets.*

'Won't they check you emptying the sacks?' asked Eric.

Bird shook his head. 'No,' he said vengefully. 'Since that bastard screwed me over that delivery, he knows he can get away with it again, so why bother? Nowadays, his men check there's no empty sacks lying on the lorry when I arrive, and count the empty sacks as I leave. That way he knows I can't get my own back on him.' He looked at Stark, curious. 'What's he done?'

'I'm afraid I can't tell you,' said Stark.

'Must be something big if there's this many of you,' said Bird. 'Before we go in, what about the money?'

Stark took four five-pound notes from his wallet and handed them to Bird, who checked them before putting them in his pocket.

'Right,' he said. 'Let's go.'

They put on the overalls, then Bird handed them each a large coal sack and took them to where his lorry was waiting. The back of the lorry was loaded with sacks of coal, with a space left for them to hide.

'Park yourself in there and I'll put a few sacks in front of you,' said Bird.

They climbed up on the flat-bed back of the lorry. Eric slipped into his coal sack and hopped to a space, where he settled, pulling the top closed over his head. Stark being larger, struggled to get into his sack and only managed it with difficulty. Already, he could feel his leg muscles complaining at the way his body was being squashed up.

He could hear sacks being moved and felt their weight against him as Bird hid them.

'Right,' said Bird. 'No noise.'

Thankfully for Stark, the journey was a short one. The lorry jolted all the way to Red Tops. When it pulled up, Stark heard voices – Bird's and another man's – then the lorry moved on, finally juddering to a halt a few seconds later. There was the sound of the rear tailboard being dropped, then Bird opened the top of Stark's sack.

'Stay limp,' he ordered.

Stark was cramped and every joint in his body ached. He felt himself being lifted up, then carried. He was dumped on a hard concrete floor. As he struggled out of the sack, he spotted the ladder leading up to the loft. He climbed it while Bird departed, carrying the empty sack. Bird returned with the sack containing Eric, and soon Eric had joined Stark in the loft.

'So far so good,' commented Eric. He shut the trap door, plunging them into darkness. 'Our eyes will soon get used to it,' he assured Stark.

Stark nodded. He'd spent enough nights in Flanders hiding in outbuildings and barns to be aware of that.

Below them, Bird continued his delivery, emptying the sacks on to an ever-increasing pile of coal, before they heard the door to the coal shed finally slam shut.

'Did you see the inner door?' asked Eric. 'The one that goes into the house?'

'Yes,' said Stark. 'But I didn't check if it was locked.'

'No need,' said Eric confidently. 'If it is, I've got me tools.'

Stark struck a match and swiftly checked the time. Five o'clock. Three hours to go.

They sat in silence in the dark, intent on not talking or making a noise of any sort in case it might be heard. But, as time passed and they didn't hear any sounds from either inside the house or outside, Eric obviously decided they were safe enough, because he whispered, 'I believe you're not a football fan, sir.'

'I enjoy a good game,' whispered back Stark. 'It's just that I don't have a particular affinity for any club. None of my family were that interested; they all concentrated on work. There wasn't the time or the money to go to games.'

'We lived right near White Hart Lane,' said Eric. 'So it was easy for us. My old man used to take me. Or, if he wasn't around, one of my uncles.' He fell silent, then added with deeply felt anger, 'We was the only North London team. Until the Arsenal moved in. The Woolwich Arsenal. The clue's in the name, sir.' He sighed. 'It should never have been allowed.' And with that he fell silent to brood on this great injustice.

With his eyes grown used to the darkness, Stark was able to check his watch at regular intervals. He sat, waiting, as he had sat and waited so many times during the war. At least this was different, he told himself. Then, death could come from anywhere: from a massive shell, a hail of bullets from a machine gun, poison gas. Here, nothing would happen until they went into action against five armed but hopefully unsuspecting guards.

The problem was getting Amelia out safely. And, somehow ensuring there were no repercussions against Sarah and Stephen.

I should have brought a gun with me so I could kill Glenavon and Cavendish, he reflected. Dead, they wouldn't be able to exact revenge. Had he been wrong to come here unarmed?

He'd had this idea that he could arrest them, put them on trial and expose the stinking corruption in the higher levels of society. But would it save Sarah and Stephen?

He checked his watch again. It showed nearly eight o'clock.

'They should be sitting down to dinner now,' he whispered. 'Time to make our move.'

The two men took off their coal-stained overalls, then lifted the trapdoor and descended into the coal store. Eric went to the door and tested the handle. It was locked.

He took a long, thin patterned piece of metal from his pocket, inserted into the lock and jiggled it around. There was a click, and he turned to Stark, a satisfied look on his face. 'Piece of cake,' he whispered. 'I'll leave you to find the lady while I let the others in. I'll be quick as I can, but it depends where the guards are.'

Stark opened the internal door. A short passageway led to the kitchen, from where he could hear the sounds of pots and pans being moved around. He crept to the end of the passage and peered in.

The cook had her back to him. He could see she was serving fish on to four plates. Four? He hardly thought that they would let Amelia join them at dinner, so who was the fourth person? Had Churchill not succeeded in keeping the Prince of Wales away?

The cook loaded the four plates on to a large tray and headed for the dining room. Stark took the opportunity to slip into the kitchen, and was just about to make for the open door that led to the stairs when he heard footsteps approaching. He ducked down and took cover in a small curtained alcove, which contained a broom and a dustpan and brush. He peered through the curtain and saw that the cook had returned, still carrying the tray laden with the four fish plates. From the look of frustration on her face, he decided that they must have waved her away, not yet ready for the fish course.

She took the fish from the plates and put it into a warm oven, and then set to work preparing vegetables.

I'm going to have to do something, said Stark. *I don't want to be trapped here.*

Then he became aware of voices coming through the wall of the alcove from the dining room.

'A new world order,' said a voice in clipped English, but with a German accent.

So, Hitler speaks English, mused Stark.

The next voice disabused him: it was a voice speaking in German that veered between smooth and silky and rough and hectoring. Stark caught some German words he recognized, those for France and Russia and Jew. Then the previous voice, speaking English with the German accent, chimed in. Hitler's translator – the fourth person.

'We, as Germans, are happy to make the initial attacks on France and Russia, but it is vital that England does not come to their aid.'

'I don't think you have any reason to think that England will want to come to the aid of the Bolsheviks,' came the voice of Glenavon. 'The whole country loathes them after what they did to the Tsar and the royal family.'

'But France . . .' began Hitler in German.

'If our plan succeeds, there will be no backing for a war in support of France. Not again. Not after the losses this country suffered last time.'

'And you won't be waging war against France,' came in Cavendish. 'You're just recovering lands that were wrongly taken from Germany as a result of the unjust deal at Versailles.' Stark could hear the smug smile in his voice as he added, 'Of course, when the French try to fight back, Germany will have to defend itself. But I can't see France holding out against German forces, not without the support they had last time.'

Quietly, Stark eased his shoes off. When the time came for him to make his move, he didn't want to arouse suspicion by leaving easily spotted coal-stained footprints over the carpets.

'And you are certain that the British and American govern-ments will remain neutral when that happens?' he heard the translator say.

'Speaking for America, absolutely,' said Cavendish. 'There is no desire in Washington for us to get involved in another European war.'

'And, as far as this country is concerned, our organization, the British Union of Patriots, has made huge inroads into all levels of government,' added Glenavon. 'We have key figures holding important positions in the Commons and the House of Lords. Influential people who can sway the vote in Parliament. And we have the power of the press, which I can assure you, from my part, will urge the great British public to support Germany as the victims in this case. And if not actively support Germany militarily, with the dreadful memories of the last war being so vivid, they'll at least vote to remain neutral.'

'And we have the feather in our cap to persuade the public,' said Cavendish, and again there was that same smugness in his voice. 'None other than the future King of England. He certainly doesn't want a repeat of what happened before.'

'He fought bravely in the conflict,' put in Glenavon. 'As you did yourself, Herr Hitler. He won the Military Cross. You, the Iron Cross. Two brave warriors with one common purpose: peace between our nations, and a new order for Europe and the world.'

'You are sure he will agree to an alliance?' asked Hitler in German.

'That will be up to you, Herr Hitler, to be your persuasive self when he comes here tomorrow evening,' said Cavendish.

'The omens are good,' said Glenavon. 'Remember, our two nations have a common ancestry. Our royal family are German – the Saxe-Coburg-Gothas. I'm sure it was some fool like Churchill who persuaded the King to change their name to Windsor. Completely unnecessary.'

There was the tinkle of a bell ringing in the kitchen. Through the curtain, Stark saw the cook go to the oven and take out the fish, and put it on the four clean plates. She loaded the plates on to the tray and once more headed to the dining room.

This time, Stark made for the door and was immediately out in a hallway, at the foot of the stairs. He stood, straining his ears for footsteps or movement upstairs, then mounted the stairs.

With the plan of the house secured in his mind, he located the room where Peters said Amelia was being kept prisoner. A key in the lock seemed to confirm it.

Stark turned the key. Amelia was sitting on the bed, and as she saw him enter the room she leapt to her feet. 'Paul!'

'Sshh!' Urgently, he put his finger to his lips.

She was already across the room and in his arms. 'What are you doing here? How did you get here?'

'I'll tell you later. Right now we have to get out.'

'No. Right now you have to put your hands up.'

Stark and Amelia jerked round to look at the door, where Cavendish stood pointing a pistol at them.

THIRTY-NINE

'It's just like a movie!' smirked Cavendish. 'The brave but incompetent hero coming to the rescue of his lady love. And failing.' He jerked the barrel of the gun at them. 'Downstairs.'

As Stark and Amelia walked past Cavendish, Stark debated hurling himself at the American and trying to wrest the gun from him, but Cavendish had moved to a safe distance.

Stark and Amelia walked down the stairs, as Cavendish called out, 'Come and see who I've got!'

Three men appeared from the dining room: Glenavon, Hitler, and a short, thin bespectacled man who Stark guessed to be the translator. They stared at Stark, stunned. Stark noticed that Hitler and his translator, in particular, looked worried.

'I was heading for the bathroom when I thought I heard voices,' said Cavendish.

In German, Hitler angrily demanded to know who this man was.

'He is Detective Chief Inspector Stark,' said Glenavon grimly. 'A pest, whose days have come to an end.'

Hitler snapped something, still angry, and the translator said, 'He has come here for Herr Hitler! We have to leave!'

With that, Hitler stormed up the stairs.

'Wait!' Glenavon shouted after him. 'He didn't even know you were here! He came for the woman!'

Suddenly, they heard the sound of gunfire from outside.

'What the hell!' burst out Glenavon. He swung to Cavendish. 'Kill the pair of them!'

Glenavon rushed up the stairs in pursuit of Hitler and the translator.

Cavendish pointed the pistol at Stark, then at Amelia. 'Not yet,' he said. 'If we're under attack, I might need you as a bargaining chip. Who's out there?'

When Stark didn't reply, Cavendish lowered the gun and fired. Amelia screamed and fell to the floor. Stark dropped down beside her, shocked.

'That time it was her leg,' said Cavendish. 'The next one is in her guts. A bad way to die.'

'Soldiers,' answered Stark, taking his handkerchief and making a tourniquet just above the wound. The bullet had torn through her leg and come out the other side. 'I don't think the bone's broken,' said Stark, trying to comfort her.

'How many soldiers?' demanded Cavendish.

'Thirty,' said Stark. 'You haven't got a chance. Give yourself up.'

'So I can hang?'

'The American government will protect you. They'll take you back to the States where you'll be safe. You said so yourself.'

Cavendish shook his head. 'I'm not falling for that, Stark. You've worked hard to get in here. You're not going to let me get away. And soldiers don't bargain.'

He aimed the pistol at Stark's head and pulled the trigger. Stark tensed for the bullet, then realized the gun had just clicked. Either it was an empty chamber or it had jammed. Stark threw himself at Cavendish, swinging a punch that smashed into Cavendish's face. Cavendish reeled back, blood pouring from his nose. He tried to bring the gun up, but Stark chopped down on his wrist, and the gun fell from Cavendish's hand. Stark grabbed Cavendish by the head and slammed the American's head hard against the banisters, then slammed it again.

Cavendish tumbled to the floor. His face was a mask of blood. He pushed himself up, crawling along the carpet, dripping blood. Suddenly there was the sharp report of a shot and Cavendish slumped to the floor.

Stark looked up and saw Noble holding a smoking pistol.

'We wanted him alive!' shouted Stark.

'Why?' demanded Noble. 'So he can talk his way back to the States where he's safe? No way!'

Behind Noble, Danvers and the five soldiers had appeared.

'You all right, sir?' asked Danvers.

'I'm fine,' said Stark. He pointed to Amelia, who was sitting up, her face a mask of pain. 'Lady Amelia needs treatment,' he said. 'She's been shot in the leg.'

'Broken?' asked Fred.

'I don't think so, but I can't be sure,' said Stark.

'Barney, take the lady to the car and take care of her,' ordered

Fred. He looked down at Amelia. 'Barney's a whizz with first aid.'

'Sergeant, give him a hand,' said Stark.

Danvers nodded. He took a second pistol from his pocket and held it out to Stark. 'I thought I'd bring another, sir, in case you changed your mind,' he offered.

Stark hesitated, then took it. 'Thank you, Sergeant.'

As Barney and Danvers went to Amelia, Fred demanded from Stark, 'Where are the others?'

'Glenavon, Hitler and his translator went upstairs. I think Hitler is going to make a run for it. There's another set of stairs at the back of the house.'

Fred ran for the stairs, followed by Eric, Pete and Joe, guns drawn.

Stark hurried to Amelia, who was being lifted up by Barney and Danvers. Her face was deathly white and she was biting her lip against the pain. Stark squeezed her hand.

'Trust them. They'll take good care of you.'

'The garage,' grunted Noble. 'In case Hitler's making a break for it.'

Stark and Noble followed Barney and Danvers as they carried Amelia out of the house. As the others headed for the main gate, Stark and Noble made their way to the side of the house, heading for the footpath that led to the garage. They turned the corner, and immediately there was the sound of gunfire and bullets slammed into the wall beside them. Hastily, they ducked back into the cover of the house.

'I thought we'd got all the guards,' said Noble.

'Cover me,' said Stark.

Noble levelled his gun from behind the cover of the wall and opened fire at the unseen gunman, while Stark darted for the cover of the nearest apple tree in a low, crouching run. Once there, he peered into the darkness, trying to work out where the gunman had hidden himself. He fired a shot into the darkness. There was an answering shot which tore into the tree, showering him with splintered bark. But his wild shot had served its purpose: he had located the flash of the hidden gun. Stark fired again, this time breaking cover and running for a tree nearer to the gunman, letting loose another bullet as he ran. Three shots fired: he had three left.

The gunman had fallen quiet. Either he was playing for time, having worked out Stark's plan to try to pinpoint his position, or he was reloading. How many bullets had he fired, Stark wondered. He was certainly close to his six. But then that depended on the type of gun he was using.

Stark dropped down and crawled to the next tree nearer to where he hoped the gunman was. He was halfway to the tree when there was a shot, and dirt and grass flew up just in front of his face. Immediately, he fired two shots in rapid succession. At the same time, Noble opened fire, a volley of bullets hammering into the darkness. Stark thought he heard a cry, and then a thud.

He waited, listening, then he ran forward, gun pointed, zig-zagging as he moved, just as he had done so many times as he ran from trench to trench across mud, stepping on the bodies of those who'd fallen. This time there were no mutilated bodies of fallen comrades, no barbed wire or thick mud to obstruct his run, and he almost stumbled over the dead body sprawled on the ground beneath a tree. The pistol had fallen from the man's hand. The man lay on his back, and in the darkness Stark recognized him as Herbert Jolly.

He heard footsteps behind him, then Noble joined him.

'Classy shooting,' murmured Noble. 'You or me?'

Suddenly, with its engine roaring, a car hurtled towards them from the direction of the garage, its headlights momentarily blinding them as it headed towards the main gates. Stark saw that the gates had now been opened. Stark ran towards the car, letting fly with his last shot, but his bullet ricocheted off the windows. So Glenavon had used bulletproof glass.

There was a burst of gunfire from the car and Stark felt a bullet tear at his sleeve, and he automatically dropped down. Then the car was gone, out through the gates. There was the sound of shooting from beyond the wall.

Amelia! thought Stark, alarmed.

He ran to the open main gate. No shots were fired at him. Half turning, he saw Noble following him.

Stark burst out into the street. The two cars they'd come in had been parked just outside the back gate, and both were wrecked, their windows shot out and the tyres flat. A figure was lying in the road, and as Stark ran towards the cars he saw Danvers scramble to his feet.

'Lady Amelia?' burst out Stark.

'She's in the car,' said Danvers.

The rear door opened and Barney stumbled out, gun in hand.

'Amelia!' called out Stark.

'I'm all right, Paul!'

Stark felt a wave of relief wash over him as he heard her voice.

'The car came past us like a bat out of hell,' said Danvers. 'Barney was putting a bandage on Lady Amelia and I was keeping watch. I got a shot in, but the bullets just bounced off. Bulletproof. Then they opened up as they went past. It was the tyres that did it. We couldn't go after them.'

'Hitler got away?' asked Noble.

'He did,' said Stark.

'It might have been a decoy, sir,' suggested Danvers. 'He might still be inside.'

Stark shook his head. 'I saw the way Hitler reacted. Trust me, he didn't want to waste any time in getting away.'

'So what do we do?'

'I'll put out an alert for all ports and airports,' said Stark. 'But it's my guess he arrived by private plane. In which case, we need to get Glenavon to tell us which airfield he used.'

As Stark headed back to the main gate and the house, Barney called after him, 'When you see Fred, will you tell him what's happened with the cars? He'll know what to do.'

Inside the house, he came across Fred and Eric coming out of a room carrying bundles of files and papers.

'What are those?' he asked.

'We were asked to bring in every bit of paper we could. Especially whatever was in the safe,' said Fred.

Of course, thought Stark. *Churchill*. 'Where's Glenavon?' he demanded urgently.

'Dead,' said Fred.

'Dead?'

Fred nodded.

So, no chance of finding out which airfield Hitler would be using.

'Our two cars outside are wrecked,' he said. 'Barney said you'd know what to do.'

Fred nodded. 'Thank you, sir. I'll make a phone call.'

'After I've made mine,' said Stark. 'I've got to put out an alert to try to stop Hitler getting away.' A thought struck him. 'What about the cook and the servants?'

'Joe and Pete are looking after them in the drawing room,' said Fred. 'We've tried to reassure them that we're not going to harm them, but I don't think they believe us.' He grinned. 'But don't you worry about them, sir. They'll be taken care of.'

'Not in the same way Lord Glenavon was, I hope,' said Stark acidly.

'No, they'll be fine. Innocent civilians,' said Fred. 'Hurry up and make your telephone call, sir, so I can make arrangement for us. We don't want to be here any longer than we have to.'

FORTY

Stark sat in the waiting room outside Churchill's office, reading the report in *The Times* of the previous night's action. According to the paper, police had been called to Red Tops, the home of Lord Glenavon, following reports of shots being heard.

> Police officers discovered the dead bodies of Lord Glenavon and Edgar Cavendish, an American film producer.
>
> Detective Chief Inspector Stark – who played a heroic part in saving the life of the King during the recent assassination attempt – was summoned to the premises and soon ascertained that the culprit appeared to be a German man who had been staying at Lord Glenavon's home. This German had apparently fled the scene and is now being hunted by the police. At this stage few details are known about the suspect.

The report continued in this vein but contained few actual details. There was no mention of the dead bodyguards or the wrecked car. No mention of Amelia.

Stark picked up the *Daily Telegraph* and the *Daily Sketch* which had been left on the table. Both of them carried only the barest of details in their 'Stop Press'. Again, they both went with the story that a German man had shot dead Lord Glenavon and Cavendish, and had then fled and was being hunted. None of the newspapers named him; he was just an anonymous German.

The front of the *Daily Target* consisted of a picture of Lord Glenavon, which filled the whole page, with the banner headline 'Lord Glenavon slain'. Inside, where the story expanded, there was no mention of a 'German killer', nor of Stark being called into investigate. Mainly, it was a eulogy for the life and work of Lord Glenavon.

A young man in a black coat and pinstriped trousers appeared in the doorway of the waiting room. 'Mr Churchill will see you now, Chief Inspector.'

Churchill was studying the newspapers as Stark entered. He put them aside and gestured Stark to a chair. 'You missed the bastard,' he growled.

'You gave orders for them all to be killed,' accused Stark.

'If a rat sneaks into my house, I don't negotiate with it. I kill it before it infects the whole house.'

'I could have arrested them!'

'But you didn't! Hitler got away! And if you had caught him, what would you have got him for?' demanded Churchill. 'Illegal entry? Then what? Deported?' He shook his head. 'The man is dangerous, Stark. I said so before. He needs to be stamped out. This was our opportunity. Unfortunately, you missed it.'

'And Cavendish and Glenavon?'

'Dangerous men. Traitors. In Glenavon's case, not enough evidence to go to trial. And Cavendish would have gone back to America.' He shook his head. 'Johnny Fairfax deserved to be avenged.'

'What about the papers your men took? I presume they were lists of prominent people associated with the BUP?'

'Papers better in my care than in anyone else's.'

'Your men knew exactly what they were after, and where to look. They knew where his safe was. I'm assuming you must have been a guest at Red Tops some time.'

'Once or twice. It's always wise to check out the opposition.'

'There is a corruption within the police service that goes right to the top. Those papers will include the names of superintendents and inspectors who are part of a conspiracy to replace the legitimate government of this country with a fascist dictatorship.'

'*Possibly* part of such a conspiracy. Many of them are well meaning, well intentioned. The trick is to sort out the wheat from the chaff. Who is really a danger to this country, and who might see reason.'

'You're forming your own cabal. Top policemen. Top people in the military.'

'Any politician worth their salt seeks out alliances within the structures that run a country. Without that, you have anarchy.'

'You used me.'

'You forget, Chief Inspector, *you* came to me. You got what you wanted. Lady Amelia freed. Cavendish and Glenavon's threats to you and your family neutralized.' He tapped the file. 'And I think I can assure you that any other threats to you and your family from that quarter will be nullified. And I hope you agree that is something I can achieve more effectively than you.'

Stark studied Churchill thoughtfully. The man was right. Churchill was the ultimate politician. A man who did deals. At heart, though, he shared Stark's principles. There were some he wouldn't do deals with – dangerous bigots such as Hitler, or Cavendish and Glenavon.

He nodded and got to his feet. 'Thank you, Minister.'

Amelia was lying on a settee when Stark arrived at her home. She started to get up as he followed Mrs Walker into the room, but Stark waved for her to stay where she was.

'How's the leg?' he asked.

'Forget my bloody leg, come here and kiss me!'

Stark sat down on the edge of the settee, studiously trying to avoid bumping against her bandaged leg.

'For God's sake, I won't break, Paul!'

'But your leg . . .'

'Is sore, but that's all.'

She pulled him to her and kissed him hard. 'God, I've missed you! Why didn't you come back with me last night?'

'It was more important that you got medical treatment.'

'Yes. Who was that? Some mysterious doctor. No name given.'

'Someone Churchill knows, I expect. He seemed to be the one pulling the strings.'

'They were going to kill me – Glenavon and Cavendish.'

'I know. That's why I came for you.'

'Were Bobby and the American chap . . . '

'Donald Noble.'

'Yes. Were they all right?'

He nodded. 'I'm seeing them both later today.'

She gestured towards the day's newspapers. 'I see you're the only one that gets a mention,' she commented. 'Are they building you up as some kind of hero?'

'I did lead the rescue,' he pointed out.

'Yes, but it's not very fair to Agent Noble and Bobby, is it?'

'I think Agent Noble will prefer not to have his role in the action publicized. He's working undercover for the American government, remember.'

'And Bobby?'

'I will make sure that Sergeant Danvers receives proper recognition,' he assured her.

'You sound so stuffy!' she laughed. 'How long are you staying?'

'As long as you'll let me. Stephen and my mother won't be coming home until tomorrow.'

'Then take me to bed,' she whispered, hugging him close.

'But what about your leg?' he asked.

She bit his ear. 'I'm the lover of a great warrior,' she teased him. 'I feel no pain.' And she laughed. Then she added, 'But if you're not feeling up to it . . .'

He put a finger to her lips to silence her, then lifted her up from the settee and carried her to the door.